mr. heartbreaker

Piper Rayne

Cover Design and Illustrator: Buerosued

1st Line Editor: Joy Editing

2nd Line Editor: My Brother's Editor

Proofreader: My Brother's Editor

about mr. heartbreaker

I made a deal with my brother a long time ago to never date his teammates.

Technically, Rowan Landry, the hot as hell center for the Chicago Falcons, is no longer my brother's teammate. Or his best friend. Their college days are long behind them, and they barely talk now.

Also, I'm not dating him—we're just sleeping together. There's a difference.

Except there's not a lot of sleeping going on, and neither one of us wants to stop what we're doing.

It's all fun and games until my brother is traded to the Falcons, because Rowan doesn't know I'm the new goalie's little sister. Oops.

Mr. HEART-BREAKER

one

Kyleigh

"THAT'S TOTALLY HIM." ALARA ELBOWS ME, CAUSING my wine to slosh over the glass's rim.

"And?" I down what's left in my glass, then set it on the now-soaked ivory linen tablecloth.

"Come on. You act like I don't know you. He's the *it* hockey player right now." She stares at Rowan Landry, the Chicago Falcons's new center, who's standing at the open bar.

Sure, I know of him. He's been all over the news since his trade to Chicago. And Alara isn't wrong. I *love* hockey players.

Thank you, Conor.

That button was installed early since I was carted around to hockey games starting at the age of four. I practically grew up in ice rinks, watching my older brother Conor play, but it wasn't until I hit twelve years old that I developed crushes on my brother's teammates. How could I not? There's just something so rough and tumble and alpha about hockey players. It's hard to explain, but they're my weakness, plain and simple. And Rowan Landry is the best of the bunch.

Not only is he the best center in the league, but he also has this arrogant, mysterious persona that sucks me in like a riptide in the ocean.

His dark hair is a little longer, wavy, and although it's styled tonight, if you Google him, you'll see it looking unkempt and like he just got thoroughly fucked in most pictures. I can't be the only woman who wants to be the one to give him that hairstyle.

"I see why they call him Magic." Alara rests her chin in her palm, her body slumping forward. "He could have been in the movie *Magic Mike*."

"Want a glass for your drool?" I slide my water glass over in front of her. "And they call him Magic because he skates so smooth and flawlessly on the ice."

"He sure is." Her eyes stay trained on Rowan. I don't judge my friend. He's hard to look away from.

"Why is he standing at a bar alone though? Maybe it isn't him. Why aren't people bombarding him?"

I'm totally downplaying my interest. I swore to my brother years ago that I'd never date any of his teammates after he went on and on, insisting that there was too much room for complications, and if things went sour, it could ruin the comradery on the team. But we never clarified that I couldn't sleep with his past teammates. Technically, Rowan was Conor's teammate in college, so I feel like the statute of limitations is up on this one. Still...I think Conor would be pissed if he ever found out.

"Too bad you have Justin or else you could go for him." I nudge Alara.

She rears back, her gaze straying away from Rowan completely. "If only this were last year." Alara laughs, and her gaze travels back to Rowan as he asks for a refill from the bartender, pulling out his money clip and dropping a bill into the tip jar. "I'd never sacrifice what I have with Justin for one night of fun."

"Justin is great." He really is. One day, I'll be at their wedding, I have no doubt. Still single and in the same position I'm in right now, but I doubt a hot hockey player will be only a few feet away from me, getting drunk.

"He is. I should call him. He looked lonely when I left tonight."

"Thanks for being my plus one." I swing my arm around her shoulders.

My mom should have been the one here, not me, but she sent me in her place—again. She always sends me to weddings when she's custom-designed the bride's dress. She and I have worked so closely with them by the time the final fitting comes around, the bride is gushing about how much they want my mom to be there to watch her walk down the aisle. Mom's usually much too busy, so I go in her place. The thought of my mom makes my chest ache, so I push away any thoughts of her.

"I'll always be your plus one."

Except at her wedding, where I'll have to scrounge up someone.

"Do you mind?" Alara grabs her purse hanging off the back of the chair, eyeing the exit.

"Go."

She looks around. The meals haven't come out yet, so I have a while before I can say my goodbyes and sneak out. "I'll only be a few minutes."

Alara and I have been friends since college. We were those lucky freshmen who got paired in the same room, and it was kismet. We were best friends from the start. And I see the look in her eye. Watching someone get married, seeing the bride and groom all lovey dovey, has made her miss Justin. I'm going to bounce soon anyway.

"Seriously, go see Justin."

"No," she says, fighting like the rock star best friend she is.

"Really. I'm fine now. I'm going to slip out soon anyway." I lift my empty glass and realize that if I want another drink, I'll have to go to the bar.

Alara follows my line of vision and giggles. "Go nail the hockey player. You know you want to."

It's tempting, and everything I know about Rowan Landry says he doesn't do serious. Okay, so I read all the hockey blogs and posts. Sue me. It's only to make sure no one is talking shit about my brother, who plays for the Florida Fury. No other reason. Especially not to read about other hockey players and their reputations. Definitely not.

"Nah." I wave off her suggestion.

Her perfect dark eyebrows raise. "Yeah, okay." She chuckles. "Be sure to text me where he takes you when you leave with him." She stands, slinging her purse over her shoulder, smiling.

She really does know me too well.

"I'm not pursuing him. I'm cutting myself off."

There's a secret I haven't told Alara yet because she's in that perfect love bubble with Justin, and if I tell her what I found right before I came here, her faith in monogamy and a perfect marriage would be shattered, just like mine was.

I squeeze my eyes shut for a beat, willing the vision of my mom and another man to go away. Maybe my dad got a haircut and grew three inches—who am I to say what a plastic surgeon can do in a week's time? There has to be some explanation other than what seems painfully obvious.

"Good luck with that." She leans down and hugs me, squeezing me tightly. She only does that when she thinks something is wrong. Am I that transparent? "If I weren't going home to a great guy, I'd be heading to the bar." She eyes the path right to Rowan.

"Go get laid," I say, shooing her away.

"You too." She laughs, walking toward the exit.

So far, none of the guests seated at my table have sat down, but it's still early and people are gathered in clusters around tables, talking and drinking and enjoying themselves. I'd do the same, but I don't know anyone else here. I scan the room, ending at the bar, which I could have predicted. I shouldn't have to say it again, but hockey players strip me of my self-control every damn time.

Rowan is leaning his back against the bar, his elbows and forearms resting on the bar top, gaze traveling across the room. His baby blues stop on me, and I suck in a breath then divert all attention as if we didn't just lock eyes for a moment. Jesus, that was embarrassing.

Way to play it cool, Kyleigh.

I grab my purse and take a sip from my water glass, then stand, wishing I knew someone here, so I didn't have to sit here by myself looking pathetic.

I head toward the door. *Look down. Keep your eyes on the ground.*

I glance up only to ensure I don't bump into a waiter and cause a scene. A vision of chicken and beef meals flying races through my mind. Maybe I can sneak out now and email the bride saying I came down with something. She doesn't know I used that excuse twice in the last four months.

As I reach the doors, I take one more glance over my shoulder. I mean, seeing Rowan Landry in the flesh, out in the wild, with no one surrounding him as though he's the latest zoo exhibit is too good not to pass up one last time.

I peek over, and damn it, his gaze is still on me.

Shit. Shit. Shit.

I probably look like a stalker. I'm one of those women Conor's always complaining about. The ones who admire creepily from afar but never approach him. Why do I care what Rowan Landry thinks of me? I'm not some puck bunny who wants to have his baby or wants to snap a picture to post on socials or show my friends. I grew up around boys like him who became hot professional hockey players. I'm not intimidated by his fame. I'm only interested in him for the distraction he's sure to give me tonight.

I press my teeth into my bottom lip. He tilts his head as if asking what move I'm about to make. Am I going to run and hide? Or am I going to go over and play?

Yeah, this is a bad idea, but I've had one hell of a shitty day. I deserve a little reward for not crumbling into the fetal position.

So instead of acting like a scared little mouse, I straighten my back, pivot, and saunter over to the bar. Consequences be damned.

two

Kyleigh

When I approach, I ignore Rowan, but I feel his gaze follow me as I step up to the bar—just far enough away from Rowan that he doesn't think I'm a sure thing. "Pinot, please."

The bartender grabs a new glass and swipes a bottle from the table behind him. I open my purse while I wait for my drink.

"I've got it." Rowan steps up beside me, pulling out his money clip and dropping a twenty in the tip jar.

"Oh, no. You don't have to do that." I take out my own twenty.

The bartender smirks between us, likely hoping for a double tip.

"If I can't buy you a drink, it's the least I can do." Rowan tips back the clear liquid in his glass, and I watch the way his throat bobs when he swallows. There's something sexy about it. The ice clinks against the glass when he sets it on the bar.

I tuck the twenty back into my purse. "Unnecessary, but thank you."

The bartender slides my wineglass across the bar, and I grab hold of the stem.

"Are you on the bride or groom's side?" Rowan asks.

A man steps between us at the bar and looks out the corner of his eye at Rowan but doesn't say anything about recognizing him. Then he glances my way, noticing that we're turned toward one another. "Oh, sorry, did I step in the middle of something?"

"Yes," Rowan says at the same time I say, "No."

"Oh." The guy's cheeks grow pink. "Then I'll just..." He steps back, looks right and left, and walks to the other side of me. "Stand here, I guess." His gaze moves to Rowan as if asking his permission.

The new guy is so close to me on the other side, it forces me to breach the distance I kept between Rowan and me on purpose.

"Come with me." Rowan nods toward one of the high-top tables scattered near the back wall.

"Excuse me?" I sip my wine, staying put.

The bartender snickers quietly, Rowan's narrowed gaze darting to him.

Stepping closer to me, Rowan lowers his head, his lips millimeters from my ear. "Please."

Tendrils of my hair move from his breath, and damn, treacherous goose bumps trail up my spine, but I somehow manage to abstain from a full-body shiver. He draws back, moving away from me, raising his eyebrows, asking me again what move I'm going to make.

Rowan turns his body, giving me a pathway to the table, and I see that the bartender has filled Rowan's drink without him asking. I guess when you're tipping like he is, and you're who he is, you don't have to do a lot of asking.

Is that why he didn't think he had to ask me to step over to a table with him? A man like him is probably used to getting what he wants.

It's as if I can feel the bartender and the man behind me waiting to see what I'll decide. But let's be serious. Would I really turn down Rowan Landry's invitation to talk privately?

I stand there, pretending to weigh my options for a moment, before I take my wine and walk past Rowan. Once I'm at the table, I pivot to face him, and he's already placed his drink on the table. I stare at the vibrant green lime at the bottom of the glass so I don't have to look into his eyes.

"So, bride or groom?" he asks again.

"Guest."

He chuckles. A low, soft rumble in his throat that pulls a smile from me and makes me wonder if that's what he might sound like in bed.

Being the sole object of his attention is unnerving, so I sip my wine to do anything but concentrate on him. "I was invited by the bride. You?" I swallow another gulp of wine, and I catch him staring at the glass, which is now almost empty.

"Guest."

I reward him with a half grin. "Not the groom?"

He chuckles again as if the idea is absurd. A girl could get addicted to earning that warm laugh. "No."

His affirmation is typical of guys like him. As if he'd burn the altar down before stepping up to it.

We stand silently assessing each other for a few moments. Surely cocktail hour will end soon.

"I've known him since high school," he says.

"My mom designed her dress."

"I just reconnected with him when I moved to Chicago."

He can't believe I don't know who he is. *Moved* here? More like traded here. But I'll play his game—for a while.

"So, we're both kind of outliers?"

He nods slowly. "I guess so."

"What table number are you at?"

Rowan pulls his table card from the pocket of his expensive suit and twirls it around in his hand. "Twelve."

I give him a fake pout. "I'm at fourteen."

"I guess that tells us where we stand in their lives." He drops the card on the tablecloth and picks up his drink. "I wasn't going to come."

"I'm probably not staying."

He shifts his stance so that he's facing me, his left forearm and elbow on the table. I down the rest of my wine, gaze steady on the guests mingling around us.

"Am I that unbearable?"

I glance in his direction, setting my wineglass on the table. "I don't even know you."

His blue eyes glitter with amusement as he twirls his glass with his fingers. Long, thick fingers I can't help but notice. "What do you want to know?"

I shrug. "Nothing in particular."

His eyes become intense and a little predatory, but I try to act unfazed. Am I really trying to play hard to get with Rowan Landry? He probably already thinks he has me. I don't need to know his favorite color or what superstitions he has before a big game. I want him to rock my world for one night. That's all.

"I'm room 1498," he says.

"And?" I arch a perfectly sculpted eyebrow.

"Figured the way you were eye-fucking me earlier, you'd value that piece of information."

I abandon my empty wineglass and turn to face him so we're chest to chest, only a few inches apart. "You're Rowan Landry, so no, I wasn't eye-fucking you. My friend pointed you out, that's all."

"So, you know who I am?" A smug look washes over his face.

"Really? You're surprised? You're in a Chicago hotel. Your trade to the Falcons was broadcast everywhere. But if it'd make you feel better, I can pretend."

The tips of his lips turn up, and his tongue slides along his bottom lip. Shit, is that something he did as a distraction to take my thoughts off course and only think about having that tongue between my legs? If so, job well done. It totally worked.

He shakes his head. "So, you know me. Now I need to know you. What's your name?"

That question snaps me back to attention. Shit. There's no possible way he'd remember me from when he and Conor played together. I was a nerdy high school girl, and he never gave me the time of day. I met him maybe twice. But I've heard his name occasionally from Conor, so maybe it's the same on his end. Then again, Conor can be self-absorbed and probably never talks about me.

"Leigh," I say, using a shortened version of my name to be safe.

His eyes lock on mine for longer than I'm comfortable with, as if he's assessing whether I'm telling the truth. This is a one-night thing. Who the hell cares? I'll never see the guy again. I'll be one of many in a long line of women who bed Rowan Landry, which is exactly how I want it.

"Nice to meet you, Leigh."

"So formal after just telling me I was eye-fucking you. Do you want to shake hands like business partners now?"

He shakes his head and studies me for another second. "I like you."

"Thanks?"

"Do you like me?"

The look on his face is so genuine, as if he wants to know

if he has a shot with me. "What's not to like? You're Rowan Landry."

The smile drops from his face, and he picks up his glass. "Want a refill?"

He takes my wineglass and steps away from the table without waiting for me to answer. I watch as he goes to the bar and sets the two glasses on the bar top while the bartender grabs new ones.

Rowan almost looked upset by what I said, which doesn't make sense. Every hockey player I've ever known has gotten off on the accolades and compliments of who they are in the hockey realm. I thought it would boost his ego a little and seal the deal that I'd end up in room 1498 in the next fifteen minutes. Maybe I should've just gone home instead of detouring over to the bar.

He returns and slides my wineglass over to me. His fingernails are clipped and clean and well-manicured. I blink to stop the image of them plunging inside me or twisting my nipples. Why I am so damn horny right now?

"Thank you, I could have gotten—"

"It's no problem." He sips his drink. "Do you think you can forget who I am for a half hour?"

I'm still in the game. "Only a half hour?"

He turns away from me, staring at the crowd of people as the DJ announces that it's time to eat. "I guess you're saved by the beef wellington. It was nice to meet you, Leigh."

He steps behind me, oddly close, and I close my eyes when his arm brushes along my back.

Let him go, Kyleigh. Just leave. Go home and masturbate to him if you need to.

"Wait," I say, unable to stop myself.

He turns around to face me.

I'm probably going to regret this. "I had a guest."

He slides his hands into his pockets, and I realize he left his drink behind. "Yeah?"

"She had to leave, so I mean, if you want, you could sit at fourteen with me. I get that twelve is higher on the list." I roll my eyes playfully, but his gaze remains on me, as intense as ever. I should've kept quiet. "Don't feel obligated..."

"I don't."

"Okay." I pick up my wineglass. "Table fourteen, then?"

His fingers cover mine as he takes my wineglass from my grip. Then he holds out his arm for me. "Table fourteen, then."

I slide my arm through his. What is going on? This was supposed to be a wham bam, see you never. Not share a meal and clink glasses while we watch the happy couple make out at the head table.

He pauses at the table's edge at the exact place I was sitting when our eyes locked, except he takes the spot where my wine spilled and holds out the chair for Alara's seat.

How did my predicted one-night stand turn into my wedding guest?

three

Rowan

I planned to make an appearance during cocktail hour and hightail it out of there with the excuse of being sick.

Jack was my best friend in high school. We played on the same hockey team for years, and when my mom couldn't go on the road trips, Jack's family took me. Jack decided to stop playing after high school, having bigger dreams than playing hockey professionally, and that's when our lives drifted in two different directions. Sure, every once in a while we'd call or text, but he was on his way up the corporate ladder, and I was busting my ass to get where I am today.

He's been in Chicago for four years, and the minute I got traded, he called me. We've gone out for a few drinks, and I met his bride, Mila, when he had me over to their trendy, newly built house in the city. They're a great couple. Mila makes Jack happy. So I'm happy for them.

But when I got the wedding invitation, I wanted to

decline. I ignored it as I do most things I don't want to deal with. Until Jack called me and put me on the spot.

Usually I'd let any call I don't want to answer go to voicemail, but I was expecting a call from my agent and answered without checking as I was hustling groceries up the stairs of my building. He told me he really wanted me there, and I said I didn't want my appearance to overshadow his day, take the attention away from him and Mila. But he said he'd take care of it and mentioned that his parents really wanted to see me, which piled on the guilt because they did so much for me since I had a single working mom. So here I am at a wedding alone, not knowing anyone except four people. Five now, if you count the hot brunette sitting next to me.

I'm not sure what Jack did, but no one has approached me for a picture, an autograph, or even to shake my hand.

But I agree to sit with Leigh, the woman I met at the bar after stealing glimpses over my shoulder during the cocktail hour. The eyes of the others assigned to Leigh's table are on me as they pull out chairs and sit down around us. I purposely position myself facing Leigh with my arm slung across the back of her chair while the DJ announces the bridal party, then the happy couple makes their entrance.

"So, what did you pick?" I ask her once the music is back at a normal level. I'm unsure how to keep this conversation going with six other people acting as if they can't hear us, but intently listening to every word.

"Beef wellington. You?" She sips her wine.

It seems like a nervous habit. She picks up her wineglass every time her cheeks flame pink. I haven't figured her out yet. When she was about to leave the ballroom, I followed her with my eyes, hoping she'd look over. When she did, I challenged her, thinking she'd come to the bar, I'd get her a drink, and we'd be up in my room within half an hour.

But she stood just far enough away from me at the bar to

tell me that she's not that easy to hold on to. My biggest problem is that I love a challenge. For the entirety of my life, all someone had to tell me was that I didn't have it or I'd never make it. I wasn't fast enough or quick enough or smart enough. Tell me I can't do something, and I'll work tirelessly to prove you wrong.

The problem is that the same mentality has been transferred to women. And I feel like this woman has my blueprint.

"Same, but I might be getting your plus one's meal."

She cringes. "Salmon, I think."

Oh, hell.

"And from the look on your face, I'd say you're wishing you were at table twelve," she says.

"Nah, it's just that my trainer has me on this diet, and I'm eating salmon three times a week right now."

Her lips tip up. She's got a helluva smile. One that knocks me off my axis. "You can have my beef wellington, and I'll take your salmon."

"I'm fairly sure I can secure a beef wellington."

"Excuse me." The woman sitting next to me taps my shoulder.

How am I supposed to get this woman to my room if I can't have a conversation for five minutes?

Leigh glances over my shoulder and raises her eyebrows.

I turn in my chair and find that the woman is probably in her midsixties, with a kind smile. I glance down and see a piece of paper and pen on the table. "Hi."

She leans in close, her attention darting to the head table where Jack and Mila sit as if they're the proctors during an exam. "I know we're not supposed to acknowledge you, but my grandson is a huge fan of yours. He's already bought your jersey and talks about how you'll turn the Falcons around."

I scour the table and see that all the other guests are watching us. If I sign that paper, I'm going to have to sign more stuff, then the pictures will start. Soon it'll be a cluster-fuck, and the clinking of glasses for Jack and Mila will be over-shadowed by the attention being paid to me. There are only a few ways I could go with this, but damn, I remember when I was a kid and dreamed of running into my favorite player. If my grandma had brought a signature home to me, I would've been ecstatic.

I pick up the pen. "What's his name?"

Her entire face lights up as if I just handed over her first grandchild. "Really? Oh, you're a sweet boy." She leans in closer as I put pen to paper but doesn't lower her voice. "I told my daughter those stories were gibberish. Just gossip."

My head tilts, and I stare up at her through my eyelashes.

Leigh snorts and covers her mouth with her napkin.

As far as I know, there's no bad press about me. I've been cordial to every Chicagoan who has approached me on the street since I arrived here. What could people be saying about me?

"I'm sorry?" My forehead wrinkles.

She leans forward and smiles at Leigh. "My daughter said she's heard you're a real heartbreaker. That you're a love 'em and leave 'em kind of guy. But I've been watching you and your date this evening." She winks.

I want to shake my head. Love 'em and leave 'em? I never loved them in the first place, so there's no leavin' 'em.

"I see it in the way you look at her," she says, placing two fingers to her eyes then pointing them back at me.

Yeah, okay. Whatever. This woman is off her rocker. Leigh and I just met.

"And your grandson's name?" I change the subject, not wanting to entertain this woman's false observations.

"Aster."

I scribble the name with my signature below. "There you go."

"He's going to be so happy. Thank you." She looks past me at Leigh once more. "Don't worry, he won't break your heart. I can tell."

I don't react because I learned long ago that your nonverbal communication says much more than what comes out of your mouth. One nasty look or annoyed expression gets you bashed on social media within a minute or less. I place my arm around Leigh, my palm landing on her warm shoulder.

"I might just break his," Leigh says, laughing and picking up her wineglass.

The older lady laughs and takes her husband's hand next to her. "Or you two could be lucky like us. We met at a funeral and hit it off."

"Now there's a meet-cute," Leigh continues the conversation, selling us as a couple by placing her hand on my thigh.

Fuck, her fingers are a mere six inches from my dick, and he wants badly to puff himself up and make up the difference.

I get it, buddy.

The clinking of glasses finally interrupts our conversation. Everyone turns toward Jack and Mila, watching as they come together for a kiss.

"They're adorable," Leigh says. "She told me how she crushed on him pretty hard for a long time."

I turn to look at her, and our faces are close as if we're a real couple. Our eyes lock, my blue meeting her brown, but neither of us pulls away.

"Jack said he noticed her but wanted to prove himself to her first."

She shrugs as though she's not buying it.

The salads are delivered, and thankfully the other table guests are involved in their own conversations.

"I thought it was admirable." Which is true. I mean, I know Jack. He's a go-getter, has a bunch of life goals in a checklist in chronological order by age that he hopes to reach.

She leans her body into mine, and unlike the grandma on my left, Leigh knows how to lower her voice. "It's nice, sure, but if a man wants me, I hope nothing will hold him back. That all he could think about was me until he had me all to himself." She straightens, and I miss the way her long hair tickled my neck.

"Are you suggesting I throw you over my shoulder fire-fighter-style and carry you to room 1498?"

She laughs. "I'd settle for a more subtle exit, but once we're in the elevator alone, it'd be game on."

Yeah, she's got my blueprint.

"You say the word, and I'll make our excuse."

She eyes the table. Sure, they're talking with one another, but she sees, as I do, what people think are sly glances our way. "After dinner. When dancing starts, you can make your move, Mr. Heartbreaker."

I lift my wrist to check the time. I can hold myself over for another hour, max. But the urge to impress this woman erupts inside me. None of the bullshit lines will work on her. "An hour of torture. Pain before pleasure. Got it."

She stabs her fork into the lettuce on her plate. "Torture?"

"I'm being polite in abiding by your wishes, but for the next hour, having my mouth between your thighs will be the only thing on my mind."

Her lips part slightly, and a lust-crazed aura washes over her face. The exact expression I was hoping for. "Well, eat fast then."

"Sure, right now I will, but up in room 1498, I'll be taking my time."

"Jesus," she murmurs, stabbing the innocent lettuce again.

Oh, tonight is going to be fun with a capital F. Emphasis on the F.

four

Kyleigh

THE WAITSTAFF TAKES AWAY OUR PLATES, AND people get up from the table. It might have been the weirdest dinner I've ever sat through. Everyone was acting as if Rowan Landry wasn't at our table, and he was engaged in regular conversations regarding weather and the best places to eat in Chicago.

"It's weird that everyone is acting like you're a regular Joe," I whisper as the last couple gets up and heads over to another table to chat with some other guests, leaving us alone.

"I think Jack is paying them under the table."

"Really?"

He turns toward me, as he has every chance he's gotten— his arm slung over the back of my chair, his body facing mine. His strong thighs are snug in a pair of slacks. *Just get me to room 1498.*

"I was apprehensive about coming, but Jack said he'd take care of it. I didn't ask many questions."

"Who is he? A mob boss?"

His lips tip into a smile. "More like an executive at a cheese company."

"One of the top cheese companies." Every fitting, Mila went on and on about how he works at the biggest cheese manufacturer in the world.

"I think Jack prefers it to be called a dairy company."

Both of us look over at the newlyweds.

"They are a cute couple," I say.

"They'll make the perfect suburban couple who will find happiness in an affluent neighborhood and raise their two kids who will want for nothing except for maybe a dog."

"Can't dirty up their perfect house."

"Maybe they'll eventually cave after the kids do some cute presentation begging for one, but it will be one of those golden doodles?"

I shake my head. "Definitely not a mutt from the shelter."

He chuckles. "Or heaven forbid, a stray."

"They'll live the American dream."

"Date nights every Saturday," he says.

"Home by ten. She'll get ready for bed—"

"And he'll go down to his man cave and watch—"

"Porn," we say in unison, facing one another and laughing.

I used to think that could be me someday. I've had a few friends over the years say they're city girls who will raise their kids in the city, but they've all slowly migrated to the suburbs. Now, instead of Sunday brunches with mimosas, I'm hitching a train to attend baby showers and first birthdays.

"The kids will get older, and she'll resent him for not picking up his socks," he says, distracting me from twirling my wineglass and wondering if I'll ever trust in the sanctity of marriage again.

"He'll try to grab her boob when they get into bed, thinking that will turn her on."

He leans closer to me, lowering his voice, and I can't help but inhale the woodsy masculine scent of his cologne. "I promise to tweak your nipples, too."

"Then what are we waiting for?" I laugh.

He continues our game. "She'll stop giving him blow jobs."

"He'll never have perfected getting her off with his tongue."

"Why does he have to be a shitty lover?" He sips his drink, the lime bobbing in the glass.

"A selfish and lazy lover. There's a difference."

He tilts his head. "Well, she's never in the mood."

"Because he stopped romancing her."

"Her buying him a pair of golf shorts isn't exactly romancing him either."

"She hasn't gotten flowers other than her birthday and their anniversary in five years."

"Five years?" His teasing smile is prominent, and butterflies lift from a deep sleep in my belly.

"He's taking her for granted just because she decided to stay home and raise their kids."

"And she regrets the decision to give up her career, despite her daily schedule juggling and organization of the house, she's working at an executive level but getting paid in sticky hands, hugs, and kisses."

I sip my wine then keep the glass in my hand. "She loves the quiet time after she's gotten them to bed. And then he comes home, and she warms up his dinner and watches him eat the meal she prepared three hours earlier while he tells her how bad his day was, never asking about hers."

His head rears back. "You're really painting Jack as an asshole."

"You're not too nice to Mila. She's working her ass off, but she's invisible to him now."

"Truce?" He lifts his glass to mine.

I clink my wineglass to his tumbler. "Sure. I'm sure they'll be different."

His gaze diverts over to them as the DJ announces their first dance. "I hope so, for their sake."

"So, you're not big on marriage?" I ask.

"Not right now. You?"

I think back to this afternoon, seeing my mom's lips on a man who isn't my dad, and my stomach rolls over. I have to suck back the tears that want to form in my eyes. "No."

He lifts his wrist and looks at his expensive watch. "Well, dinner's over."

"That it is." I down the rest of my wine and place my glass on the table.

"I think I've been a good boy." He rises from his chair and towers over me, holding out his hand.

"You've barely touched me," I say, standing so close our chests practically touch. My nipples pebble in response.

"I was afraid I wouldn't be able to stop if I started."

Holy hell, this guy has the lines. We both know the score tonight. I go up to room 1498, we get all sweaty and get one helluva workout. Then we part ways, never to see one another again.

I'm not a prude, I've had one-night stands before. Not a ton. Surely not as many as him. But tonight, I need to get out of my head and not think about the impending implosion of my parents' marriage. Not that I wouldn't be angling to sleep with this man even if my mother wasn't betraying my father.

"You go first. I'll sneak out in a few minutes."

He tips his head down to my neck, a move I'm really starting to love. "Be quick. Knock three times when you arrive."

I rear back and tilt my head up to look into his blue eyes.

"Am I not the only woman you gave your room number to tonight?"

His tongue slides across his bottom lip. His eyes are filled with lust. "You're the only one I see tonight."

"If you didn't know already, I'm a sure thing. You don't have to use those lines on me."

"I don't have you in the elevator—yet."

He turns and heads across the room, stopping to talk to a couple. They hug one another, the woman staring at me over his shoulder. They talk for a few minutes while Jack and Mila's dance draws to a close. He approaches them as they exit the dance floor, shaking hands with Jack and pulling him in for one of those man hugs. Then he hugs Mila.

So many people shift their attention to Rowan as he winds his way through the crowd, ignoring me and exiting the ballroom. I wait for the father and daughter dance to begin before I grab my purse and slowly make my way to the exit.

My heels click on the hotel's marble floor as I walk the length of the hall to the elevator. As I press the button, I'm surprised by the lack of people waiting for the elevator, but I guess it's early for a Saturday night. The elevator doors slide open, and I step inside, pressing the button for the fourteenth floor.

Just as the metal doors begin to close, Rowan's large body slips inside. He presses my back to the wall, his hands on my cheeks, and his lips crash down on mine. I make a noise of surprise at his firm, pressing lips.

His hands shift to the bar on either side of my hips, locking me into place and pushing me against the glass elevator wall. I inch up on my toes, my heels slipping out of my shoes to meet him halfway. To feel the strength of him. To smell his addictive cologne. To taste his citrus breath after a night of drinking vodka tonics.

Rowan Landry is every bit the kisser his fangirls believe he is. His calloused hands slide up my body, holding my head in place while his tongue slips past my parted lips, gliding into my mouth.

I melt into his strong hold, my mouth opening for him. He tilts my head slowly, moving me to a better angle, allowing his tongue to dive deeper, and I whimper when his hands leave my cheeks and fall to the small of my back as if he can't get me close enough to him.

I could kiss him for eternity. He's mastered the art of the slow, easy kiss that moves seamlessly to demanding and wanting.

He ends the kiss, and I shift forward, not wanting him to stop, but his lips travel to my jaw, casting small kisses toward my ear. "I can't wait to get you out of this dress."

My hands cradle his waist, sliding under his suit jacket. His muscles are rigid, even through the layers of clothes. Lust pools between my thighs. "How am I going to do my three knocks?"

He chuckles in my ear, igniting a wave of shivers. "Just give me time to ensure the other women I picked up tonight aren't in my room." I draw back, and he chuckles again, his palm gliding down my arm until my hand is in his. "Come on."

As if we're in a movie, the doors open, and we stumble down the luxurious hallway with spiral-patterned carpet and crystal sconces, unable to stop kissing and touching one another. My eyes clock the room numbers as we pass, my stomach filling with a buzzy sort of excitement the closer we get to his room.

Once we're outside room 1498, he stops with his back to the door, pulling me toward him, and his kisses turn me into a wild mess. He's so smooth. Using his free hand, he retrieves his key card out of his suit pocket and presses it to the door to unlock it. I watch the small light turn green, and he pushes the door open for me to enter first.

I raise my eyebrows and walk into his room. "If I find a naked woman in the bed, I'm leaving. You won't have a catfight on your hands."

There's a small black suitcase on the luggage stand, the bed is made, and the bathroom doesn't appear to have been used. I stare at the perfectly made bed and the tall skyscrapers of Chicago lighting up the night sky outside the window.

"Too bad. I was hoping to see a wrestling match." He comes up behind me, his hands landing on my upper arms. His voice is low as if we're not alone.

"Who says you'd be worth me scratching some woman's eyes out?"

"Because your nipples have been hard all night. Unless that was because of someone else." His hands slide around to my back, finding the top of my zipper. "May I?"

I suck in a breath and nod, stepping forward a little so he can unzip my dress.

He lowers my zipper, and it feels as though the sound vibrates off the walls in the quiet room. This is it. I'm going to sleep with Rowan Landry.

Once it's lowered, I hear him suck in a rush of breath, and I really hope it's because he can see the top of my thong.

"Fuck," he murmurs.

I turn around and lower one of my straps then the other, letting the top of my dress fall to my waist, revealing my strapless black bra.

His gaze falls to my chest, and his Adam's apple bobs. "You're so damn gorgeous."

I reach back and unhook my bra, dropping it to the floor.

His eyes light with arousal and his gaze roams my body as he strips off his suit jacket, removes his tie, and pulls his shirt out of his dress pants. Stepping closer, his hands cradle my neck, his thumbs running along my jaw before his lips descend on mine.

It's as if someone shot a starter's pistol because now that we're behind closed doors, our kiss is deeper, more urgent. Each of us takes turns dominating the kiss, and we meet one another with the same intensity.

His hands slide down under my dress, his palms grabbing my ass and pulling me closer to him. He's hard against my stomach, and heat pools between my thighs. I push my dress all the way down to better feel his length.

Once I'm in just my heels and a thong, he steps back, his heated gaze tracing down my body, chest rising and falling with his deep breaths. Watching his avid appreciation for my body makes me ache between my thighs. This. This is what I needed.

I bring my hands to the top button of his dress shirt, but he takes the opportunity to mold his palms to my breasts, his thumbs running over my nipples, and I find I can't wait any longer. My fingers slide under each side of his shirt, and I tug it open, buttons flying in all different directions.

His chest is beyond impressive. I soak in his rippled muscles and the light dusting of hair that leads under his pants. I manipulate his belt, the button of his pants, and the zipper over his bulge. Pushing them down, I find he's wearing a pair of black boxer briefs that stretch snugly around his muscled thighs.

I don't get nearly enough time to admire him because he yanks me closer, his hands grabbing my ass, and I lift, allowing him to pick me up, wrapping my legs around his waist. He carries me to the bed and sits on the edge so that I'm straddling him.

"Keep the heels on," he says before taking my nipple into his mouth.

Fuck, who gave this guy a list of all my turn-ons? I need to make the most of this night because I'll never have it again.

five

Rowan

I DON'T USUALLY SLEEP AROUND THESE DAYS. I'VE
had my share of one-night stands, but most of those were
during college and my early years in the league. They just don't
satisfy me like they used to. So picking up Leigh tonight is
unexpected for me.

I only got the hotel room because it's Saturday night,
which means my teammate Tweetie, who lives above me, is
probably having people over, and I could use some peace and
quiet and wasn't sure how late I'd end up staying at the
wedding. We start training camp next month, and it's time to
get my head back in the game.

I push all that shit, all the worry about my first full season
with the team, away because I have a knockout straddling my
lap wearing only a thong and a pair of killer heels. It's been a
long time since I've been as attracted to a woman as I am to
Leigh.

Her short nails run along my scalp, fingers winding
through my hair. I suck her pert nipple, twirling my tongue

around the pebbled tip. Leigh's moan spurs me to keep going, my hand lifting to her other bare breast and tweaking her nipple between my thumb and forefinger. Her fingers tighten in my strands, tugging lightly.

I run my free hand across her silky skin, up and down her spine. She straightens, and I pop my mouth off her tit and kiss the valley between her breasts, staring up at her through my eyelashes. Her dark hair falls on either side of her face, her caramel-colored eyes piercing through me as though she can see into my soul.

When I flip her over so her back meets the mattress, she squeals, and I pull her thong off. Then I stand between her open legs, pushing my boxers down my legs and grabbing a condom from my bag. I fist myself, tugging up and down. I can't remember the last time I felt this out of control, desperate to be inside of a woman.

"You still good?" I ask, wanting to make sure I'm not pushing things too fast.

She sits up and takes the condom wrapper from my hand. Staring me in the eye, she rips it open with her teeth, her gaze never straying from mine. "Is this clear enough for you?"

She takes out the condom and places it over the tip of my cock, her thumb and forefinger sliding it down my length. My dick twitches from the first touch of her petite hands.

"Hell," I mumble, bringing my hand between her legs and gliding my finger along her center. Her legs open wider, granting me access, and I tease her opening with the tip of my finger. Wetness coats me, and I slide my finger forward, circling her clit. "All ready for me, huh?"

She wraps her arms around my neck, pulling me in for a kiss. She doesn't wait for me to take control, her tongue licking along the seam of my lips to open for her. And I'm not an idiot. I want her to take whatever she wants from me, so my lips part. Her tongue slides into my mouth, meeting mine with the same feverish urge I feel.

I push one thick finger inside her, and her breath hitches, her torso rising and falling. I swallow her moan, plunging my finger in and out of her before adding another when I think she's ready. I want her dripping by the time I fuck her.

She strokes her tongue against mine, and I curve my fingers inside her. She dips her head back with a moan, and I admire her swollen lips. Her body is flushed in the prettiest shade of pink, and I want to cast a line of kisses along every inch of her flesh.

Her back falls to the bed, my fingers slipping out of her, and I place one knee on the mattress, my hand splaying her thighs open, giving room for my hips.

She wraps her arms around my chest as I kiss her right below her navel and travel north, across her stomach, up through the valley of her tits, to the hollow of her neck. She rocks her head back, giving me the access I want, and I lick up her throat and over her jaw, opening her wider with my knees and falling between her legs.

The tip of my dick pushes against her opening, and her back bows off the mattress. "Please, Rowan."

My heart is racing, my balls heavy while I try to act cool, as if I don't want to take her to the hilt like a fucking animal. I slide into her an inch or two at a time, and once I'm fully seated, we both groan, the satisfaction of finally getting what we've been teasing one another with the entire night.

She's tight and wet and hot—basically perfect. Her short nails rake up and down my back as I give her body a moment to adjust.

I withdraw and sink back into her. She moans, and my mouth falls to her collarbone, her neck, and her ear. Her scent, the sound of heavy breathing, the warmth of her thighs around my waist—all of it spurs a desire inside me that I've never felt before.

Usually by this time, I'm just trying to get the woman off so I can come right after her, but with Leigh, I find myself wanting to draw it out. I want her to leave this room never the same, but I don't have time to delve into that foreign feeling because I don't want to miss a second of having her under me and feeling her soft skin pressed along my hard muscles.

I rise up on my hands, pushing and pulling my hips in and out. With every thrust, she meets me with the same intensity. Leigh pushes at my shoulders, and I willingly flip over, never turning down a woman who wants to ride me.

Expertly, she straddles me, guiding me into her, and places her hands on my chest. Her tits jiggle while she circles her hips in a rhythm that drives me crazy. I want to take control, but I want to commit to memory the vision of her with her head rocked back, her eyes closed. I use the opportunity to watch her take what she wants from me without apology. It's sexy as fuck.

I grow harder inside her, my hands falling to her hips, helping get me as deep as possible.

Her eyes pop open, and she locks her gaze with mine as I drill my cock up into her. A drop of sweat slips down between her tits, toward her stomach. I follow the path, admiring her toned body. Her fingers clench over my chest, scratching me, and her mouth parts, a strangled cry slipping out from deep in her throat. Jesus, this woman is amazing.

I slide my hand between her legs, circling my thumb over her clit. Her back arches, and she gasps.

"That's it. Take what you need." My voice is rough like the waters of a stormy ocean.

I watch her reach the threshold, then tumble over into a state of sheer bliss. Her body stiffens, her eyes flutter, and her pink lips part slightly. She's fucking beautiful when she comes.

I slow my thumb and stop thrusting until the last wave of her orgasm slips away from her. Then I flip her over again and take the control I wanted.

I pummel in and out of her, sweat slick between our bodies, my balls drawing up in anticipation of my release. Her fingers thread through sweaty hair as I bury my head in her neck, breathing her in. My need hits a level I can no longer control, and I spill into the condom on a groan then collapse onto her, bringing my lips to hers. Our kiss is somehow languid and earth-shattering at the same time.

After I grow soft inside her, I roll onto my back, both of us still catching our breaths. I excuse myself to go to the bathroom, remove the condom, and start the shower.

Letting the water heat up, I go back out to the bedroom to find Leigh lying on her back, staring at the ceiling. "You okay?"

She circles her head toward me, her caramel eyes meeting mine. With a small nod, she slides up the bed, still naked, not attempting to cover herself, and smiles. "How could I not be?"

I like to think I'm a perceptive guy. Sure, I've been burned by first impressions like most people, but it feels as if maybe she's hiding something. But I'm not going to pry because I'm not sure I'll even see her after tonight. And tonight isn't about having a heart-to-heart. We're up here to get one another off, enjoy one another's bodies, have a good time, and move on.

So, I'm not going to ask her if she's okay. Instead I ask, "Shower?"

She slides her long, tan, toned legs over the edge of the mattress and walks over to me without an ounce of shyness. I wonder if she knows what a turn-on her confidence is. "I get to shampoo you first."

She slips into the bathroom as my eyes follow her, watching her ass, already planning on taking her from behind next time. I'm not sure one night with her will be enough.

six

Rowan

I WAKE UP TO AN EMPTY BED AND AN EMPTY BOX OF condoms.

A small stream of light filters through the break of the curtains into the quiet room. I sit up in bed, the sheet resting over my legs and lap. The shower isn't going, and all her clothing that was discarded haphazardly last night is gone.

She's gone.

I don't have to look at the hotel notepad to know there's no number with a note that says, "call me."

We both knew the deal. This was a one-night thing, but I can't deny that I enjoyed spending last night with her more than I anticipated. Usually I'd welcome a woman being gone without any complications, so I'm not sure what this melancholy feeling is.

I get out of bed, head into the bathroom, and turn on the shower, but the minute I do, a memory from last night is triggered—Leigh pushing me against the wall, one of her legs over my shoulder as I got her off with my mouth. Fuck, she was so responsive.

Once the water warms, I step under the stream and close my eyes, washing the memory of her off me, along with our mixed scent from hours and hours of sex. At this point, I'm not sure if I should find some other woman to erase Leigh from my mind or seek Leigh out, which feels impossible anyway. We live in a city of almost three million people.

I could ask Mila for her contact information, but she and Jack are leaving for their honeymoon this morning. Mila convinced him to take a two-week trip to Fiji, but we all know his laptop will be nearby the entire time.

It doesn't matter anyway. Leigh and I had an agreement before coming up to the room. Neither one of us was looking for anything more than last night.

I finish showering and get dressed, dropping a tip for the maid on the dresser. I take a moment to stare out the window at Chicago, pushing away all my anxiety about what I need to prove to the Falcons' fans this season. Coming into a team and being the new guy who replaces their favorite player is hard in any city. Most fans know Jennings was losing his stamina and had little time left in the league. We played together here at the end of last season, but as of this season, it's me the fans and the organization will look to as their star player. The pressure to make sure I keep them on my side is like a slow drip poison inside me that I can't find the cure for.

Grabbing my shit, I walk out of my room, looking back as if I'm afraid that once I step out, the memory of her won't linger in my head any longer.

What the hell am I doing? It was a one-night stand. Get a fucking grip, Landry.

The door clicks shut, and I walk down the hallway toward the elevators. Another flicker of memory accosts me when the doors open. I need to get the hell out of this hotel, then she'll be gone from my mind.

I stand in the corner, shutting down all thoughts of her swollen lips after I kissed her right against the glass wall to my right.

What seems like a lifetime later, the doors slide open. After mumbling a good morning to the reception staff, I step out of the lobby. The doorman opens the door for me and flags down a taxi.

The taxi pulls away from the curb, and I stare at the outside of the hotel, certain that last night with Leigh was the best sex I've ever had. From the moment I saw her across the room, I was drawn to her. Yeah, that's all it is. Leigh was the best sex I've had, and our chemistry was insane. That's the only reason she's still holding my thoughts hostage.

Twenty minutes later, because of traffic, the taxi pulls up in front of my building. I toss the driver some bills and step onto the sidewalk.

Another damn sign that says The Nest is taped to our black iron security gate. Our building used to house three football players from the Chicago Grizzlies, which got it coined as The Den. So when Tweetie, Henry, and I moved in, it was coined The Nest. Women write their numbers or leave notes—stuck up with chewed bubble gum—about how much they love us, how they want to hold our sticks and be our lucky charms.

I walk right by the pieces of paper flapping in the warm breeze and open the gate, then make sure it's closed and secure behind me. Tweetie, one of our left wings, has the top floor unit, while I'm on the second. One of our right wings, Henry, is the level above the ground floor bar with his son, Bodhi.

I climb the stairs, and when I'm about to open up my door, I hear Tweetie's door open above. He barrels down the stairs with energy I find surprising given that he's the old man in the league. I'm always surprised by how fast he recovers from his parties.

"Magic! You missed one helluva get-together last night. More than one girl was asking for you." He smacks my shoulder.

"I had my friend's wedding."

He eyes my bag and pushes his chin-length blond hair behind his ear. "And you spent the night?"

"Yeah." I don't give him any more information than he needs, but his eyes bore into mine as if he's looking for more. "What?"

"You hook up with a bridesmaid who's always a bridesmaid and never a bride? Those are always the best. Desperate to please."

I shake my head but can't help laughing.

"You did."

I punch the code into the keypad and step into my apartment.

"Come on, we're going to breakfast." He picks up my bag and tosses it into my condo.

"Tweetie!"

"Bodhi wants us to go to that pancake place again." He nods toward the stairs.

"I'm exhausted," I say, not in the mood to join the Sunday brunch rush.

"You need to replenish those calories." He remains outside my door. He's wearing joggers and a Chicago Colts shirt that he bought since the top of our building is fitted with a rooftop bar and stadium seats that overlook the Colts' baseball diamond.

My stomach growls, and he gives me his classic look that says get your ass moving, we're going. I might as well just go with them—it'll help me get Leigh out of my head anyway— so I throw on my baseball cap and lock up my condo.

"By the way, those notes are getting worse, and every time I tear down the sign for The Nest, someone puts one back up. Bodhi lives here, and he doesn't need to see that shit." I'm hoping Tweetie will eventually see that for Henry's sake, we need to make our building a better place for Bodhi to grow up. The kid is only six years old.

"Season starts soon, and it'll cool down." I side-eye him and he chuckles one of his full belly laughs, then raises both hands. "I can't control the women."

He's right, but the parties aren't helping. I give him a look.

"Okay, I'll cool it with the parties. I gotta detox for the next few weeks if I don't want to suck at training camp anyway."

Tweetie doesn't have to worry. Sure, he's one of the older guys on the team, but he made his reputation a long time ago as one of the best left wingers in the league. Everyone loves him. He's one of those balls-to-the-wall players who always gives one hundred percent. I just had no idea the guy could party like he does. He's like Peter Pan and doesn't want to grow up.

We reach the second level as Henry is opening his door, Bodhi coming out with his small football.

"Hey, Bodhi," I say, holding out my hands for him to throw me the football.

He throws it to me, and I examine the small Grizzlies ball with all three of the players' signatures who used to live here. "Man, Damon Siska, Miles Cavanaugh, *and* Cooper Rice? Pretty awesome, bud." I toss it back to him.

"Cooper's way of keeping us happy since he's been getting complaints." Henry eyes Tweetie. "Trying to keep the good tenants, I think."

Tweetie laughs, and I walk down the stairs with Bodhi.

I'm not sure how Henry does it. This is my first year

playing with him, but what happens to Bodhi when we travel? I guess I'll find out soon enough.

"You're both giving me hell about having fun. I just told Magic I'll slow down, okay?"

I open the gate to the sidewalk, and Bodhi walks through it.

"Some woman knocked on our door last night," Henry tells me, and I glance over my shoulder.

Henry shoves Tweetie and gives him a look that says, straighten out, asshole.

"Sorry about that, Bodhi," Tweetie says. "We're just four bachelors living in a building from now on."

I look at Bodhi, and he raises his eyebrows as if he doesn't believe him. I'm not sure I do either.

"Maybe I should've shacked up with some other players," Tweetie says as we stop at the light.

"There's still time," I say, and he tries to put me in a head-lock, my hat falling to the ground.

"Walk sign." Henry grabs Bodhi's hand, and they cross the road.

"Thanks, Daddy, I have eyes," Tweetie says, using Henry's nickname.

It's not really original, but the description fits. I'm not sure about all of Henry's story and why he decided to adopt, but I haven't asked since he's never offered the information. But even without Bodhi, I think that Henry would be the father figure on the team. I mean, he adopted a kid as a single professional hockey player. Who does that?

Henry flips Tweetie off behind his back, and Tweetie laughs. The man takes nothing seriously.

"So, who's the woman?" Tweetie asks me when Bodhi and Henry end up a few people in front of us.

Henry always makes it clear that we don't talk about the

women we bed in front of Bodhi. This is common sense, but then again, Tweetie can forgo common sense sometimes.

I'm not a kiss-and-tell asswipe, so I give him limited information. "She was a guest at the wedding."

"Duh. And?"

"And nothing. I hooked up with her." I shrug.

"So, it was a one-and-done."

I nod, turning the corner toward the breakfast place. I could probably ask Tweetie. From what I know, he's never had a serious girlfriend. "Hey, what are your thoughts about marriage?"

He laughs, causing people to look at us, and I lower the brim of my hat. I am not in the mood to be recognized today, although it will probably happen since I'm with two other players.

"I don't have any thoughts about marriage because I never think of it."

"Have you ever been in a serious relationship?" I ask.

He doesn't answer immediately, and I notice that he's trying not to step on any cracks as we walk the sidewalk. "Uh... once."

The tone of his voice makes me think I shouldn't pry, so we walk for a few minutes in silence, something I didn't think Tweetie was capable of.

"What? You think this woman from last night is the one?" he asks when he breaks the silence.

"Hell no." I don't. "But I wouldn't mind a repeat."

He knocks his shoulder with mine, and I almost run into an elderly woman holding a bag of groceries.

"It won't be as good the second time," he says. "I've been there. Just move on."

"We didn't exchange info, so I couldn't find her anyway. At least not until the bride returns from her honeymoon in a couple of weeks."

"Well, think of it this way. If she wants to, she can find you."

Fuck, he's right. I didn't even think about that. Maybe there's a chance after all.

We catch up to Henry and Bodhi right outside the breakfast place, and they hold the door for us. It's so crowded in the small waiting area, I pick up Bodhi and hold him at my side while Henry talks to the hostess and name-drops me like an asshole to get us seated faster.

I shake my head, pretending I'm not really with them, but the hostess glances in my direction. Then a few of the people waiting turn to stare at all of us. If you follow the Falcons, you know who we are.

"Can we go look at the guy making the pancakes?" Bodhi asks.

"Sure."

I weave through a few tables to get over to the window where you can watch the cooks making the pancakes, but when I'm almost there, a waitress zips in front of us to drop off an order at a table. My gaze stops on the woman sitting in the booth. She's not in a dress and heels anymore, and she's not wearing any makeup, her hair thrown in a messy bun. But it's Leigh, I know it is.

Is this some weird sign from the universe?

seven

Kyleigh

AFTER I LEFT THE HOTEL ROOM EARLY THIS morning, I went back to my apartment, showered, and changed.

Alara called to tell me that we were going for breakfast because she wanted all the details from the night before. Of course, we headed to our favorite pancake house that we haven't been to in a while.

"So?"

I hold up the menu so she can't see the blush I'm certain is pinkening my face. Last night with Rowan was something I've never experienced before. The man is talented with everything from his fingers to his mouth to how he uses his dick. He aims to please, that's for sure. I choose not to think of where he learned all his moves because it probably came from a long line of women before me. By the time we ran out of condoms, he told me to ride his face, and I'd never come so hard in my life.

"There wasn't a lot of conversation," I say from behind

the menu. I'm acting as if I'm not going to get the pancakes and strawberries like always.

"That's the best kind of night." Her perfectly manicured nail lands on top of the menu, and she brings it down. "You're holding out on me."

I shrug. "What do you want to know? His dick size?"

She moves her head side to side. "Yeah, because he's Rowan Landry. Is he as gifted in that department as he is on the rink? But at the same time, no, because if you two ever got serious, that would be weird."

I scoff at her. "We're not going to get serious."

She stares at me for a long time, sipping her orange juice through her straw. I shift in my seat. This is Alara's way of getting things out of me.

"We didn't exchange numbers or anything. Plus..."

Her mouth hangs open. "What did you do?"

I hate that she knows me so well. "I might have given him another name."

"What?"

The people at the table beside us turn immediately from Alara's loud mouth.

I lean in a bit over the table. "He played with Conor back in college. I didn't want to give him my real name."

"So, what name are you going by now?" she asks with a grin.

I set my menu down and grab a creamer for my coffee. "Leigh."

"Leigh?"

"Yes. Leigh." I nod, assured that it doesn't matter.

"But your name is Ky*leigh*," she says as if I don't already know that.

"Yes." I stir my coffee. "But no one calls me Leigh."

"But..." She waves off the topic. "Okay, whatever, so you're Leigh to him. You had fun though?"

"Of course."

"I think it's more than that."

I sip my coffee and stare at her over the rim of my mug, swallowing the hot liquid. "Listen, just because you're happy with Justin doesn't mean it's for everyone."

She leans back in the booth, her eyes never leaving mine. Alara is in school to be a psychologist, and I hate when she uses the shit she's learning in school on me. "I'm sorry, when did you become so anti-relationship?"

I haven't told Alara about what happened with my mom.

I haven't told anyone.

I was going to call Conor today, but why should I blow up his entire belief in a happily ever after, even though the man is still enjoying his bachelor ways?

"You're hiding something," she says.

"You're a pain in my ass."

"Actually, I'm your best friend. The one you're supposed to share everything with."

"You said you didn't want to know his dick size," I say, trying to use humor to deflect.

"Stop being cheeky. Now tell me."

The waitress comes over and takes our orders, but it doesn't distract Alara from her mission. Once the waitress walks away, she's leaning back in the booth, waiting for me to start talking.

"Last night before the wedding, I saw my mom with another man."

There. It's out in the universe. It's no longer my secret, and I can no longer convince myself that I was seeing things. That it wasn't real.

"What?" Her mouth drops open, and her eyes widen in disbelief.

Her parents are divorced, and it was nasty before she turned eighteen. The reason she wanted to become a therapist was to help kids through divorce because of the tug-of-war she felt as a kid.

Tears prick my eyes as I tell her what I saw. "On my way to the wedding, I stopped at the boutique and had to go upstairs because I forgot the card my mom had given me for Mila and Jack. As soon as I walked in, I saw my mom's office light on, so I thought I'd joke with her about why I was attending in her place because she said she was busy and how she needed to start declining the invitations. But..."

Alara takes my hand, and I nod, swallowing the lump in my throat.

"She was sitting on her desk, and there was a man standing between her legs, kissing her. He was pulling her blouse out of her skirt."

"And it wasn't your dad? You're sure?"

I shake my head.

She squeezes my hand. "That sucks so bad, Ky. I say we confront her."

I laugh, but it's weak at best. "Alara."

"I'm serious. If my childhood taught me anything, it's that you need to go to your mom and tell her what you saw. I'm assuming you grabbed the envelope from your office and snuck out the back?"

I nod.

"I would've run in there and tore the bastard off my mom."

I shake my head, but I can't help but laugh at the image she's putting in my head.

"You can't just ignore it, Ky." Her eyes are full of sympathy and understanding.

Alara knows how close I am with my mother, even if she drives me crazy sometimes. We work side by side, and it's devastating to find out she's not the person I thought I knew. I feel so betrayed. I can only imagine how my dad will feel when he finds out.

"I know, but I'm not sure I'm ready. I mean, how could she, of all people, do this? She's used our family, her 'perfect' marriage"—I put the word perfect in air quotes—"to sell her bridal designs and brand the business. Do you know how many photoshoots we've done as a family to benefit the business? Ones where she and my dad look so in love? Her perfect Nilsen family. I didn't know I was helping to perpetrate a lie. What a joke."

She doesn't say anything but blows out a breath.

She knows, as well as I do, how much my mom has marketed us as one big happy family. It's an essential part of the brand at this point. Brides think it's good luck to have their dress designed and made by us because of it. And now I find out that none of it's true.

"I'm really sorry."

I nod. "Anyway, last night was a great distraction to keep me from thinking about all of that."

"But you'll have to—"

"I know, but I'm not ready. I need a day or two to process it."

"But don't just bury it, Ky. That's not healthy."

I divert my eyes to get away from this conversation. Alara is always who I tell big news to, but now that I'm saying it out loud, I'm not sure I was ready to believe and accept it myself.

That's when I see *him*.

"Oh my god." I move to pick up the menu but remember it's no longer on the corner of the table because the waitress took it after we ordered. I scan the table, pick up a napkin, and put it over the bottom part of my face.

"Um..." Alara looks over her shoulder and turns back around, laughing hysterically, drawing attention to us. "You're not being inconspicuous, you know. If anything, you're making yourself more obvious."

"I left his hotel room early this morning in order to dodge the awkward morning thing." I slide to the far end of the booth, hoping to stay hidden.

"And did the walk of shame through the lobby."

I drop the napkin and throw a creamer at her. "What am I going to do?" She turns around again, and I throw another creamer at her. "Stop looking!"

"Who's the little boy? He's cute. I didn't know Rowan Landry was a single daddy." She raises her eyebrows up and down several times.

"He's not. Henry Hensley is."

She rolls her eyes at me. "You really need to stay off the hockey blogs."

"I didn't learn that from the hockey blogs. You know I love the sport. I grew up with it, so how can I not know so much about it?"

"Want to sneak out the back?" she asks.

As I'm about to say yes and leave some money on the table, Rowan walks my way. "Damn it."

I'm guessing he's taking the boy to the glass wall where all the kids want to watch the chef flip the pancakes. He usually makes a show of his art, making pancakes into shapes and figures.

"He's coming this way, isn't he?" Alara's amused smile makes me almost pick up another creamer, but I refrain, too scared to move in case I draw his attention to our booth.

"Here you go, ladies." Our waitress cuts him off in the aisleway, and he has to stop with the boy in his arms who's still eyeing the window. "Pancakes and strawberries." She slides me my plate. "And the waffle flight." She puts Alara's dish in front of her. "Enjoy. I'll be back to check on you."

The damage is done because Rowan is staring at me. The

slow grin that grows on his face brings to mind all the times he made me come last night. I had an amazing night with him, and my body reacts as if I didn't get enough.

"Leigh," he says as if he's been waiting to run into me for a year instead of mere hours.

"Hey." I lift my hand.

He steps up to the edge of our table. The boy doesn't give us any of his attention, staring over Rowan's shoulder at the pancake man. Our eyes lock for a moment, neither of us saying anything or acknowledging the awkward coincidence.

"Hi, I'm Alara. Saw you last night but never properly introduced myself." She puts out her hand, which tears his focus off me. I want to kick her under the table like a toddler, but at the same time, I'm thankful.

"Rowan." He shakes her hand.

"Landry. The Falcons' new center," the boy in his arms says. "I'm Bodhi Hensley. My dad is Henry Hensley. Right wing."

Alara laughs and shifts her hand to him. "Nice to meet you, Bodhi. I'm Alara, and this is..."

"Leigh." I wave, and Alara giggles.

Rowan's gaze seeks mine out again, and god, the man is even more gorgeous in the daylight. Even in a T-shirt and joggers, the definition of his body is obvious.

"Who are your friends?" A guy I know is Tweetie comes by holding his arms out for Bodhi, and he goes willingly.

"Take me to the pancake man, please," Bohdi says.

"In a second, bud. Rowan needs to answer my question." Tweetie Sorenson is standing next to Rowan Landry. I could pinch myself.

"This is Leigh and Alara." Rowan points at me then Alara.

"Hey, ladies, I'm Tweetie." He grins at us, then looks back at Rowan. "I meant who are they to you?" His smirk says he's purposely being a shithead to Rowan. He looks between Rowan and me, waiting patiently.

"Leigh is a friend."

Alara coughs and pretends she's choking and needs a drink of her orange juice. Tweetie clocks her response and seems to put the pieces together.

"Leigh, I'm curious, were you at a wedding last night?"

"She sure was," Alara answers for me.

"Ah...you're the reason for my buddy's smile this morning."

"Go show Bodhi the pancake man," Rowan says, obviously unamused.

"That guy isn't giving me half the show this here is." Tweetie stands firm, but he's so tall, Bodhi can still see the man making the pancakes.

"What's going on over here?" Henry Hensley comes over.

"I suddenly feel like the it girl in high school." Alara sips her orange juice again, her eyes pinging between each pro hockey player circling around our booth.

"We're going to need a table for six," Tweetie says to Henry.

"Oh no, we have our meals already. You guys enjoy your breakfast." I wave off his suggestion, but Henry's already walking over to the hostess stand.

"Let me show you what it's like the morning after you sleep with a Falcon. Rowan here is at least going to buy you breakfast." He winks and puts his hand around Rowan's neck and squeezes.

"I'm game," Alara says with a bright smile.

I whip my head in her direction, forehead wrinkled. "What? No."

"You did leave before I could buy you a meal."

I look over, and Rowan hasn't stripped his gaze off me,

raising those eyebrows just as he did at the bar, challenging me to say no.

He knows as well as I do that last night was exceptional. But I'm not sure we could ever recreate it. A night like that is meant to be forever instilled in the memories one takes with them through life.

"I'm sure your body is just as spent as mine and Rowan's. Coach always says you need to replenish those calories you burned." Tweetie gives me a smile I don't trust because it looks like trouble. Mostly the fun kind.

How did I get swindled into a breakfast with Rowan Landry and his teammates, thus ensuring I'm going to have to do a second walk of shame this morning?

eight

Kyleigh

HENRY WORKS SOME SORT OF MAGIC, AND WE'RE SAT at a table in the back corner. Rowan's carrying my plate over, and Henry is carrying Alara's.

"Just so you know, I'm taken," Alara says when we sit down.

I stare at her with a what the fuck expression.

She shrugs. "Justin would want me to tell them."

"He'd also want you to get autographs." The first time I met Justin, we talked about Rowan's trade and what it meant for the Falcons going forward.

"Understood," Henry says, picking up his menu and not giving Alara a second look.

"Not that you're not hot and shit, but I can tell you're definitely a serious relationship kind of girl." Tweetie gulps down his water in three swallows.

"How can you tell that just by looking at me?" Alara challenges him as she does with most things.

"I was disappointed when I woke up this morning," Rowan says, leaning close.

The first thing I notice is he's not wearing cologne. I loved it on him last night, but the scent of his masculine soap is even better.

"We ran out of condoms," I whisper back.

Alara eyes me over her waffle flight.

"What's that?" Bodhi asks Alara, almost sticking his finger in her whipped cream.

"Be careful, bud," Henry says, tugging him back into his seat.

"It's called a waffle flight. Each waffle has something different. This one has strawberries. This one has bananas..." She points and names the other two. She's so good with kids, but I guess that's what happens when you're training to become a child psychologist.

"Oh, I want one of those." Bodhi looks at his dad, and Henry opens his mouth.

I'm trying to focus on the table conversation rather than the way Rowan's bicep keeps brushing against mine.

"There are drug stores on every corner," he says.

Alara, Henry, and Bodhi are in a conversation about the waffle flight, and thankfully Tweetie, who was eyeing Rowan and me pretty hard, gets up to take a call, his phone held to his ear.

"Let's not call last night more than it was," I say in a low voice, then fork my pancake, feeling uncomfortable eating before they've even ordered, but happy for the excuse to not have to give my full attention to Rowan.

Alara passes Bodhi her untouched waffle flight, so now it's just the kid and me eating. This is the weirdest breakfast.

"I want to see you again." Rowan picks up my plate and sets it on the edge of the table.

"What are you doing?" I reach for the plate, but if I go too far, I'll end up stretched out over his lap.

"They're cold now. You deserve hot ones where the butter melts and soaks into the fluffy goodness. This way I can keep you here a little longer."

I sigh and hold up my coffee mug to the waitress walking by, needing something to distract me. She pours my coffee and fills Henry's cup. He asks her to pour Tweetie one too. Rowan asks for a chocolate milk.

"You drink chocolate milk?" Alara asks, not disguising how funny she thinks that is.

"I want a chocolate milk, Daddy." Bodhi looks up at Henry.

Henry looks to Rowan with a thanks-a-lot expression.

"What? It's full of calcium." Rowan shrugs.

Henry nods to the waitress, who pretends she doesn't know who they are and disappears.

"You're killing me. Be an adult and drink coffee." Henry brings his mug to his lips.

"Sorry." Rowan sips from his water glass.

Like some creeper, I so want to watch Rowan's Adam's apple bob. As soon as that thought hits me, I know that I need away from his masculine energy. It's doing a number on me.

"Did you hear me?" Rowan asks me.

"Yeah, you're opting for a kid's drink rather than an adult beverage. Why?"

"You know what I'm talking about." He turns in his chair, his arm slung over the back of mine, and memories of last night rush through my head. "I want to see you again."

"Oh yeah, um..." I try to turn away to ask Bodhi how old he is and if he likes cars or dinosaurs, anything really.

"Leigh." That snippet of my name warms my body, even if I wish it didn't. "You can at least look me in the eye if you're going to turn me down."

I swivel in my seat, and holy shit, he's really close to me. My knee bumps his muscled thigh. "Why?"

"Because at the risk of sounding cliché, last night was too good to not have a repeat."

I open my mouth and close it, my teeth nibbling on my bottom lip. "I'm not sure we can recreate that."

"So it was good for you too?"

I should've known this is what would happen with an athlete of his caliber. They're used to getting what they want and don't back down from defeat easily. Then again, I haven't outright said no. And there's a reason for that, I suppose. "Is that even a question?"

"I figured you enjoyed yourself, but you dodging seeing me again makes me think I need another shot to really prove myself."

The waitress comes over with Rowan's and Bodhi's chocolate milk, then Tweetie returns to the table, and we all order, including Alara and me. Once the waitress walks away, Alara grabs Tweetie's attention, asking him about the upcoming season. I know it's for my benefit—she usually reads a book while I scream at the television.

He goes on and on about how it's going to work so well with Magic at center and Daddy at his right. How their line is set up for success.

Rowan's fingers run along the back of my neck, and I suppress a shiver and turn back to him.

"Sorry," he mumbles.

"It's okay."

He removes his hand from my neck and places it on my thigh. "This okay too?"

His fingers wrap around my thigh, his thumb running circles. That thumb might as well be on my clit for the effect it's having on me.

I turn and shield my mouth with my hand next to my cheek. "I'm not sure I know what we're doing?"

"Yeah, you do."

His blue eyes sparkle, and my heartbeat picks up pace. He's right, I do know what's going on. I could lie and say I don't want another night with him—God, or even two—but he'd see right through it.

"So what? You want to just go to the bathroom and bend me over the sink?"

"I was thinking the alley, get your back scratched up from the brick."

A current of warmth rushes through my body.

"Okay, we've given you two enough time to talk out why she left your limp dick this morning. Time to join the table conversation." Tweetie snaps his fingers between our faces.

Rowan practically growls and picks up his chocolate milk.

"So, Leigh, tell me why you look so familiar." Tweetie places his crossed arms on the table and leans in closer to me.

"Um..."

Shit, I rack my brain to try to remember if Conor ever played with Tweetie. Conor's with the Florida Fury now, and Tweetie played for the Fury, too, but Tweetie was already in Nashville before Conor got there. There's no way our paths should've ever crossed.

"She has that look. You know, where everyone thinks they know her." Alara pulls his attention off me.

"No, she doesn't," Rowan says. "There's nothing ordinary about her."

My stomach does a swoosh as if I'm on a rollercoaster.

Tweetie scrunches his eyebrows at Rowan. "Okay, man, you need to tone down the stalker vibes."

"I think it was sweet," Alara says, smiling at Rowan. "It's okay to like my girl. She's awesome. But you have to share her."

"Oh, Magic doesn't share. I do, however." Tweetie winks at me.

"Yeah, not my thing." I'm not sure what to make of this guy.

Rowan's fingers wrap tighter around my leg and slide up closer to the apex of my thighs. I straighten my back and force myself to take a deep breath. I'll never make it through breakfast at this point.

"Can we remember innocent ears over here?" Henry chimes in, and we all look at Bodhi, who is busy piling waffles into his mouth.

Tweetie turns his attention back to us. "So, Leigh, what do you do besides my boy here?"

"Funny." I give him a half-assed smile.

"Inappropriate," Henry says, looking up from his phone.

"I'm in school to become a child psychologist." Alara raises her hand as though she was asked the question, and I can't thank her enough for taking the spotlight off me.

"That's great." Henry pockets his phone and starts a conversation with her about why she decided to get into that line of work.

Which leaves me with Tweetie and Rowan. I drill a hole into the pancake man's peripheral. I want my pancakes now.

"You a Falcons fan at least?" Tweetie asks.

"I am."

"You from Chicago?"

"I am." He doesn't need to know anything else about me.

"Who's your second favorite player since Rowan is probably your first now?"

"Why don't we cool it with the inquisition?" Rowan says before finishing his chocolate milk.

"Hey, I'm trying to get to know the girl better, okay?" Tweetie brings his coffee mug to his lips. "You should be happy I care so much. Her bff isn't vetting you." He glares at Alara, but she's too busy talking to Henry to hear him.

"Last I checked, we're not dating," I say.

"Yet," Tweetie says.

"Excuse me?"

"Yet. I see it. My boy really likes you. You must have one magic pussy."

"Sorenson," Rowan clips out his last name.

Tweetie laughs. "Jokes. They're just jokes. But seriously, I feel like it's oddly coincidental we all end up at the same breakfast place after she left your sorry ass in bed this morning, no?"

I can't really deny his point, so I say nothing. Rowan doesn't either.

Our food comes out, and I'm happy for the distraction of pancakes. Rowan ordered an omelet with hash browns and a side of pancakes. He pulls the pancakes in front of him first, grabbing packets of butter, and puts a pat under each pancake.

Tweetie is busy with his head down in his meat lover's breakfast. He's got bacon, Canadian bacon, and sausage in some skillet concoction.

"You're really serious about your pancakes, huh?" I ask.

Rowan's gaze lifts to mine. "Give me yours." He pushes his plate aside and pulls mine in front of him, doing the same with the butter. "This is the most important part—the bottom pancake gets two butters."

"You're adding a lot of calories to my breakfast."

He doesn't respond, continuing to add the butter, then he lifts each pancake and puts syrup on each one. Not a ton where it soaks them, but just enough that there won't be one bite without the right amount of syrup.

"Here you go." He slides the plate in front of me.

"He's letting you see his neurotic pancake perfection. That's, like, fourth date shit, man." Tweetie eyes my plate of pancakes.

I cut into them, forking off a piece. I feel Rowan's eyes on me, and I turn to him as the sweet goodness explodes in my mouth. Hell, he's onto something.

He nods at my plate. "You'll never go back, right?"

I nod and continue to eat with everyone.

After we finish, Rowan asks for the check and goes up to pay at the counter. He returns with a bouquet of Dum Dums and holds it out to me. Tweetie tries to reach in, but Rowan smacks his hand.

"I always get first choice," Bodhi whines.

"Not now, kid, Rowan is smitten." Tweetie thumbs in Rowan's direction. "Let him try to impress her."

"I like the root beer ones," Bodhi says.

Rowan reaches into his pocket and pulls out two, handing them to Tweetie to give to Bodhi.

"Thanks!"

"Two?" Henry shakes his head.

I examine the bouquet of candy and pull out the blue raspberry one. He passes the rest around and pulls another out of his other pocket. It's a blue raspberry one.

"Another coincidence," he says, tapping his Dum Dum to mine before taking the wrapper off and putting it in his mouth.

I've never wanted to be a lollipop more in my life.

We finally all get up so another group can have our table. A few patrons stop the guys to shake hands and wish them luck this season. Henry, Tweetie, and Rowan are all polite, and once we're on the sidewalk, I figure we'll be saying our goodbyes. I'm surprised by the disappointment in my chest.

Rowan takes my hand, pulling me away from the group. "What are you doing for the rest of the day?"

"Um..."

"Come home with me," he says, and I sigh. It's so tempting. "I have a full box of condoms," he smirks, and my core clenches involuntarily.

"I gotta go!" Alara waves to me. "Call me later."

"We're heading home," Tweetie calls, and the three of them walk away.

I watch all their backs walking down the street.

"Rowan, I'm not looking for—"

He presses a finger to my lips. "Me either." He steps closer. "Just...I want more...that's all."

And I'm sure that is all he wants. Why would I even think he'd want a relationship?

"Okay," I say, and he raises his hand for a taxi. "We can walk."

He opens the taxi door, waiting for me to climb in. "No, we can't."

He gets in next to me, his hand on my thigh again, and gives the taxi driver the address, shutting the door behind him.

As much as I want to go to his place, my gut says this could be a really bad idea. Because I'm not really a Friday night girl. I *do* like relationships. Well, up until my mom decided to ruin hers.

nine

Rowan

THE TAXI TAKES ALMOST AS LONG AS IF WE'D walked—because of lights and Sunday tourist traffic—but I didn't want to risk Tweetie walking with us and saying something that would have Leigh turning around and walking the other way. He always means well, but sometimes he needs to know when to shut the hell up.

The driver pulls up along the curb right across from my place at the address I usually give so they won't know exactly where I live, although it's fairly well known at this point. At least by the true puck bunnies.

He pulls away, and I spot Tweetie, Henry, and Bodhi ahead on the street, stopped and waiting to cross at a light. They're busy watching the people pouring past on their way to see the Colts game. I'm sure all three of them will go upstairs to the rooftop and watch the game.

I slide my hand into Leigh's, weaving through the cars inching forward. Sure, we earn a few horn honks, but we Frogger our way through, and we reach the other side safely.

Once we're behind the iron gate that has black mesh winding through it so we're not visible, I press her back to the concrete wall, my lips crashing down on hers. I haven't felt this starved for a woman since...last night in the elevator.

She welcomes me, arms wrapping around my waist, tugging me closer. Her tongue dances with mine, and it isn't nearly enough to satisfy my need for this woman. It's even worse now that I know what's waiting for me once I get her undressed.

I yank my lips off hers and lower myself, picking her up fireman-style, and climb the stairs to my apartment.

"A girl could get used to this," she says, lightly smacking my ass.

I grab her tight ass in my palm. I don't know what's happening, but this woman has me by the balls, and she doesn't even know it.

I key in the code to my condo and open the door, walking to my kitchen. I lower her ass to my counter, place my hands on the sides of her face, and kiss her again. Her lips, her taste, they're so addicting.

"This is such a bad idea," she says when I sprinkle kisses along her jaw. "It was supposed to be a one-night stand."

"I can't find it in myself to care." My hands splay on her thighs, opening her legs for me to step in between.

She opens willingly, her hands tugging at the hem of my shirt, pulling it up my torso. I back away and help her. Her eyes zero in on my muscles, her fingers running down every ridge.

"Are you even for real?"

It's hard not to puff my chest out in pride when she says that. Instead, I take her hand and lower it over my groin. "Very real."

She palms me, running her hand over my hard dick. "No doubt about it."

I lean forward, loving her hand on me, and place my palms on either side of her hips on the counter. My lips find hers, and I inch forward, giving her more access to me. Our tongues tangle and explore one another in an easier rhythm than when we were downstairs.

I groan when she moves her hand off my dick, but she tucks her fingers under the waistband of my joggers and grips me. The skin-to-skin contact undoes any willpower I had at trying to play it cool.

I strip my lips off hers and grab her T-shirt, pulling it up over her head. She releases my dick for a second to shed the barrier between us but returns it right away.

"I'm gonna combust if I don't get inside you." I grab her by the ass and carry her against my chest into the bedroom.

Her teeth lightly scrape along my shoulder, and when I drop her on the bed, she bounces on the mattress before climbing up onto her knees. She brings her hands to either side of my joggers and tugs them down to my ankles. Then she does the same with my boxer briefs. My dick springs free, and she looks up at me through long dark eyelashes.

I place my hand on her face, my thumb running along the length of her plump bottom lip. She's so beautiful, but she'll be even more so with my dick in her mouth.

She leans forward, her hand anchored to the base of my cock. Her eyes never leave mine as she swipes her tongue over the pre-cum on the tip.

"God, you're something," I say, my brain unable to find the right words.

She continues to stare up at me while she lets a slow drip of saliva slip out of her mouth and down onto my dick. The move is so fucking sexy, my dick twitches in her hand, and a slow, easy, satisfied smile tilts her lips. "I kind of like this control."

My fingers thread through her dark strands. "It's all yours. For now."

Her perfect white teeth nail down her bottom lip, and her chest rises and falls with a deep breath. "Promises, promises."

"I make good on my promises, you can bet on that."

"Another thing we have in common. I finish what I start."

She goes to work on my dick, and she takes her time. I watch her, my fists tightening as she takes my entire dick inch by inch down her throat, inducing a choking sound, and that hardens my cock even more. She glides me back out just as slow, and my head rocks back from the euphoria her warm, wet mouth brings me.

"Look at me," she says in a sultry voice, but shit, the demanding note in her tone kicks my ecstasy up another level.

I straighten my head and our eyes meet. She's running her saliva up and down my dick with her fist while her other hand plays with my balls. Leigh is a fucking rock star at getting me off.

"Shit, you're too good at this," I say, sliding my thumb into her mouth and wetting her bottom lip. Her lust-filled eyes undo something inside me. Maybe because it feels like she's enjoying this as much as I am.

"Maybe it's just beginner luck."

She doesn't wait for me to answer. Instead, she sucks me down firmer. The moans slipping from her throat as she works me over are sounds I'll play on repeat in my brain later.

Watching her back arch, I really wish I would've taken off her bra and leggings so I could indulge in the view of her naked body. Maybe smack her bare ass. Next time.

Shit, will there be a next time?

I push aside all thoughts of that and enjoy the feel of her mouth on me, the wetness, the warmth, the sucking sensation, and the way she plays with my balls. Just when I'm scrambling for something to think of to keep myself from coming, she swipes her finger behind my ball sac and presses there gently. I inhale a sharp breath.

"I'm gonna come." My fingers are back in her hair, tightening on her strands from the intense desperation to unleash my cum down her throat.

She doesn't stop, and when the first burst of my seed releases, she sucks the tip in her mouth, taking all of it. My shoulders fall, my muscles relax, and fucking hell, she swallows it all and cleans me up with her tongue. Once she's done, she sits back on her heels looking mighty satisfied with herself. As she should be.

"Get the rest of your clothes off," I practically growl. "Ass on the bed. Legs spread. Pussy out."

She sits down, and I love the fact she still takes off her leggings and panties. "You don't have to pay me back."

I step out of my joggers and boxer briefs, putting a knee on the bed. "Somehow I think you're just being polite."

She lies down, sliding her head up to my pillow. Seeing her on my bed makes my pulse quicken, but I'm not going to think about that right now, because her pretty pink pussy is right in front of my face.

I situate my shoulders between her thighs, running my finger along her clit. "Let's just hope I have the same beginner's luck."

She laughs, and I swipe the length of her with my tongue, causing her to sober up, rise up on her elbows, and watch me get her off. Which I do in record time, I may add.

Three hours later, I soften inside her, and she falls off me and onto her back, both of us catching our breaths.

I'm still figuring out a way to get her phone number when she slides off the bed and goes to the bathroom. "Be right back."

I take the time to remove my condom and tie it in a knot,

grabbing some Kleenex next to the bed and wrapping it inside before tossing it in my trash can.

Leigh comes out of the bathroom and picks up her underwear and leggings.

"You're leaving?"

"I'm sure you have things to do." She doesn't look at me when she answers.

Not really, but I shouldn't tell her that.

"The Colts are playing. We could go to the rooftop," I offer.

What the hell is wrong with me? Isn't this what every guy wants—a quick and easy out?

She looks at me from the corner of her eye, covering her delicious pussy with her pink underwear and her tits with a matching bra. "Maybe we should talk."

Then she disappears into the kitchen and returns with her T-shirt. She continues to get dressed, and I watch her cover up a body I can't get enough of. My dick is raring to go again, which seems crazy, but the chemistry between us is insane.

I put my arms behind my head, leaning against the headboard. "I think we should exchange numbers."

She sort of laughs, but there's a tension to it that I don't like.

"Is that a no?"

She turns to me at the end of the bed, pulling a ponytail holder out of her purse and securing her hair back. She unwound the elastic in her hair earlier at some point, and I have no idea where it is. Apparently she doesn't either. "You're Rowan Landry. You can go down to that street and have a line of women."

"I don't want a line of women."

She sighs. "We agreed to nothing more than sex."

"Did I change that by asking for your number?"

She looks away for a beat then returns my gaze. "What are your expectations if we exchange numbers?"

"I'm not sure, but I already know that you haven't walked out that door yet, and here I am, wanting more of you."

Her hand falls to her stomach, and her throat bobs when she swallows. "So, you'd use it to hook up only?"

I get out of bed, grab my joggers, and step into them. I don't miss the way she watches me the entire time. She feels the same. I just need to convince her that this is the perfect situation.

"Neither of us want anything serious, so it seems pretty easy to me—you wanna fuck around, text me. If I wanna fuck around, I'll text you."

"Easy as that, huh?"

I place my hand on her hip, drawing her closer. My lips go to her neck, kissing up to her ear. "This is new for me too, but I just know that I'm not done with you."

"Rowan," she says, but there's no fight in her tone, which keeps me going.

"Are you going to make me beg?" I whisper against her flesh.

"I should." Her arms wrap around my shoulders, her fingers fiddling in the back of my hair. "Strictly sex then. No fancy dinners. No date-like atmospheres."

I chuckle and suck her earlobe into my mouth. "Deal."

I draw back from her, and our eyes meet, both of us smiling.

"Now I need your phone."

She digs into her purse and hands it to me. We exchange numbers, then I walk her to the door.

"Text me if you're horny?" I say, unsure how to end this encounter.

She laughs. "Please never say that again."

I wrap my arm around her waist and pull her into me, my

lips meeting hers for one final kiss. I'm not ready for her to go, but pretty soon I'm going to look like a clinger.

I open my door for her and find Tweetie coming down the stairs from his apartment. He stops, stares, and laughs.

"Done already?" He lifts his wrist, but he doesn't wear a watch, so it's just for show. "Do I need to apologize for my boy?"

"Fuck off." I glare at him.

Tweetie holds out his arm. "I can escort you to the gate."

Like hell he will. "I've got her." I take her hand and step out of my doorway.

"No shoes? No shirt? You trying to get the puck bunnies all hot and bothered?" He laughs and jogs down the steps, lifting his arm when he walks out of the gate. "See you soon, Leigh. I'm sure of it."

I shake my head and walk Leigh to the gate. After she's secure in a taxi, I walk back up the stairs. It's going to take all my willpower not to text her in an hour.

ten

Kyleigh

I'M STILL STUNNED OVER THE FACT THAT I HAVE Rowan Landry's cell phone number in my phone, and I'm supposed to call him whenever I want to fuck him. It's a power trip, I swear. I want to text him this morning just to see how serious he is about this agreement.

Instead, I'm on my way to my mom's storefront with her coffee order. It's time that I confront her about what I saw, as much as I'm dreading it. Rowan was the perfect distraction this weekend, but I can't put it off any longer.

That's not to say that my stomach isn't a ball of nerves. I'm so full of anger and sadness and shock that I'm not sure how this is going to go.

My mom has her own bridal boutique in downtown Chicago. Although she's been approached by major companies to design for them, or to sell the brand to them and have her work as the creative director, she's stuck to the boutique wedding experience. She believes the dress makes the wedding and that every bride deserves to feel her most beautiful on her wedding day. She used to sew them all herself until business really took off, and now she employs some seamstresses to fulfill her vision.

It's been an amazing experience, working alongside her since college and watching her fit brides, talk about the design, and interpret exactly what they want, even if they don't know it themselves. I've seen so many brides cry just from looking at her sketches and fabric swatches before the dress is even made. I've looked up to Mom all these years and figured maybe I would take over one day, but now, I'm not so sure. Because it all feels like a lie, and I can't imagine that would ever change given what she's done.

Her usual eighties music is playing when I walk in the back door. I push back the dread of what I saw a couple days ago.

Instead of going into my office and dropping my purse off, I go right to her office. No one else comes in until ten, so I have enough time to talk to her in private.

She's wearing her usual loungewear, although it costs more than some of our clients' wedding dresses. Maybe not exactly, but close. She'll change into her pantsuit or a dress if a client is coming in. Sitting at her drawing board with her glasses on, she has one hand on a scrap of fabric, examining it.

I knock lightly to avoid startling her. "Mom."

She doesn't turn around. "Come and look at this, Ky. Is the lace too old-fashioned for this dress?"

I steel myself, drop the coffee holder on her desk, and walk over.

Her dark hair that matches my own is pulled into a low bun. I resist the urge to yank the holder out of her hair and tug her to the floor. How could she do this to our family?

"I need to talk to you."

She swivels in her chair and lowers her glasses, obviously

hearing the hitch in my voice I always have when I'm upset. "Okay, but what about the lace?"

"I don't give a shit about the lace."

Her head rears back. "Kyleigh." She tries to give me her mom tone that used to work on me.

"I came here on Saturday," I say. "I forgot the card for the wedding, and I came here."

I grab my iced coffee from the holder and slam my straw down to free it of the paper, then aggressively place it in the cup and suck down a big gulp. There's so much I want to say, but I'm here for answers.

"Okay, what does that have to do with the lace?"

I tilt my head at her and narrow my eyes. She slides off her stool and walks over to her desk, taking the coffee out of the holder.

"I'm waiting," I say.

"Was the wedding terrible? I don't understand why you're so..." She twirls her finger at me. "Like this."

My heart rate picks up, and I feel the blood whoosh through my neck. "I'm like this because of what happened before the wedding." I raise my eyebrows at her, but she settles into her chair, sitting cross-legged, seemingly oblivious.

"Because you were rushed, and you forgot the card?"

"Mom!" I shout. "I saw you."

"You saw me when?"

"Saturday night. Stop playing games. Just tell me who he is."

Her porcelain face falls, and she swallows, setting her tea on the desk. "I wasn't here on Saturday evening."

"You're going to sit there and lie to me? You were kissing some guy. Some guy who wasn't Dad! He was pulling your blouse out of your skirt." I squeeze my eyes shut to rid the image from my mind.

She says my name as if she wants time to explain, but all my patience was used up while she was playing stupid.

"How could you destroy our family?" I point at our family picture on the wall, part of a photoshoot she made us do last year. My heart hammers, and my blood feels hot. Tears well in my eyes, and I feel hollowed out. "You just took a knife and sliced it through that canvas. I hope he was worth it."

"You don't understand. He's not important."

Her words make me see red. "He was obviously important enough to you that you risked us! You risked Dad!" I turn around and head for the door.

"Kyleigh!" she calls. "Did you..."

I whip around. "Tell Dad? No. You're going to tell him, and if you don't, I will."

Then I walk out of her office and continue walking right out of the building. Once I'm outside the back door, I rest my back to the brick wall, bending over and taking a few deep breaths.

There was so much more I wanted to say, but my anger got the best of me. All the things I practiced saying were forgotten.

My phone vibrates, and I dread pulling it out, thinking it might be my dad, but I see that it's Alara telling me she's here for me and to give my mom hell. Best friend for life.

I stare at my phone and just want to disappear. I want to get on a plane and fly somewhere no one can find me. I don't want to think about how everything I've ever known and thought was true is just one big lie. But if I go to my apartment, Mom will come and try to talk to me. I need to go somewhere she'd never look until I can gather myself together.

I find the contact I saved last night and text Rowan, hoping like hell he's home.

You busy?

The three dots appear immediately, and I walk away from the boutique toward the street.

> Just finished my morning workout. Be back to my place soon. Horny?

> Stop saying that, but...

> You're horny. It's okay. You'll have to ride me. I'm spent.

My stomach pitches, wishing I was already riding him.

> How long?

> I love this eagerness. Half hour.

> Meet you there.

I order an Uber and climb in, giving them the address. I watch the people on the streets of Chicago, guessing they've all had better Monday mornings than I have, but as the Uber makes its way toward Rowan's, I already know this is exactly what I need to escape.

eleven

Rowan

Last night, I did my grocery shopping for the week, watched some film clips to prepare for the upcoming season, and constantly checked my phone in case I missed Leigh's message saying she wanted my dick again. Sadly, she didn't, but this morning she does.

Which makes me question what she does for a living that makes her available on a Monday morning.

I'm just leaving the locker room at the space my agent, Jagger Kale, found for his clients in Chicago. He got all of us together and chipped in to outfit the space with the best equipment. This way we can work out in privacy without people snapping pictures or interrupting us.

My phone rings, and I see a number I don't recognize. Letting it go to voicemail, I pocket it as Tweetie pushes through the gym's front door.

"Did you hear?" he asks me.

I really don't want to sit here and entertain Tweetie when I have Leigh on her way to my place. But I don't want to tell him why I have to rush off because I just don't want to hear about it.

"The Falcons might have Conor 'Pinkie' Nilsen."

My eyes widen. He's the best goalie in the league right now, and I had the privilege of playing with him back in college. "I didn't even know they were going after him."

"We're way too good of an offensive to not have a great goalie. Conor would be a great pick up."

I feel bad for Erickson, because if Conor is in, Erickson is either out or becoming a second-string goalie. "Erickson isn't bad."

Tweetie crosses his arms and gives me that toughen up look. "He's not. But when Jennings retired, maybe Erickson should've too. We'd be unstoppable with Pinkie."

I still remember when Conor earned the nickname. Most people think it's because he lost the top of his pinkie finger during a game, but it was first coined from Pink Floyd's "Another Brick in the Wall" because his skills in the net are amazing, as if he's a brick wall and nothing can get past him.

"It's not official yet?" I ask.

Tweetie shakes his head. "Not yet. I'll let you know when I hear."

"I gotta go." I slide to the side to walk around him, but he steps in front of me before I can pass.

"Where are you going?"

I shrug, trying to keep my expression neutral. "Home."

He examines me for a minute, and I'm not sure what he's thinking. There's no way he knows Leigh is coming over.

"Ruby was outside at Peeper's, putting up a for sale sign for the business. She said now that baseball season is almost over, she feels like she'll get a better price than if she waits. So... if you see her, tell her not to sell it to some person who wants to turn it into a café or some shit."

"Why don't you buy it if you care so much?"

He laughs. "Shit, it'd be filled with women every night, and I'd be in debt from buying them drinks. A bar isn't something I should ever entertain." He pats me on the back. "Go get laid."

"I don't know what you're talking about." I walk toward the door, not looking back at him.

"I'm your best friend. You have that look on your face."

"You're my best friend?"

"Don't deny it and hurt my feelings." He disappears into the locker room, and I walk out the door, allowing it to lock behind me.

On the curb, I pull out my phone, waiting for my Uber, and see that the number that called earlier left a voicemail. I look at the transcription and see that it's Conor, so I dial up the number, walking away from the door toward the corner.

It rings once before Conor picks up. "You sending me to fucking voicemail, Magic? Do our college years mean nothing?"

I chuckle. "Where are you calling from?"

"Shit, I keep forgetting. Is that why people aren't picking up for me? Some girl got my number and spread it around, so I had to get a new one last week."

For a second, I wonder if maybe I shouldn't have given Leigh my number.

"So, I might be coming home," he says.

I forgot that he's originally from Chicago. We were so close in college, but once we went into the league, we drifted apart. We don't really see each other unless we're playing one another.

"You want to come to Chicago?"

He hems. "I don't know. I love this fucking team, and I mean, Kane Burrows knows the importance of a goalie. But the opportunity to come home to my family and play with the best line in the league? I think I'd be crazy not to try to make it happen. I'll miss the Florida weather though, that's for sure."

"You think it's going to happen?" I stop at the corner, looking down the street to see if I can spot the Uber.

"Kane and Jana pulled me into their office this morning. They're such a great team, which is another plus for me to stay here."

Jana and Kane are married, and while she's the acting owner, Kane is the coach. Their reputation in the league is unsullied.

"Sounds like a tough decision."

"It is. I'm trying to get through to my family, but no one's answering. Not even my sister. I want their advice, you know?"

"They still live here?"

He chuckles. "Hell yeah. But I wanted to talk to you about the team. Like Tweetie and Hensley? They're good guys? What's the culture like in the locker room?"

We talk about the team dynamic for a few minutes. I know Tweetie would try to sell us to him, but Conor's gotta do what's best for him. And if that's Chicago, that's awesome. I'd love to have him back as a teammate and hopefully become as close as we were in college.

"All right, I'm gonna go talk to Kane and Jana to see where everything's at. Act surprised when you see it on *SportsNight*."

Perfect timing, as my Uber pulls up in front of me. "Hope to see you in a Falcons' uniform this year."

He laughs. "See ya, Magic."

We hang up and I get into the Uber, texting Leigh that I'm running late.

I'll be a few minutes late. There's a café a block away on the corner if you want to wait there.

I'm downstairs at the bar.

Isn't it a little early for drinks?

She snaps a picture of a beer mug with ice in it and a dark liquid that I think is coffee.

Judging me?

No.

Although I hope she isn't already drinking.

I've got to get my energy up if I'm going to do all the work today.

Truth. Tell Ruby to make you an espresso.

Putting ice in the mug was putting her out, and she wasn't afraid to tell me. If I order an espresso, I fear she'll send me packing.

Yeah, she's a tough one.

I like her.

You like me more though, right?

Hmm...better hurry before she wins me over.

I know my worth.

??

I have the skills you want.

Skills?

> My mouth, my fingers, my cock…

Such a filthy mouth.

> You love this filthy mouth, especially when it's between your legs. Now down that coffee because I'm not killing time when I get there. You're up in my condo and on my bed on all fours.

Bed? So boring. (a GIF with a woman yawning)

> That's it. Game on. Better order a second coffee.

Promises, promises.

> Just wait…

That's the problem. I am.

I shake my head and stare out the window with a smile, wishing Chicago traffic wasn't so fucking terrible. Just the flirting texts have gotten me hot. I need to get to my place to quench this thirst for a woman I've only just met.

I push away the thought that this is trouble, because I'm not going to listen to my brain right now. My dick has turned my brain off and is overriding all attempts to make contact with common sense. All I can focus on is Leigh.

twelve

Kyleigh

When I arrive at The Nest, there're a bunch of old receipts posted on the gate with chewed up gum. Names with phone numbers are written in girly scripts, all promising a good time.

My gut twists with the thought of all the competition for Rowan's attention, but it's not because I'm invested in this relationship. The sex is just too good to pass up, obviously.

"Who are you?"

I turn at the sound of a woman's gravelly voice. She's a smaller woman with red hair that looks as though it's probably dyed that color. Her gaze flits over me, and she doesn't look impressed by what she sees.

"I'm just waiting for someone." I thumb in the direction of the gate into the building.

She sighs. "You're kind of early, aren't you? Season hasn't even started." She crosses her arms. Although she's four inches shorter than me and a few decades older, I'm intimidated.

"Oh no...I mean, I'm not..."

She walks closer, her eyes narrowing on me. "Oh…"

"What?"

"Did one of them hurt you? I'm sorry, sweetie, but I've owned this bar a long time, and you're just one broken heart in a long line of them. The last few years, I had hoped that these professional athletes weren't the classic 'one girl one night and another the next.' But this new group." She stares at the gate and sighs. "Even that single dad on the bottom isn't looking for a good woman."

"Yeah, it's not like that."

She takes me in again. "Your eyes are red like you've been crying. It was Landry, right?"

Jesus, she's good. I could very well be here for Henry or Tweetie. How did she figure out I'm here for Rowan? "That's not why I was crying."

She nods but clearly doesn't believe me. "Unfortunately, he's the heartbreaker. No surprise. He's too good-looking, and when they're too good-looking you can't trust 'em."

"Honestly, I'm not upset over Rowan."

"Rowan, is it?" She takes me in again, then waves me toward the bar with a dated sign above it that says Peeper's Alley. "Come in. I own the place, and I'm not open, but I have some coffee brewing."

I look at my phone and see that there's nothing from Rowan yet, and it's already been a half hour. I should leave and go home, face my mother, but I'm not ready yet.

So I follow her in.

She turns around right when we get to the door. "Ruby, by the way."

"Hi, Ruby…Leigh." I continue the lie of my name since she seems to know the guys who live here. I see a for sale sign on the window right before we walk in. "You're selling the business?"

The bar is, for lack of a nicer word, old. It's a classic bar with seating around the bar and a few small tables sprinkled through the room.

Ruby rounds the bar and grabs the old-school coffeepot, pulling out a mug. "Cream or sugar?"

"Actually, do you have some ice?"

Her lips tip down, and she sighs dramatically, grumbling about how young people ruin everything sacred and holy, even coffee.

I'm ready to say never mind, but she grabs a beer mug and fills it with ice, dumping the coffee over the ice. Not exactly like my favorite cold brew, but I'm not going to complain since she's nice enough to get me off the sidewalk where I look like one of the Falcons' puck bunnies.

"Are you in the market?" she asks, and I look behind me, unsure if I missed something in our conversation.

"For?"

"A bar." Her tone is filled with annoyance. I'm pretty sure it doesn't take much to earn her ire.

"Oh, no, I'm a fashion designer," I say, but as the words leave my mouth, I wish I could take them back. I don't want to design shit right now. Sure as hell not a wedding dress, which is the craft I've been perfecting under my mom's guidance for the past five years. I'm not even sure I believe in the sanctity of marriage right now. How can I work with brides and look them in the eyes, feeling as though I'm setting them up for disappointment?

She hems again, which I realize is something she does when she's trying not to outright judge.

"Why are you selling?" I ask.

She pours herself a cup of coffee and rests it in front of her. Her movements are smooth as though she's spent the majority of her life behind the bar.

"I don't like change." She shrugs. "And everything around here is changing. Becoming something I don't want. I have no interest in slinging fancy cocktails and catering to an uppity crowd, but that's what you have to do these days to survive."

I nod, understanding how much things have changed over the years.

My phone vibrates in my purse, and I pull it out to see that my brother is calling me. I send him to voicemail. My mom has probably called him and involved him in this. As if he's going to calm me down or try to convince me I didn't see what I did. She just needs to tell my dad. Until she does that, I don't want anything to do with her.

"Dodging someone?" Ruby asks before sipping her coffee.

I shake my head. "Just my brother."

She nods. "He's probably ready to kick Landry's ass, huh?"

"No. I told you, it's not like that."

She grabs a stool from under the cash register and pulls it closer to sit across the bar from me. "You look like a good girl. Don't get involved with those egos up there." She nods toward the ceiling. "More than half the women are looking for Landry when they come in here."

"Can I tell you a secret, Ruby?" I figure I'll just tell her because I need her to get off this whole Rowan-is-breaking-my-heart thing.

"Sweetie, I was born to hold people's secrets. Bartender oath number one."

I sip my iced coffee. "We're not romantically involved."

"You and Landry?"

I nod. My phone buzzes again, and I'm ready to send Conor back to voicemail but see it's a text from Rowan, telling me he's going to be late. I text him back.

While I wait for his reply, I set the record straight with Ruby. "I just met him a few days ago, and we're really just..."

Her head rocks back, but she still doesn't look pleased when she looks at me again. "You know his nickname, right?"

I giggle. More at Rowan's texts than Ruby asking me if I know his nickname. Of course I do. "Magic."

"*And* Mr. Heartbreaker."

I cover my heart. "No breaking this heart because it's not involved in our arrangement."

She hems again. I'm starting to hate that sound coming out of her.

I go back to my phone and continue to text Rowan, laughing at what he's saying. I have to say I love flirting with him. I'm kind of impressed I haven't second-guessed every word I write, worried about what he might think of me.

"That him?" Ruby asks.

"Yeah." I snap a picture of the coffee Ruby made for me and feel myself smiling like a goon.

She hems.

"What?" I ask with exasperation, putting down my phone.

"Nothing."

"Ruby, just say what you want to say." I have a feeling if I don't let her, we'll keep going around in circles.

"You don't look like a girl whose heart isn't involved."

She's so wrong, but my parents brought me up to respect my elders, and I don't have to prove anything to Ruby anyway. She'll know I was right when this ends with Rowan, and I'm still very much intact. Maybe he'll be the one who's a little broken up.

"Why don't we set that topic aside and talk more about you selling this establishment?"

"You interested?" she asks me again.

"I wouldn't know the first thing about running a bar."

"It's easy. A pretty face like yours would sell the drinks, no problem."

I laugh. "I feel like you're sweetening me up."

"You have this look about you like you're about to go through a change."

"Are we back to the heartbreaker stuff?" I sip my coffee, checking the time on my phone, wondering where Rowan is.

"No. It's something else. A booty call doesn't show up at ten on a Monday morning. And your eyes are red and swollen from crying. I've been giving you hell about Landry, and you haven't cracked and told me what really has you so upset."

I suck back the tears threatening to fall. "I..."

"Bartender oath," she says.

"I found out that my mom is cheating on my dad."

Whoosh, a huge boulder on my shoulders loosens, along with a flood of tears.

Ruby pushes a bar napkin over to me. "You're not the first with that story. Although it's usually a wife or husband complaining or confessing about the cheating, not a daughter."

I blot my eyes, swallowing past the dryness in my throat and trying not to appear in distress. "I just confronted my mom."

"Before you came here?" Ruby asks.

I nod.

The door opens and a filter of light streams into the dark bar. I quickly wipe my eyes.

"Landry," Ruby says, "I kidnapped your girl, and she's going to buy my bar."

I don't turn around to look, but I hear him walk across the room.

"Buy the bar, huh?" He doesn't take the stool next to me but stands beside me.

"Ruby is trying to persuade me."

"It takes a tough woman to kick out all these girls fluttering their eyelashes at the guys who live here." Ruby finishes her coffee and takes her cup back to the coffeepot. "Coffee?" she asks Rowan.

"Nah. Sorry, Ruby, we have somewhere to be." He holds

out his hand for me, and I swivel on my stool to face him. Rowan is dressed in shorts and a T-shirt, hair still a bit sweaty. "Unless you want to stay here while I shower."

His tongue runs across his bottom lip, and I squirm.

"Just go get it on. I don't need to hear your weird foreplay." Ruby shoos us with her hand, never turning around.

"Thank you, Ruby. How—"

"Go. It was nice meeting you. Let me know when you want to buy the bar."

Rowan shakes his head as I climb down from the stool.

"You'll be the first one to know," I say with humor.

We say our goodbye and walk out of Peeper's Alley to the street as a car pulls up curbside. A man gets out with a drink carrier holding two iced drinks. Rowan walks over and thanks the man before walking back over to the gate and typing in the security code.

"What are those?" I ask once we're secure behind the gate.

"These?" He holds them up.

"Yeah."

"Iced coffees."

"Two of them?"

"They're my favorite." He smirks, and we climb the stairs.

"Is one of them mine?"

We reach his door, and he presses in his other security code. "I'm undecided because I was told not to do anything nice for you."

"Did Rowan Landry order me an iced coffee?"

He pushes the door open with his foot and holds it open for me to walk through first.

"No." He takes an iced coffee out of the holder. "Rowan bought you an iced coffee."

My stomach does a somersault. I should probably stop using his first and last name like he's some icon I'm sleeping with. I wish I was confident enough not to wonder out of all the women he's had, why does he seem to keep wanting me?

"Thank you, Rowan," I say, accepting the straw he's offering. "I'll let the gesture slide this one time."

"You will, will you?" He puts his coffee on the counter and stalks toward me, backing me into the corner between his kitchen and family room. His foot lands between my legs, and I part my legs to make room for his thick thigh. "I'm glad you called."

"Want to go to the bedroom?"

He shakes his head. "I'm taking a shower, and you're coming with me."

He picks me up, and I yelp, almost dropping my iced coffee. I'm beginning to like being in his arms too much. He carries me and my iced coffee into his bathroom.

Yeah, I'm glad I called too. He's just what I need to forget about my problems for the day.

thirteen

Kyleigh

"You sure like to carry me places." He lowers me down his body until my feet land on the tiled floor.

"Is that a problem?" His hands go to my blouse and manipulate the top button, making his way down.

"I didn't say that." I sip my iced coffee and set it on the counter.

"Do you have to get back to work at some point today?"

Do I? Hell no. I'm not sure when I'll be able to be face to face with the woman who took a grenade to our family.

I shake my head, and that satisfied smile of his shines.

He concentrates on his task, and when he gets a glimpse of my bra-covered breasts, his breath hitches, and it makes my core tighten, as does the way he looks at me. It's as if he can't believe I'm here. He brings out a wanton side of me I never knew existed. And it's not because he's Rowan Landry. It's because he wants me as much as I want him, and he's not shy about showing it.

Rowan pushes my blouse off my shoulders, and I help him

free my arms one at a time. He carefully holds it by the collar and hangs it on a towel hook.

Thankfully, he steps back and turns on the water, stripping his shirt off on the way back over to me. My hands go to the button of my pants, but his hands land over mine. "That's my job."

I hold up my hands, more than happy to let him undress me.

"Then let's quicken this pace." I grin at him, admiring his muscled chest.

"Patience." He steps closer, his face nuzzling in my neck, kissing the top of my shoulder. "You know I make good on my promises."

He runs his knuckles down my ribcage, igniting a path of goose bumps before he dips his fingers past the waistband of my pants, running the tips of his fingers along my waist.

"Rowan," I say, really wanting to increase this pace to get him inside me.

My button flicks open, and he lowers my zipper at an excruciatingly slow pace. Then he hooks his hands on either side of my pants and wiggles them over my hips, but he doesn't let them fall to his floor. Instead, he guides them down my legs and waits for me to step out of them. After hanging them next to my blouse, he steps back, and his gaze runs up and down my body.

He doesn't say anything, and I don't cover myself because the avalanche of lust filling his eyes is all I can see. Without looking away, he toes off his shoes, discards his socks, and pushes down his shorts and boxer briefs, standing in front of me naked.

No wonder he's Mr. Heartbreaker because the man was gifted not only with an untouchable amount of skill on the ice, but he's gorgeous as well. From his defined hard muscles to his sculpted jawline and piercing blue eyes, he's the epitome of any woman's dream guy. And he's lowering himself...wait, he's lowering to his knees in front of me. Oh shit, he's going to...

I straighten my back along the wall, trying to calm my nerves. I'm not sure why, since he's gone down on me before. He runs his nose along the silk of my panties, and his eyes close. God, I've never had a man make me feel so desired.

His fingers run along my hips, and he tugs my panties down my legs, waiting for me to help him remove them completely. Then he swings my one leg over his shoulder and slides his knees along the tile, shifting closer.

My hands go to his hair. It's a little sweaty from his workout, which feels erotic as hell for some reason. He swipes his tongue along my center, and my back arches off the wall with a moan. Reaching up, he pulls down the cups of my bra, his hands molding to my breasts, and his thumbs crest over my nipples. Resting his chin on my stomach, his eyes focus on me.

"Fuck, you're delicious," he says, lowering his face back between my legs.

He swipes with his tongue and twirls it over my clit, pinching my nipples at the same time. My head hits the wall from sensory overload. He works me slowly, his hands dropping from my breasts, then I feel a finger tease my entrance.

"Eyes open," he whispers.

I look down the length of my body. He smirks before swiping his tongue over my clit again and plunging one of his thick fingers inside me.

It's all too much. The man is perfection.

He pushes another finger inside me while his mouth manipulates my clit. The delicious stretch has me pulling him closer to gain the friction my body demands.

Rowan groans, working me over, playing with my entrance, switching up the rhythm, and it drives me right to the edge.

He withdraws his fingers, and I whimper, but he turns us, guiding me off the wall and over to the counter. "Get up."

I slide onto the bathroom counter while he remains on his knees. Swinging my legs over his shoulders, he pulls me forward so half my ass is hanging off the counter. Then he devours me. There's no other word for it. He's uncontrolled and wild, bringing me somewhere I've never been with a man between my legs. I need more. More of his tongue. More of his fingers. More friction. More *him*. My moans and whimpers mix in with the steam from the shower, the bathroom now more like a sauna.

My orgasm hits me like a freight train, and my chest bolts forward, my legs tightening around his head, but Rowan holds me down on the counter, slowing his movements as I ride out the waves of my orgasm on his languid tongue.

He rises from between my legs, and his lips meet mine. I taste myself on his tongue, feeling his dick press against my opening. Rowan reaches over my shoulder, opens a cabinet, and blindly reaches until a box falls out.

He pulls away from me with a groan. "I have to have you." He rips open a condom, running the latex down his rigid length.

"How do you want me?"

Rowan slides my hips off the counter so I'm standing again, but his hand goes to my cheek. The kiss he gives me is so intense that I'm eager and ready again by the time it's over.

He pats my hip and directs me to bend over the sink, making heat unfurl in my belly. He undoes the clasp of my bra, then his hand runs down my back to my ass and back up, sliding around to the front of my neck and lifting my face to stare at him through the mirror.

Fuck. If I could take a picture right now of the two of us, I'd sleep with it under my pillow every night. Pull it out whenever I needed some happy time with my vibrator.

Me naked and bent over for his viewing pleasure with him standing behind me, hand on my neck, his muscles flexed and tense. The look in his eyes is one of pure male satisfaction and dominance. As if he's a king lording over all his subjects. All of that mixed with his sweaty hair and the steam filling the room is a wet dream come to life.

No wonder he's Mr. Heartbreaker. He's breaking hearts because he's too good at this sex thing, and those women are probably mourning the loss. I'll probably cry when this is over too.

He inches forward, removing his hand from my neck and using both hands to spread my ass cheeks. I have the brief thought that maybe I should be self-conscious, but he licks his lips, then bites down on his lower one, and I've never felt more desired.

He slides his thick length inside me. "Fuck." It comes out in a way that sounds as if he almost can't believe how good it feels.

When he withdraws and slams back inside me, his fingertips delve into my flesh as he controls the rhythm, fucking me hard and fast. There's nothing else to call this but fucking— not making love or fooling around or sex even. He's taking his pleasure from me with no apologies and delivering my own.

My nipples rub along the counter with every push and pull, the friction turning them into hard points. He doesn't relent, slamming into me like a man possessed. I happily go with him, rubbing the condensation off the mirror when it becomes too much to see him anymore. I want to watch him devour me. Commit it to memory.

Our heavy breathing and grunting fill the room as our climaxes rise to an uncontrollable limit. My core tightens around him, and he groans.

Just when I can't take any more, he does something with his hips that takes him deeper, and I explode, my pussy clenching around his cock. His fingers press into my flesh so hard I wouldn't be surprised if there are marks left behind, which I'd welcome.

Rowan comes inside me, grabbing at the back of my hair. When he's spent, his sweaty chest falls to my back as my arms give out, and I flatten against the counter. He kisses my spine three times before sliding out of me. I miss him immediately.

I stand up and catch my breath while he takes off the condom and tosses it in the trash can.

He guides me into the shower, and as we each wash each other, what happened earlier this morning comes to mind for the first time since we met up today. I'm thankful he never asked me about my red-rimmed eyes.

But of course he didn't. We're not dating. We're fucking, that's all.

fourteen

Rowan

I'M AT OUR WORKOUT FACILITY, LIFTING WEIGHTS AS I do every morning, but in reality, I'm killing time before Leigh texts me. For the past two weeks, we've developed a routine. An unhealthy one where we see each other every day. One where most of our time together is in bed, or against a wall, or with her on a counter or bent over a piece of furniture.

This obsession I have with her can't be healthy, but I can't seem to find it in myself to care.

I'm grabbing a set of dumbbells when I spot Easton Bailey, the shortstop for the Chicago Colts, walk in. He's one of Jagger's clients too.

"Hey, man. My season is about to end, and yours is about to begin." He chuckles and drops his bag on the floor, then sits on the bench.

"Plan a vacation yet?" I ask, putting down the dumbbells and sitting on the bench across from him.

Easton Bailey is newer to Chicago too. He's spent only a few seasons on the Colts. The best part of my apartment is being able to see him play from the rooftop. There's a reason he won the Gold Glove award last year. His fielding is spectacular. Chicago loved him as soon as he stepped on the field. I know Miles Cavanaugh didn't have the same luck when he came to play football for the Grizzlies. Chicago fans are hard to win over.

"I'm gonna head home to Alaska first."

"Had enough sunlight?"

He chuckles. "Yeah, and the Chicago winter isn't cold enough for me."

"I'm sure the moose and the polar bears miss you."

He shakes his head. I'm sure it's not the first time someone's made a joke at his expense about him being from Alaska.

"You should come visit. There's always room in our igloo."

I laugh and run a towel down my face. "Let me know which dog sled to take, and I'm there."

"Fuck you," he says, taking off his ball cap and running a hand through his hair. "If I knew where you were from, I'd give it back to you."

I cover my heart with my hand. "That hurts. You don't care enough to know where I grew up?"

"Sorry. I'm not a puck bunny who knows your favorite color and favorite meal."

"Bailey!" Tweetie comes in, always one to make an entrance, and I see Henry behind him.

Ever since school started, it's like we have Henry back. I'm not complaining about trips to Six Flags and the zoo with Bodhi, but I'm sure it's nice for him to have some adult time. Then again, I'm not a dad, so maybe he's upset Bodhi's in school.

"Oh hell, I swear you have a tracker on me," Easton says. He thumbs over his shoulder. "This guy shows up at the club

I'm at last weekend, sliding into my VIP, drinking all my alcohol."

Tweetie claps him on the shoulder. "You should be thanking me. That girl you left with was one I brought into the VIP area."

Easton scoffs. "You're acting like I don't have game. She was eyeing me all night."

"Because you're Easton fucking Bailey. Every girl in the place was eyeing you at least once. I mean, after they saw the redhead at my side."

Easton smirks and shakes his head at me. "That ego needs to be taken down a few rungs."

I roll my eyes. "Tell me about it. He lives above me."

"Shit, I'd be worried the floor was going to give." Easton grins.

Henry sits next to me while Tweetie stands in front of the mirror, flexing. He kisses both of his biceps. If I didn't know the guy, I'd probably hate him. But he's joking, and he's been a great friend and teammate to me so far.

"You think I'm the bad neighbor, Bailey? You should hear the moans coming from Magic's place lately. He's about to nail down a girl he met at a wedding."

"Screw you." I shake my head at Easton to not believe Tweetie.

"You're never available anymore, and I know you're with her." Tweetie gives me a look inviting me to tell him he's wrong.

"You sound like a jealous girlfriend," Henry says, moving toward the weights.

"I'm a jealous friend. You're raising a kid, he was my wing-man." Tweetie thumbs at me.

I point at Easton. "Guess you're his wingman now."

Easton holds up his hands and shakes his head. "Fuck no. I can't keep up with the old man."

"Old? Who the fuck are you calling old?" Tweetie poses like a bodybuilder, and we all laugh.

"Tell me you don't do that in front of the women," Henry says. "I can see you naked and flexing like it's going to turn her on."

I fall back laughing because the vision is clear in my head.

"There's only one thing I need to flex, and let's just say the response I usually get is that it won't fit."

"Are you sure they're not thinking, where is it?" Henry bobs his head right and left as if he's looking for something.

"Fuck off, Daddy. A woman would have to dust off cobwebs to see your dick."

Easton's head volleys back and forth between them. I'm sure it's the same with his teammates and the ball busting.

"When was your last STI test?" Henry raises an eyebrow.

"Do I need to put you in separate corners?" Easton asks, standing and putting his hands out like a referee.

They both laugh.

"Shit no, Tweetie would go ballistic in a ring," I say.

Tweetie flexes his shoulders, happy for what he sees as a compliment. "It's all in brotherly love, right, Daddy?"

"Sure. I gotta get to working out before I have to pick up Bodhi. You done, Rowan, or are you staying?"

I look at the clock and see that it's getting close to my time with Leigh. "Nah, I'm out. You three have fun." I turn to Easton. "When Tweetie starts foaming at the mouth, it's time to call the police."

"Gotcha." He gives me a mock salute.

"Go have fun with your regular pussy," Tweetie says, flipping me off, but I head to the locker room, ignoring him.

I pull out my cell phone.

On my way.

At Ruby's.

I'll swing down to get you first.

Perfect.

I'm on my stomach on my bed, and Leigh is straddling me, her ass on my ass and her hands massaging my shoulders and back. My shoulder's been sore, and I winced during sex, so she told me she'd give me a massage.

"Are you looking forward to the season?" she asks.

My cheek rests on my hands and the silky smoothness of her palms feels so much better than any trainer's hands. "Honestly?"

"If you want to tell me."

"It's a little nerve-racking."

She runs her hands down the sides of my ribs and back up, digging the heels of her palms into my muscles.

"You're feeling the pressure?" she asks.

I nod but don't answer.

"Everyone loves you. Chicago can't wait to see what you can do during a full season for the team." She kisses the back of my neck. It's a gesture that would've scared me a couple weeks ago, but today feels oddly comforting.

"Until I fuck up. Until I don't do my job. Until I don't get them the Cup they're expecting at the end of the season. I was traded late last season, so the team's fate was pretty much already sealed. This season, everyone's going to be looking at me to make sure we end up where we want to."

She sighs as if she's watching one of those dog commercials where they talk about them being abused and not fed. Why the fuck did I admit that to her?

"There's a reason you were traded here. There's a reason they believe in you. I'm sure all the pressure you're feeling is hard to deal with, but you've already bonded with your teammates, built the chemistry between you, and you're getting a fresh start when the puck drops on that first game. You're going to be fine."

I roll over but hold her hips to keep her on top of me. "You sound like you know hockey."

A look crosses her face, but it vanishes too quickly for me to ask. "Just good at pep talks, I guess," she shrugs.

I run my hands up the sides of her torso. "Your turn now."

She shakes her head. "I'm good."

"I want my hands on you, and you're probably sore, so this way we both get pleasure."

She giggles, slides off my lap, and rolls onto her stomach on my bed. I get up on my knees, crawling between her legs. I bend one and lift it up in the air, kissing her ankle.

"This isn't like the normal massages I get."

I chuckle and continue a path up her leg. "It's a special one."

"Does it have a happy ending?"

"That'll be extra." I kiss all the way up her leg before lowering it and grabbing her other ankle.

"What if I leave a big tip?"

"Trying to swindle yourself a deal?" I ask, twisting her ankle to inspect her tattoo.

It's a black anchor on the side of her ankle. It's little, but sexy.

"Why an anchor?" I ask, moving my lips up her legs. Every inch of her is delicious and addictive.

"I went through a rough patch in college. My friends all went to a tattoo parlor. I wasn't going to get one, but then I started looking. One of the artists came over and I was talking to him and said that if I got one, I wanted something with significance. Not just something I picked out from a book. He asked me a few questions and brought up the anchor when I said I was considering dropping out of school. It just felt right."

"Why? What does it mean?"

She sighs. I'm not sure if she doesn't want to tell me or if it's because my lips are on her inner thigh now. "For me, it's about resilience and getting through the tough times. A reminder that I'll get through them."

"May I ask what the tough time was back then?"

I know I shouldn't. It's not my business when we're just messing around with one another, so if she says no, I can't fault her.

"I wasn't making it in college. I felt lost at my drawing board. Like I shouldn't be there. I had no fresh ideas. My professors kept calling me in and asking what the problem was. I didn't think I had what it takes."

I hate that I have to ask her the next question because though I could sculpt her pussy from memory, I have no idea how she supports herself. "What did you go to school for?"

She laughs, and I move up to massage her back. I've never really given a massage to anyone, but her muscles feel tense and constricted.

"Sorry, that's weird. I guess I never told you. I went to school for fashion design."

"That's impressive. So, you're creative, huh?"

"I'm not sure about that anymore. But yeah."

I should offer some advice like she gave me a second ago. We're both clearly at a point of our lives where the uncertainty of the world we live in has us feeling a little off balance. "Are you struggling with a design or direction?"

She doesn't say anything at first, and I watch her back rise and fall with a big breath. "I guess so."

"Well, I'm sure you'll figure it out."

Again, I'm met with silence, so I continue to do what I do best for her and distract her from the outside world like she does for me.

"Are you sore?" I whisper in her ear.

She rolls over to face me. "No."

"Perfect." I grab a condom from my dresser and allow us both to forget our worries.

I've never felt more found than being lost in her.

fifteen

Kyleigh

"H{\small AVE} {\small YOU} {\small TALKED} {\small TO} {\small YOUR} {\small DAD}?" R{\small UBY} {\small ASKS}, handing me a creamer.

When I showed up here this morning, Ruby surprised me with a container of cold brew she bought at the grocery store. Sure, she put it on the counter unopened and said it was on sale and that was the only reason she bought it. I smiled, opened it, and poured it into my beer mug filled with ice. Maybe she's more open to change than she thinks. Baby steps.

"No, but I need to. I haven't been to work in two weeks, and I assume if my mom had told him already, I would've heard something about it."

"You gotta rip off that Band-Aid." She pours herself a cup of hot coffee and sits on the stool on the other side of the bar.

"Any takers on the sale of this place?" I change the subject, not wanting to think about what might be happening between my parents right now.

This friendship I'm finding with Ruby is weird, since we only meet up before Rowan comes to get me after his morning workout. At first, I tried to play hard to get with him, but now I feel as if I spread my legs every time he's around. Not that there are any complaints on either of our parts.

"No. I'm starting to think maybe I jumped the gun. I think when the boys left to move in with their women, it was a knee-jerk reaction."

"Boys? Women?" She's never mentioned having children before.

"The Grizzlies. Before this group of clowns, some of the Chicago Grizzlie players lived here. Miles Cavanagh, Damon Siska, and Cooper Rice. Cooper actually owns the apartment part of the building, and I own the bar, but don't tell anyone that. Anyway, one by one, they all found love and wanted out of the bachelor pad. I didn't want to get to know another group of boys, but..."

"Tweetie won you over?" I ask, laughing before taking a sip of my coffee.

"Sadly, he has, but it's also your boy. Plus, Hensley and Bodhi are good people. I'm just tired. I don't have those legs like you do to run around this place all day anymore." She sits up straighter and sips her coffee.

"Why don't you just get some help? Someone to work for you?"

"It's hard to find someone reliable. I put up a sign once, and all I got were young girls like you who wanted to find their way into the boys' apartments. Plus, have you looked around this neighborhood? It's turned into a trendy area, and I'm not that type of person."

The bell rings for the back door, and I assume it's a delivery. Ruby goes to answer it, and I check out the bar. Back in college when I thought I was going to drop out, I worked at a bar for a while. I had so much fun, and it brought back my creative juices because I wasn't obsessing over school every day. Maybe...no. I have some money from my grandfather's trust I just got on my birthday. It's not much, but enough to start over somewhere. But this place is right under Rowan's condo. How weird would that be when this thing is over? I'd still be an owner and have to see him coming and going with other women. No thanks.

I hear Ruby bossing the delivery guy around out back, telling him to wheel it into the storage room. She comes back and opens the register, taking out a check.

The check reminds me that I have my own rent to pay. Sure, I have a paycheck coming from my mom, but I don't think I can ever work for her again. Shit, am I really considering buying a bar?

I would never want to leave Ruby in a lurch if this thing with Rowan goes south, but right now, things are going strong.

"These delivery people keep getting lazier and lazier. Then again, I'm sure if you were out there, he would've taken it all the way to Timbuktu if you wanted him to. It sucks getting old and losing your looks." Ruby sits back down.

"Ruby, he should be doing it because it's his job."

She huffs.

"Hey, um...since I'm unsure what I want to do with my life, how about maybe I buy your bar?" She opens her mouth, but I put up my hand. "I worked at a bar in college. Sure, I'm rusty, and I'd need a lot of your guidance on the day-to-day operations. Maybe we just kind of do a trial run?" She opens her mouth, but I continue on. "I can't do anything involving my actual skillset right now. It reminds me too much of my mom."

She stares at me for a long moment, and I'm ready for her to turn me down. "You want to buy the bar? And work here when you're not fucking Landry?"

"Well, that was uncalled for."

"I can't let you make a snap decision like that."

"Jeez." I sip my iced coffee.

"Think about it for a while. We could start off with me showing you what it's like to run a bar. Maybe you can help me update it a little? I'll pay you for your time. And if you're still interested after, we can talk about you buying it."

She's right. I probably should think about it longer than five minutes.

"All right, sounds like a plan."

She nods. "Good. In the meantime, you need to talk to your dad."

I frown. "I will."

"Today." She covers my hand with hers.

When I first met Ruby, I thought she was brash and somewhat cold, but she's been kind to me in a motherly way. Though I'm not sure why, I'm not going to dissect it. I really need someone like her—who's not invested in the outcome —on my side right now because I feel like I'm lost in the desert without water and no compass to tell me which way to go.

"Okay." I nod.

"Even if you don't tell him about your mom, he's probably worried about you."

I nod.

The door opens, and right on time, Rowan walks in wearing his shorts and T-shirt and carrying two iced coffees.

"Ha, I beat you to it today, Landry." Ruby grabs my mug with the cold brew and holds it up.

That slow easy laugh of his rings throughout the empty bar, and a shiver runs along my spine. "This is her favorite," he says, holding it out to me.

I accept it and put it on the bar next to the beer mug.

"Feeling a little competitive, are you?" she says.

"Ruby, I'm sure you're great, but I have something you don't."

She shakes her head and shoos us away. "Go. I don't want to hear it." She pretends to cover her ears.

I finish my cold brew before picking up the iced coffee Rowan brought me. "Thanks again, Ruby. I'll let you know."

"Take your time, sweetie."

We walk out of the bar and toward the security gate. Rowan enters the code, and once we're behind the gate, it's game on, our lips and hands all over one another. Seriously, the day we don't do it for each other has to be coming soon, right? But today isn't that day.

An hour later, Rowan is in the shower, and I'm lying alone in his bed. Ruby is right, I need to reach out to my dad. Like the chickenshit I am, I pull out my phone to text him.

> Hey, Dad, how are you? Sorry I didn't get back to you. Saw that you called a couple times.

His response will tell me whether or not Mom told him.

> Work. Work. Work. Have a big case right now.

> I'm sorry you're working so much.

> Mom told me you guys got into it and that she gave you an extended vacation. I wanted to check in.

My teeth mash together at her lie. It's one lie on top of the other with her.

> Something like that. Don't work too hard.

Me? Never. (laughing face emoji)

> I'm serious, Dad.

I'm good. Why don't you come for dinner on Sunday? Let's talk this out with your mom.

> I think I still need some time.

Once this case is over, me and you and spaghetti?

> Of course. <3

Hang in there. You know how she gets. Has a hard time seeing the promise in other people's ideas sometimes.

I nod and want to weep for my dad because she has a hard time seeing him, her husband, because she's blinded by another man.

> Anyway, I know you're busy. I just wanted to check in.

Thanks Ky. Call me if you need me, but I'll reach out as soon as this case is wrapped up.

> Love you.

Ah...love you.

"Who are you texting?"

My phone slips out of my grasp, and I reach to grab it, but it fumbles from one hand onto my lap. I look guilty as hell.

"Jealous?" What was meant to sound playful didn't, and

now he's probably thinking I have something to hide. I do, just not what he thinks.

He gets into bed with me with a half smirk. "Was it another guy?"

"It was," I say, relieved he could tell I was joking.

"Who do I have to beat up?" He starts tickling me, and I squirm around on the mattress.

I laugh and try to catch my breath so I can speak. "Stop it. I'm super ticklish." I push him away and try to get out of his hold. I have a love/hate relationship with tickling.

"I can tell." He swings one leg over me and continues his assault. "Tell me who it was, and I'll stop."

He can't be serious. But he's not stopping, so I'm going to have to give in.

I laugh some more. "My dad," I say breathlessly.

He stops and stares at me. "No kinky weird shit?"

"What? Eww. No." I push at his chest, and he falls on top of me, taking my lips with his.

"Good because you're mine."

He draws back, and I'm not sure what the look on my face is. Surprise? Shock? Elation?

"You know, until we're bored with each other." He shrugs, playing it off.

"Totally." I try to do the same.

He lowers himself back down and kisses me again. I wish I could get those two words out of my head—you're mine. But they keep ringing out again and again, taunting me to deny that this is starting to feel like something more.

sixteen

Rowan

Tweetie, Henry, and I arrive at the hotel room our agent, Jagger Kale, booked for us. We're scheduled to have an interview with *SportsNight* to talk about the upcoming season.

Jagger opens the door of the suite dressed in a pair of slacks and a button-down shirt. "My trifecta." He walks toward us and places his hand out for us to shake.

"How's the family?" I ask.

"Good. I'll be back for your first game with my son."

"Does he play?" Tweetie takes no time before he's over at the snack table Jagger set up for us, grabbing a cookie.

"Nah, he's a gamer. But he loves to travel, so he agrees to go to a game, and I agree to go wherever he wants. It's bonding time. Hensley gets it."

"Magic will know what that's like soon enough," Tweetie laughs, snagging a small sandwich before he's even finished chewing his cookie.

"What are you talking about?" I sit on the couch, wanting

to get this interview over with. I hate doing them. The only reason I'm a little more at ease today is because Tweetie and Henry are with me, and we all know Tweetie will take over.

"Your girl. She's at your place all the damn time."

"You have nothing better to do but spy on me?"

Tweetie clicks his tongue on the roof of his mouth. "That's how often she's there. Every time I leave my place, she's either coming or going."

He's not wrong. For the last three weeks, Leigh has been all I think about, all I want. We talk, and I've been getting to know her, but I haven't asked her a lot of personal questions. Twice now, I've found her at Peeper's Alley with swollen eyes as though she's been crying.

If I go there and ask why she's upset, it'll suggest that we're more than just a hookup to each other. And I sure as hell don't want her asking me about my personal demons. She must be finding some solace in Ruby, which is odd since that woman has never seemed like someone who wants people to cry on her shoulder.

"Bodhi likes her. The other day she stopped after she left your place and helped him chalk a sun on the stairs," Henry says.

My eyebrows raise. "Really?"

Henry nods, opening a sparkling water. "She seems nice. Good with kids. And I'm guessing she's good at other things since she's kept your interest for more than a week."

I lean back on the couch and rest my ankle on my knee. "Fuck off, I'm not like that. I think you're confusing me for Tweetie. And I'm not dating her. I'm just..."

"Fucking her?" Jagger asks, sitting in the chair next to me.

"Yeah... I mean..."

Jagger holds up his hand. "You don't have to answer to me. I had my fun, but don't be an idiot and pass up the woman for you like I did. Thankfully, I got a second chance, but not everyone does." He eyes Tweetie, who turns toward the snack table, giving us his back. I'm not sure what that's about.

Leigh is beautiful, funny, and I have this pull to her I've never felt with anyone else. I've never considered dating anyone since I got into the league. Seems like a waste to me because of how much I travel. Plus, I don't want to bring an innocent person in to bear the brunt of all the doubts in my head about what kind of a man I might be to a long-term partner. Leigh's too good for that, and she seems happy to keep our agreement the way it is, so why mess that up?

"Look at him thinking." Tweetie laughs, sitting in one of the chairs with a plate full of food.

"Give him a break," Henry says. "Our boy might be realizing he's falling."

I shrug. "She's a great fuck. That's it."

The words taste sour coming out of my mouth. She's more than that. And she will be more than that to someone else after she's done with me, which will probably be as soon as my season starts since I won't be available as much.

"Okay, the interview is going to start soon, so get all nice and cozy on the couch. Tweetie, put the fucking food down, and don't hog the spotlight," Jagger says.

"That's a hard ask," Tweetie says.

We all sit side by side on the couch with Tweetie in the middle. Jagger gives Tweetie his stern dad look, the only look I've seen from anyone that sobers Tweetie up.

The interview begins via a video call, and I get the first question.

"You're the man everyone is looking at to turn things around for the team this year. How does that pressure feel?"

I tap my ankle, a telltale sign that I'm nervous. "Of course there's pressure, but I'm confident I can contribute to the team, along with everyone else, and earn us a better result this year."

"Especially with the guys to your left. They're calling you the Trifecta."

I look at Jagger, who points at himself, obviously the one who coined the phrase.

"We're definitely a force to be reckoned with, but there are a lot of talented players in the league. At the end of last season, we jived on the ice, so we'll continue to build on that this season."

He directs a few questions to Henry and Tweetie, and they both give the regular PR-approved answers. It's all about fulfilling your role on the team. How there isn't any drama between teammates. How we're poised to do well this year.

"We heard that you all live in the same building," the interviewer says.

Henry chuckles. "Yeah. We do."

"And that your fans have coined it The Nest?"

Henry and I look at Tweetie, and he raises his hand. "I did. It was The Den back when the Grizzlie players lived there, so it's only fair we take it over."

Henry groans.

"Henry, you're a single dad, right?" he asks.

He nods. "I am."

"How's that work living with Mr. Heartbreaker?"

I roll my eyes, and Jagger points at me to cut it out. I fucking hate that nickname.

Henry laughs and glances at me. "He's not too much of a heartbreaker these days."

"Or ever," I grumble.

Jagger glares at me, but I'm not going to sit here and let them take shots at the kind of person I am.

"Yeah, he's got—" Tweetie starts in.

"How about we keep this to hockey?" I say.

The interviewer clears his throat and glances off screen. Fuck this entire thing. Why do they have to get involved in my personal life?

"Sorry, but we gotta ask the hard questions the fans want answers to. You understand, right, Rowan?"

I look at Jagger. If looks could kill, I wouldn't be alive to answer the guy. "Yeah, all good."

"Well, in other news, I assume you've heard the rumors?" the interviewer asks.

Jagger pulls out his phone and stares at it. He never has his phone out during our interviews. He's always there to keep us on task and make sure to shake his head if we veer in the wrong direction.

"What rumors?" Henry sighs because it's usually some shit we can't confirm.

"You've got a new goalie."

We all look at Jagger. He holds up his phone, smiling.

"It's been reported that Conor Nilsen has been traded to the Chicago Falcons, though we're waiting for confirmation on that," the interviewer says.

"Let's go!" Tweetie shouts, and Jagger motions for him to bring the volume down.

Probably because it will appear disrespectful to Erickson, our current goalie.

"You played with him in college, right, Rowan?" the interviewer asks.

"I did, and he'll be a great asset to the team, but at the same time, Erickson will be missed in the locker room. He's a great player and mentor to a lot of us."

Jagger smiles at my answer. It's almost too rehearsed. So much so I wonder if these interviewers understand they have no clue who I am underneath this persona.

"Well, I think I speak for all of us when I say we can't wait to see the four of you on the ice this season. Thanks for taking the time to chat today. Good luck this season."

We all say our goodbyes and thank them for having us.

Once the interview is over, Jagger turns all the equipment off and sits back down across from us. "Okay, you can all thank Daddy now."

"What are you talking about?" Henry asks.

"I convinced Conor to come home to Chicago. So when you win the Cup this year, you better be kissing my ass and offering me an extra five percent on all your contracts." Jagger goes over to the snack table and opens a soda.

"You'll be kissing ours from all the endorsements," Tweetie says, joining him.

"Pretty cool, you and Pinkie together again, huh?" Henry slides over on the couch, lifting his wrist to check the time. "I gotta get Bodhi. Want to come and get a reminder of why you need to be sure you're practicing safe sex?" He chuckles, standing and straightening his pants.

"Please, Bodhi is an endorsement to have children," I say.

He blows out a breath. "Not when he gets with his friends. Some of his friends would make you run to get a vasectomy."

He walks over to Jagger, shaking his hand and thanking him.

"Daddy duty, huh?" Jagger asks.

"Yeah."

Henry leaves, and my phone vibrates in my pocket. My pulse quickens, hoping like hell it's Leigh.

At Ruby's whenever you get home.

I'll be there in twenty.

I pocket my phone and go over to Jagger, thanking him.

"You're all leaving? I was going to treat you to lunch." He holds up his hands.

"Unless Leigh's pussy's on the menu, Magic isn't interested." Tweetie smiles wide.

I'd love to smack that smile off his face, but he's not wrong. That's about the only thing I'm hungry for.

"Go. I get it. If my wife was here, I wouldn't be hanging out with you dipshits."

I say goodbye and leave the plush hotel, grab a taxi, and book it to my condo, ignoring all the signs that Leigh is worming her way into my daily life.

seventeen

Kyleigh

ALL I'VE DONE SINCE FINDING OUT ABOUT MY MOM IS ignore my real life and spend the majority of my days with Rowan. I know I'm pushing off the inevitable, but it's freeing to just be with someone for sex. At least it started that way. Now every time I'm with him, I feel a little more for him and then feel guilty that he doesn't know who my brother is.

It's been easy to dodge my mom because she hasn't even tried to call me. Good. I hope she's being eaten alive with guilt, but something tells me that's not the case. Conor has called me a few times, and I've dodged him. My dad is busy with a case. Which leaves me to push away all the anxiety I feel about what's going to happen with my parents and pretend that everything is okay. At least for the time I spend inside The Nest.

My phone rings, and Conor's name flashes across the screen. I press the button to send it to voicemail, but he doesn't leave one, sending me a text instead.

Call me. I've got huge news.

I'm busy. What's your huge news?

I'm coming home.

What is he talking about? His preseason training has to be starting soon like the Falcons'. Why would he come home? *Shit.* If he is coming home for a visit, I have to tell him about Mom.

I press his name on the contact and press the speaker button, muting the television.

"Finally have time for your big brother?" he answers.

"A minute or two, I guess."

"You're funny."

"What do you mean you're coming home? Doesn't training start soon?"

"It does." I think he's in his kitchen because I can hear a sizzling pan in the background.

"So how do you have time to come home before the season starts?"

I wasn't prepared to tell my brother about my mom. His season is about to start, and it will probably crush him just like it did me. And maybe it's a little because I know that Conor will call my dad and tell him. He'll confront the situation head-on while I tend to try to avoid conflict. We've always been opposites in the way we react to a crisis. It would be so easy to let him just take this over and handle everything with my parents. But a part of me knows that I can't place the sole burden on him. That it isn't fair.

"Yeah, I have my training in Chicago."

"What are you talking about?" Why would the Florida Fury come up to Chicago to train for the season? I grab my iced tea and take a sip, leaning back in the chair.

"I'm a Falcon now."

My iced tea sprays out of my mouth. "Wha...what?"

"I've been traded. I can't wait to tell Mom. She's gonna be so happy. Speaking of, can you go get her? She's not answering my call either."

I stand and grab a napkin, wiping down my coffee table. "I'm not at the shop."

"Why? Are you sick?"

"Conor, I need you to start from the beginning. Why would they trade you?"

He scoffs. "Jeez, sis, thanks for thinking I'm not a hot commodity. You think no one wants me?"

"No." I toss my tea-soaked napkins in the trash. "I'm just surprised the Fury doesn't want to keep you."

"Of course they wanted to keep me, but the Falcons wanted me more."

I'm not sure I understand how the trade thing works, but it doesn't matter. Conor coming home means I need to end this thing with Rowan. Profound disappointment fills my chest. "That's cool."

"Cool?"

Conor's clearly offended that I'm not jumping up and down. I'm happy he's coming home, but his return forces me to confront the two things I've been avoiding—my mom's infidelity and my situation with Rowan.

I can't leave Conor in the dark. He needs to understand what he's coming home to. Before finding out my mom was cheating, I would've been screaming with excitement.

"Yeah, when do you have to report here?" I ask.

"For training. Which means soon. I'm coming into town this week to find a place. Unless you want to offer up yours?"

"Um...no. You want to shack up on my couch?"

He talks about his agent hooking him up somewhere, and all I can think of is losing Rowan. It shouldn't be a problem since it's hardly been any time that we've spent together, and we both agreed it wasn't anything serious. It sucks to lose my one constant since my world shattered, but I can adapt. I always have. I run my thumb over my anchor tattoo.

The number one problem is telling my brother that he's not coming home to the big happy family he's used to.

"Hey, Con." I feel nauseated at having to do what I've put off for so long.

"Want to insult me again?"

"No. Um... I have to talk to you about something, and I hate to do it over the phone, but I'm not sure I have a choice."

His silence is deafening. I'm not sure what he's even thinking it could be. "Ky, what's going on?"

"So...I went to one of Mom's weddings."

"Mom's weddings? How many times has she been married?" He laughs.

I want to ask if he's preparing his dad jokes years in advance, but this isn't the time.

"You know what I'm talking about." I lower my head, pissed that I have to be the one to tell him. Damn my mother for putting me in this position. "I stopped in at the shop on my way because I forgot the card to give the couple."

"So forgetful," he jokes because he's usually the forgetful one.

"Can you not sense the seriousness of what I'm about to tell you?" I'm annoyed that he's still being Mr. Jokester when I'm dying inside and filled to the brim with anger at my mom.

"Okay, sorry. What is it?" That's the one thing with Conor. I'm not sure if our age difference was a wide enough gap that we just never fought. We did, but rarely.

"I saw Mom in her office with another man."

There. He knows. I said it. And I really hope if my mom doesn't tell my dad that Conor will be with me when I do.

Conor is quiet for a few seconds, and his voice sounds

strained when he does talk. "Okay, what's the real news? You knocked up? Get married in Vegas? Finally tell Mom you're going out on your own?"

"I'm serious, Conor. Mom is cheating on Dad."

I hear his quick intake of breath, and my gut sours. The thing I hate most in life is upsetting people. I've never been able to stomach hurting someone.

"Seriously?" The heartbreak in his tone kills me, and tears spring to my eyes.

"I am," I nearly whisper.

"Does Dad know? Did she tell him? Did you?"

I couldn't do it, but I hate telling Conor that. He's always been such a great big brother, taken a lot off my shoulders. When I didn't want to go to Mom's alma mater, Conor stuck up for me and said the School of Fashion Design at Kent State University was just as good. She's always had a soft spot for Conor, so she didn't give me a ton of grief except a dig here or there over the years.

"Conor..."

He groans. "He should know."

"I couldn't do it." It makes me physically ill to think about sitting in front of my dad and telling him that his wife of thirty-three years is cheating on him with some mystery man. It's going to blow up his life.

"Fine. We'll do it together. I'll be flying in. What did Mom tell you when you confronted her? I'm assuming you did..."

The doubt in his voice shows how well he knows me. This is where we're so different. Conor never shies away from conflict, believing everyone should get what they deserve.

"Why aren't you mad? You sound...resolved." I grab my dust rag and run it over the furniture. When I'm frustrated, I tend to get obsessive about cleaning.

"What do you mean? Of course I'm pissed."

"But you didn't really react. I was crushed. I wanted to rip that man off Mom and punch her in the face. You're just like, 'We have to tell Dad' and 'What did Mom say,' as if she could make any excuse for what I saw." I work my way into the nooks of the table to make sure every speck of dust is gone.

"It fucking sucks that she did it, but she did. Now we have to tell Dad so he can deal with it."

He's so matter of fact. I don't know if I'm envious or pissed off that he's not wallowing in grief and anger like I am.

"Conor, she just ripped our family apart and for what? Some guy who she said was no one to her." Just the thought of her sitting in her office chair and telling me he wasn't anyone brings all the rage that was so hard to push down back to the surface. It makes me wish I could go back in time and relive it so I could throw my iced coffee in her face. The satisfaction of seeing it drip down her expensive leisure wear would be worth it.

"I know, Ky. I do. And I am mad, but we're adults. This is Mom and Dad's problem."

I stop dusting and sit on the couch before I pass out. Did he just say it's not our business? "They're our parents, Conor. It affects us too. And she used us. Put us out there like some perfect family to help her business, meanwhile she's going behind Dad's back and fucking someone else!"

He blows out a breath. "Yeah, I know. We'll talk more when I get in. This sucks, but ignoring it isn't going to help. Trust me."

"I'm not ignoring it. I confronted her, and she tried to act like it was nothing. Then she told Dad she gave me a vacation. She's lying about everything. How can you be so calm?" I rub at a water ring on my side table.

"It's bullshit. It is, but I feel really far away right now to really get into this. We'll talk when I get into town."

This is the cool, calm, and collected Conor. I'm not sure where he learned to handle crises this way.

"Fine," I grumble.

"You'll come apartment shopping with me? I mean, you are on vacation."

I smile before realizing I'm still mad. There are very few people who can get me to change moods as fast as Conor. Then again, Rowan can take me from a crying mess to so turned on it takes nothing to orgasm. "Yeah, sure."

"Now say congratulations, big brother. I can't wait to have you home."

I shake my head, leaning back on my couch. "Congratulations, big brother. I can't wait to have you home."

"There's my little sister. I'll text you when I get into town."

"Okay."

"And Ky?" he says. "I love you, and no matter what happens, you always have me. But we'll get through this. I'm not sure how much shit we'll have to paddle through, but we'll come out of this."

And that's why I love my big brother. "Thanks, Conor."

"Love you."

"Love you."

We hang up and I sit on the couch, clutching my phone to my chest. I go to the text message Rowan sent me an hour ago and study it again. Guilt is the only reason I didn't respond to him right away because I know I need to tell him who my brother is. Now it's even more pressing.

Busy?

I click on the reply button, and my thumbs hover over the screen. With Conor's transfer, everything has changed. I should just send a message back to end this, but at some point,

I have to tell him. With Conor coming here, there's no doubt there will be a run-in between the three of us.

Be there in thirty.

Now I just have to walk in there and confess what I've been holding back and not allow his body and his words and his dick to sidetrack me before I can tell him who I really am.

eighteen

Kyleigh

Rowan is outside the gate when my Uber pulls up outside the building.

I tried to give myself a pep talk on the way over here. We haven't known each other for long. I should be fine with telling him we can't see each other anymore. The problem is, I also have to tell him who I am, which compounds the problem because we don't get to just part ways. We'll still have to see one another when Conor is involved, and I know I won't be able to see Rowan without remembering how good we are together.

He meets me at the Uber, opening my door and holding his hand out for me. This man toes that line between fuck buddies and making me wonder if we're dating, but I guess maybe he's just treating me with respect. Truth is, I wouldn't still be fucking him if he was kicking me out of his apartment five minutes after he came or not showing any signs of being a decent human being.

"Hey," he says when I accept his hand and step out of the car.

"Nice of you to meet me."

That low laugh I've come to expect slips out of him. "Too nice?"

"Not at all." I rise to my tiptoes and kiss his cheek. "Thanks."

His hand goes limp in mine. *Shit. Shit. Shit.* That was something a girlfriend would do.

"Let's go." I change the subject, pushing away the awkwardness as if it never happened. I tug him toward the security gate, but he doesn't budge.

"I'm actually starving, and I don't have anything at my place. Mind if we go get pizza or something?"

I can't tell if he's joking or serious, which makes me conflicted on how to answer. I haven't eaten anything all day either, so I could use some food, but that's against the few rules we mapped out when we ventured into this agreement.

"You're serious?"

He nods, not letting go of my hand. "I promise, we can go dutch so it's not a date."

"You want to get pizza?"

"Yeah. I promise not to read into it."

I roll my eyes at his joke. "Okay, but no deep dish. Takes too long."

I pull him the opposite way he's facing because if we're going, we're going to my favorite place. It might be easier this way anyway. Telling him I'm Conor's sister in public might prevent him from getting too outwardly angry at me.

"Hard bargain," he says, walking in line with me.

Now I understand the hat. He was wearing it that day at breakfast too. It's his way of trying not to be recognized. Lucky for him, my favorite place is kind of a dive, so even if people recognize him, they probably won't approach him. The clientele isn't really the selfie type.

"I like you taking control," he says, his thumb running along my pointer finger.

"Stop petting me." I go to unwind my hand from his, but he tightens his hold.

"I'm making sure you don't wander into the street."

"Yeah, I might go chase a butterfly."

I stop at the corner and look at him. He steps closer, tucking our entwined hands behind my back, tugging me into him and kissing me for everyone around us to see. I should push him away and say PDA is a boundary we can't cross, but I don't. Instead, I kiss him back, and I actually slide my tongue into his mouth.

Thankfully, a few guys in their twenties whistle when we don't move on the walk signal. Rowan ends the kiss, lowers his hat with his free hand, and we walk across the street.

We arrive at the pizza place, and I request a small booth in the back. I sit on the side of the booth that faces the door, so Rowan's back is to everyone. I don't love the hat if I'm honest. His hair is too great to be hidden.

"Right now, I want to be one of those cheesy couples who sit on the same side of the booth," he says, his foot playing with mine under the table.

"Yeah, we don't need a headline like 'Rowan Landry Fingers Some Random Girl at a Pizza Joint.'" I pick up the menu as if I don't know what I'm going to order. Rowan takes his finger and lowers the top of my menu so he can see my face. "What?"

His smile that's usually on display when I'm with him isn't there, and my stomach clenches. Maybe he wanted to come to a public place because he's already found out who I am, or maybe he wants to break it off.

"Two things." He holds up his two fingers. "One, you're

not some random girl. Two, can you please stop thinking of me as Rowan Landry?"

I sink back into the booth, cross my legs, and rest my hands in my lap. A part of me wants to ask more questions about number one, but I go right to the number two. Because he doesn't know how right he is about number one. "I'm sorry. I know who you are, obviously, but that's not why I'm doing this. You know that, right?"

He shrugs, and I sigh.

"Rowan," I whisper, "You know I knew who you were the night of the wedding. But I didn't go up to your room because of who you are in hockey or who you are in Chicago. I went up to your room because you made me laugh and the ease between us. I thought this would end that night, but it didn't. I'm not sleeping with you so I can tell people I'm sleeping with Rowan Landry, professional hockey player. It's just hard to separate you from the icon you are. Does that make sense?"

He picks up his silverware wrapped in a paper napkin and plays with the paper napkin ring with his fingers. "Ever wish you could meet someone who didn't know who you are?"

More than he knows. I smile, but it's strained. "I'm not famous."

He tosses the paper napkin ring to the side and nods. "I'm not famous either. I can go a lot of places without anyone recognizing me, but just once I'd love to know for certain that someone isn't trying to use me."

My mouth falls open, and I slide out of my side of the booth and into his. I take his head in my hands. "Is that what you think?"

He doesn't say anything.

"Hi, I'm Ellen, your wait—"

I put up my hand. "Can you give us five, Ellen?"

I'm pretty sure she goes away because Rowan's eyes land

on mine after diverting to hers for a second. "Answer my question."

"I don't think so, until you refer to me using my first and last name. Like it's out of the realm of possibility that I'm here with you. I don't like it."

I search his face for where this insecurity is coming from. Has he been scorned by someone before? Did he fall for some woman who pretended to love him because he's a professional athlete? I really hope not.

"Why are you worried even if I was? I mean, we're not a couple…"

He takes my hands off his cheeks and lowers them to his lap. "When I'm with you, I forget who I am to the outside world. I'm just a guy who met a girl that he can't stop thinking about all the time. Then I get reminded of how you might think of me, and I'm not sure…shit, just forget what I said."

My chest squeezes, and my stomach whooshes down to my feet. "Why are we forgetting it?"

His hand slides to my knee, and he lifts the edge of my dress, so his palm is touching my skin. He inches it up to my mid thigh. "Because I sound like an idiot. Asking you to separate me from the hockey player. It's just—"

I press my hand on his covering my thigh. "I get it. I do. When I'm with you, I only see you as the guy I'm fucking. The guy that…" I don't want to tell him all my internal battles to make sure I keep him in a category where I won't be hurt. Not that I love him, but I like him. A lot. And now I have to end this, tell him who I am, and see him from time to time and pretend there was never anything between us. "I wish we were different."

He tilts his head, not understanding what I'm saying.

"I kind of wish we were both in the headspace to be looking for something. That dating was an option for us. But it's not."

He frowns, and his palm glides up my leg. "I get what you're saying."

I don't miss that he doesn't say, "I wish dating were an option too." It tells me where I stand with him, which I can't argue. Regardless of whether he can't stop thinking of me, this was our deal. And I'm in no way ready to venture into a new relationship with all the crap with my mom still swirling through my head. I'm not even sure I believe in true love anymore.

His finger runs over the outside of my underwear, and we both groan. "Want to get the pizza to go before I can't control myself and finger the woman consuming me in some pizza joint?"

He's deflecting, not wanting to talk about his feelings, and I can't call him out because I'm hiding so much myself. I need to tell him I'm Conor Nilsen's sister, that I found out my mom is cheating on my dad, and that my head is all over the place, which is why I didn't tell him sooner.

Then he slides a finger under the elastic of my underwear, toying with my clit. He lowers his head, and he whispers, "I need you."

I raise my hand. "Ellen!"

We get the pizza to go, and it grows cold on Rowan's counter as we finish what we started at the pizza place. Once again, I can't bring myself to tell him who I really am.

One more day, I tell myself. Just one more day.

nineteen

Rowan

"Harder," Leigh says, her fingers tightening in my hair. "Right there. Don't stop."

She's mad if she thinks I'd stop. She's lying on her back, her legs straight up on my chest and shoulders while I'm bent over her. I can't get deep enough.

"You're fucking soaked," I say, drilling into her.

I watch the pink flush creep over her body, her nipples erect and begging for my mouth. She's always beautiful, but when I have her right before she comes, a crawling sensation races up my spine, igniting a feeling of dread that I have to commit her to memory because there might not be a next time. She could end this any time she wants.

I'm gone for her. My need still hasn't waned, only grown, in more ways than one. I want to know more about her, but she keeps herself so closed off.

"There. Shit. I'm going...Ro...wan." My name slips from her lips, and her pussy clenches around my dick.

This must be what heaven is like.

She reaches back, grabbing the pillow under her, her hands clenching the edges. I watch her muscles tense from the sheer pleasure of her orgasm.

"Jesus, you're gorgeous," I say, hammering into her double time to reach the point she's at because I want my lips on her.

I want to kiss her, let her know this effect she has over me.

"Your dick..." she whimpers, and her eyes close, her head lolling back.

"Your pussy," I say back, my climax rising to a level I can no longer push away.

I come on a curse, filling up the condom. I wish I could be bare inside her, although I've never done that with anyone. But Leigh seems to be breaking all my rules.

I fall on her, my hand cradling her cheek, my lips crushing hers. She opens, and our tongues glide along one another's, inducing another round of arousal that should've been doused a long time ago.

I grow soft inside her, but I don't want to move.

She wraps her arms around my shoulders, her short nails running up and down my shoulder blades. We take our time, not rushing to clean up like all the other times. We both seem content to lie here and bask in the glow of what we just did.

I need to squash this need. I need to figure out how to become unattached to her, but every time I tell myself she's just a woman I'm screwing, I wince because it doesn't feel that way. I want more from her.

Even now, I'm supposed to go meet up with Conor for a beer, but I don't want to leave her.

I slow our kiss and move my lips to her jaw. "Want to come get a drink with me?"

She freezes under me, and I guess that answers where she wants this thing between us to go. Absolutely nowhere.

I kiss just under her ear and slide out of her, going to the bathroom to dispose of my condom and feeling like an idiot for mentioning it. When I come out, she hurries by me to use the bathroom.

"Other people will be there." I try to smooth the waters by making it seem like the invite wasn't a big deal. "Not sure if you follow hockey. I mean, I know you knew who I was," I say through the door. "But Conor Nilsen just got traded to the Falcons. We went to college together. He's here looking for a place, and I said I'd meet him at Ruby's for a beer."

Did I really have to give her all that information? I could've said I'm meeting a teammate and left it at that.

The bathroom door opens, and she hurries past me to pick up her shirt off the floor. She tosses the shirt over her head with something that feels kind of like panic. Seeing her dressed only makes me want to unwrap her again.

She sits on the end of the bed to put on her sandals.

"Do you?" I ask.

"Sorry?" She looks up at me while she's bent over tending to her shoe. If I didn't just watch her come, I would've thought she's uncomfortable being around me.

"Follow hockey? Is that how you knew me?"

She squirms, her eyes flitting around for a beat. "A little..." She finds her purse on the floor and stands to grab it. "Actually..."

She positions her purse crosswise over her body, and the way the strap slides between her tits makes my dick twitch. One thing I've yet to do is titty-fuck her. I should probably get to that before she breaks this off.

"Yeah, I do follow hockey. I actually read a lot of the blogs." She puts up her hand. "Not because I'm some puck bunny or anything. I mean...I like hockey players, but I didn't...what I said the other night."

The way she's stumbling over her words causes me to chuckle. She sighs and stares at the floor.

"Hey." I break the distance between us and place my hands in hers at her side. "I'm not judging you."

"Yeah, but hockey blogs sound bad. But I'm not—"

I press my lips to hers to get her to stop talking. "Okay, so what are they saying about me? That I'm a waste of talent?"

She laughs and shoves me in the chest. "Honestly, I haven't been reading them since we got together. I've been..." She lets whatever she was going to say go, and I want to pry, but I have to get going. From what I've witnessed, she's going through something but hasn't shared anything with me, and I've forced myself not to ask. "Everyone in Chicago can't wait to see you play again this season." She gets up on her tiptoes and kisses me back. "Including me."

"Good. If you ever want seats..." Shit, there I go again. Another covert way of asking her to move this arrangement into something more. Or at least gives the impression that I want something more.

"I'll let you know."

I nod. We still have preseason training to get through. Why am I pushing the limits?

"Have fun with your friend," she says, wrapping her arms around my waist, tightening her hold on me.

I rest my chin on her head and hold her. We've never really hugged before, and I don't love the way this feels. It feels like a goodbye. She pulls back and stares at me. There's something in her eyes. They're void of her usual free-spirited demeanor.

"What's going on?" I frown.

A soft smile creases her lips. "There's something I need to tell you."

"Okay..."

"I'm not—" My phone rings from where it's charging in the kitchen.

I ignore it and continue to hold Leigh close. "Go ahead."

My phone stops and rings again right away. What the hell?

"They can wait. What is it?" I don't take my eyes off her.

Then the buzzer rings by the door. Conor must be here already.

She looks at the door to the bedroom. "Conor Nilsen?"

I chuckle. "You don't have to refer to us all by our first and last names."

She laughs, but it's strained and anxious. "You go ahead. Do you mind if I shower quickly? I just remembered that I'm going to meet Alara, so I should probably get the sex smell off me."

I try to find something in her body language to give me any clue as to what's going on with her. "Of course. The door will lock automatically behind you. Are you sure you're okay?"

She nods and rises up the balls of her feet, pressing her mouth to mine again. I run my hand around her head to keep her lips on mine and slide my tongue through her parted lips.

I pour every emotion I can into the kiss with the hopes she knows she can trust me and say whatever's on her mind. I know we've only been with one another a short time, but I feel closer to her than to most people in Chicago.

She closes the kiss when the buzzer goes off again. "Go," she says, pushing me in the chest.

"How long will you be out with Alara?" I ask, wanting her to come back over tonight.

"I don't know. Probably well past your time with your friend."

Point made. She's not interested in getting to know my friends or doing anything outside of what we do here. I hate the feeling of disappointment that fills my chest.

"Okay, text me the next time you get horny." My joke falls flat.

I kiss her forehead and walk toward the door, pressing the

button and telling Conor I'll be right down. I don't look at her when I head back into my bedroom.

"Why do I feel like you're upset?" she asks.

"I'm not." I pull on a pair of jeans and a T-shirt from my dresser.

"You don't seem fine." She leans her shoulder on the doorframe of my bedroom.

"Go shower so you're not late to meet Alara." I hurry up and get dressed.

She watches me until I give her one more kiss on the cheek and walk out the door. Once I'm finally away from her, I let go of the breath I was holding, wondering if she was right the first night I met her—maybe she will be the one to break my heart.

twenty

Rowan

I JOG DOWN THE STEPS, OUT OF THE SECURITY GATE, and into Peeper's Alley. Conor isn't anywhere that I can see, so I stop at the bar to ask Ruby where he's at.

"Back room," she says before I have a chance to even open my mouth. "Where's my girl?"

"She didn't want to come," I say and turn toward the back room, not interested in getting any shit from her. I asked Leigh, she didn't want to come. End of story.

Conor sits alone at the big, round table in the room that's always reserved for us and has a television to watch the games. Ruby set this up for the Grizzlies years ago, and us Falcons have taken it over as our own to get away from any fans, a.k.a. puck bunnies, who might come in looking for us.

"Pinkie," I say, patting him on the shoulder when I approach.

He turns with his beer in his hand, then he slides out of his chair and shakes my hand, pulling me in for a hug. "It's been too long."

Though we haven't been close in recent years, I can tell he's still the same guy who was my closest friend in college. The cocky dark-haired guy all the girls loved. He'd show up anywhere from class to a party and be surrounded. Sure, a lot of us would, but Conor had this way with the ladies that made him seem older, more confident. The girls just swooned over the guy. He still has the calm "take life as it comes" demeanor about him.

I sit down in the chair, and Ruby brings me my drink, setting it in front of me. "If you would've stayed for a second, I wouldn't have had to walk all the way over here." She puts her hand on Conor's shoulder. "Need another one, sweetie?"

What the hell?

"I'm good with this one for now. Thanks, Rubes."

Conor's ability to already shorten her name—which she's not a fan of unless you know her well—just confirms my earlier thoughts. The man wins over everyone.

"Thanks, Ruby," I say before she can leave the room.

"Uh-huh," she says under her breath.

Okay then. I guess I'm the asshole today.

"This place is great." He sips his beer. "I wish you had a fourth unit here. I'd move here in a heartbeat."

I nod. I have a second bedroom, but I'm a little old for a roommate. Unfortunately, the first thing my mind goes to is how I could possibly fuck Leigh all over my condo with a roommate? "It's a good setup."

"Kale's got a hookup, but it's not ready for a couple weeks. I might buy something anyway."

"What about your parents? Could you stay there until it's ready?"

He shrugs and gulps down his beer. Once he rests it on the table, he stares at the television for a beat. "That's not an option, and my sister only has a one-bedroom."

"You have a sister who lives here too?"

He side-eyes me. "You don't remember Ky?" He looks at the ceiling. "I guess she was pretty young when we were in college, right? Think you only met her a handful of times. But yeah, I could crash on her couch if I really had to, but I won't fit on it. Not to mention it's hard to bring women home to my sister's place. Probably gonna be a hotel."

"Where are your parents at?" I ask, assuming they're in the suburbs somewhere.

"They're in the city, but not around here." He sits up straight, holding his beer mug between his hands and staring inside it. "Things are rocky."

"Really?"

From what I always knew of Conor's family, it was perfect. I was jealous of the relationship he had with his parents. Care packages would always arrive, and he'd be on the phone with them a lot. My mom tried to come see me at college a few times, but it was always hard for her to get off work. Eventually, she never mentioned it, and I got used to being alone during parents' weekends. So to hear things are rocky with his parents is a real surprise.

"My sister found out my mom is cheating on my dad. Like witnessed her and the other guy making out in my mom's office."

Fuck. That sucks.

"I'm sorry, man."

He nods and tips his beer back. "Yeah, well, my sister doesn't handle things like this very well, so she's an emotional mess, and my mom is trying to act like she didn't get caught and is just ignoring it. My dad is presently in the dark, so coming back to Chicago is nice, but not what I thought it would be. At least I can be here for my sister through this shitty time."

I tip my drink back, unsure what to say.

I mean, I had a shit childhood, one that still torments me

and threatens to ruin any happiness I try to obtain, but it was that way from birth. I never knew any different. Finding out in adulthood that your family isn't the perfect one you always envisioned has to be a hard pill to swallow.

"I'm sure she'll appreciate you being here."

He chuckles. "So much so she told me she was busy this afternoon and that she'd catch me tomorrow morning. We're going to check out a lead on a place Jagger gave me, and if I don't like it, we're going to see a few other places."

"These trades are such short notice. I'm sure she's got stuff to do."

"I guess, but so far you're the only one who seems excited to have me."

"I can call Tweetie. He's hyped to have you on the team. Hell, I'm excited to be back on the same team as you." I finish my drink. I was going to call Henry and Tweetie last night, ask them to join us, but I think Conor needs some time not having to be on for everyone. "And if the apartment thing falls through, you can always crash at a hotel for a bit."

He groans. "Just the thought of spending every night in a hotel—reminds me of being on the road. But I'm happy to be back in Chicago regardless of all the shit going on. We're going to have a killer line."

"I wish I had something to make you feel better about the situation with your family, man."

He cracks his neck and looks at the television. "It's okay. It's just hard. I put on a brave face for my sister, but I don't know... I thought they were happy these days. It feels like everything I believed was bullshit. Plus, what does this mean for the future? Separate holidays and shit?"

I continue to listen, not having any advice to give him and wishing I had some wisdom like those quotes you see on social media or billboards. Something to make him feel better and give him hope it will all work out.

"It's good to be back with you. You always were such a rock for me." He finishes his beer.

"I'm not sure I remember it that way." He was the closest thing I had to family in college, a time I felt so alone. He was the one who was always there for me.

"You always had all your shit together."

I laugh. "No, I didn't. And I don't know. I mean there's this wo—" I stop talking because I'm not going to make it about myself tonight. I'm not even sure how to describe what's going on with Leigh and me. Eventually, I need to talk to someone about her.

"You losing your bachelor card?"

"Fuck no," I say. I'm not lying, but also, I'm skimming the truth. If Leigh wanted something more, I'm not sure I would say no, and that's a step I've never taken. Thinking about it makes my heart pound like my first game in the league.

He stares at me long and hard. "You cannot get all serious with someone right as I come into town. We're going to relive those college days. Between you, me, and Tweetie, we'll own the clubs."

I refrain from agreeing or saying no, instead pushing the topic to something else. "How was living in Florida?"

It's a lame question, but I don't want us to venture into a conversation about what our nights will look like. Right now, it's great being with Conor, but I wish Leigh was right next to me, or better yet, on my lap.

He tells me about Florida and how he's going to have to get used to the Chicago winters again. We talk about some bullshit topics, and Ruby gets us each another drink. By the time we call it quits, and we're walking out of Peeper's Alley, I realize having Conor back as a teammate makes Chicago feel more like home.

twenty-one

Kyleigh

"Do Mom and Dad even know you're in Chicago?" I ask Conor at the fancy steak restaurant he wanted to go to tonight. I dodged Rowan by using Alara as an excuse again, but I plan to come clean as soon as Conor goes back to Florida to pack up his stuff before preseason training.

"No. Dad called me when he heard the news. Mom sent me a text, which tells me she must assume you've told me. When I get back for good, I think me and you should see Dad, tell him, and go from there. Let's let him finish out this case first."

I nod because I don't really want any part of it, but Conor's been my shoulder to cry on, and I can't make him do it by himself. "Okay."

He cuts his steak, and I sip my wine because I don't have much of an appetite.

"So, what's your plan? If you're not going to work with Mom again, are you starting your own bridal design business?"

I finish my wine while he cuts a precise piece off his steak and puts it in his mouth. As usual, I'm delaying because I don't want to hear his reaction.

"Well, I wasn't going to tell you, but you'll find out anyway. I might be buying a bar." I clench my teeth and smile, widening my eyes with an expression like can you believe it?

I've been thinking a lot about it the past few weeks like Ruby asked, and I told her a couple of days ago that I'm interested.

He chokes on his piece of steak. I look around in a panic for someone to give him the Heimlich, but he clears the piece of meat himself and grabs a sip of water to recover. "You what?"

He clearly doesn't think it's as exciting as me.

"I don't want to design clothes, let alone wedding gowns. Pretend like everyone is getting into some happy union when in reality it's probably doomed to fail. Owning a bar would be fun." I shrug.

Conor places his fork and knife down, eyes drilling into mine. "You're going to use what money? Grandfather's trust that you just got on your birthday? Instead of using the degree you worked your ass off to obtain?"

"I was a bartender in college that one summer, remember?"

His mouth opens, and he inhales slowly as if he's trying to gain the patience to deal with me. "You were a bartender. Not a bar owner. Ky, it's a little impulsive, no?"

I shrug again. I expected this reaction from Conor. I've never been an impulsive person—or maybe I have, but I always felt my mom pushing her thumb down and would never act on it.

"It's not impulsive. I've talked to the woman who owns the bar a lot about it. I think it's the kind of change I need."

"Who is this woman? She's probably trying to get rid of a

place that's most likely pulling her down into debt. So now it will be your debt."

"It's not like that. She said we'll work together until I'm comfortable, and she wanted me to think about it. I did, and the more I do, the more I want the challenge."

He groans and shakes his head. "Don't throw your life away just because Mom did hers." He goes back to cutting his steak, and I watch his face grow redder the more he thinks about what I want to do.

"It's like a fresh start. I'll get to meet new people. Have regulars. I'm excited." And I am. Also a little scared, but I know Ruby will be by my side to show me the ropes before I officially purchase the bar.

"Come on, Ky, what are you thinking?"

"I'm thinking that I'm twenty-five. I'm thinking I'm an adult. I'm thinking that I'm able to make the decisions about what I want my future to look like."

Truly, the only downfall is that Peeper's Alley is right under Rowan's condo, but he won't be there forever. Eventually, he'll get traded or retire and move somewhere else. And I'm not making my life decisions based on Rowan. He's just a fling that's destined to end soon, so that would be stupid.

"You know how many bars and restaurants close every year? And those have experienced owners."

The waitress walks by, and I stop her, asking her for another glass of wine. Conor is driving me to keep drinking.

"How about you say, 'That's cool, sis, I can't wait to check it out?' How about you have my back on this decision?"

He leans back, wipes his mouth with his crimson-colored linen napkin, and studies me as if he's waiting for me to back down. Not going to happen. I don't let my eyes leave his no matter how uncomfortable he's making it.

"I wish you would've run it by me first."

"As if I need your permission?" I'm growing more annoyed by the second.

"Not permission, but we could talk it out. Look at the logistics. I mean, I don't even know where it's located. Who is this woman? Have you looked at the financials?"

I cross my arms and lean back in my chair. "You don't have to know because you're not purchasing the bar. I am. It's *my* decision." I point at my chest.

"Why don't you just start your own boutique? Why would you go start something new? Something you know nothing about? I'm thinking about your future." He blows out a breath and picks up his scotch glass, shaking his head as though I'm some idiot.

"Because I never want to design clothes again. All my life, I've done what she wanted. Go to fashion school? Okay, Mom. Don't go to New York, come home and work with me, I'll mentor you. Okay, Mom. Oh, you don't want to own a car in Chicago, just use Uber and take the El. Okay, Mom." I give him a glimpse of what my entire life has been like with me going along with everything Mom wanted. "Don't date Caden Sperry. He's not your type."

Okay, she was right about Caden, but I'll never tell her or anyone else that.

Conor doesn't say anything because he can't. He's always had a free pass to do whatever he wants. He played hockey, dated who he wanted, picked the school he'd attend all on his own. Never with one opinion from my mom.

"Okay, I get it," he says. "But you did enjoy the fashion design if I remember correctly? And you did go to the school you wanted to?"

I nod and thank the waitress as she drops my wine off at the table. "I did, but I can't imagine sketching anything right now. Design and Mom go hand in hand for me."

The way she holds a piece of fabric while her other hand

sketches that part of the dress to detail it perfectly? I do that now. My entire process is hers, not mine. Not the one I graduated with from KSU anyway.

He doesn't say anything for a few seconds. "Fine. When I get back, you can take me over there. I want to see it."

"Great. Thanks for seeing my side." I smile and sip my wine, my meal completely untouched.

"I didn't say I see your side. I just said I want to see it." He buries his face in his plate again, and I want to dump my wine over his head.

I don't really care what he thinks. I get that he's looking out for me, but I'm an adult now. Not the little sister he has to protect. I'll make that bar a success, just wait and see.

After dinner, Conor makes the excuse that he's going out with some guys, which I really hope isn't Rowan because I was hoping to sneak over to his place tonight. We say our goodbyes, and there's a clear divide between us. He doesn't agree with my decision, and I'm mad he's not supporting me. Problems to deal with when he returns from Florida for good.

He goes to the bathroom, and I pull out my phone, ready to call an Uber, but I text Rowan instead.

> You home?

Three dots appear, and I wait, hoping he's not going to message me back saying he's going out.

> I've been waiting…

My stomach explodes with the fireworks only he can set off.

> Fifteen minutes.

> Get ready to take off your panties as soon
> as you get here. I need to taste you as soon
> as you walk through the door.

I clench my thighs underneath the table.

I grab an Uber, and the fifteen-minute drive to his apartment feels like an hour, but once the car pulls up to the curb, I hop out.

He waits just outside the security gate, leaning along the wall and scrolling through his phone. He's in joggers, a sweatshirt, and barefoot with his slides on.

I walk up to him. "Excuse me, is this The Nest?"

His gaze lifts, and he pockets his phone, that smile that draws me in on his lips. "No, sorry."

"Oh shucks, I was looking for Tweetie Sorenson?"

His smile drops, he wraps his arm around my waist and pulls me toward him, nuzzling his face into my neck. "Sorry, he's out. You're stuck with me."

I draw back, but he doesn't release my waist. "I guess you'll have to do."

"I guess so." He turns and goes to press the key code into the security gate.

"Actually." I place my hand over his, and he turns to face me. "I want to show you something."

He tilts his head and studies me. I take his hand and guide him away from the gate, toward Peeper's Alley.

"Yeah, I'm not in the mood for Ruby. Can we just—" He stops when I pull out a key and insert it in the lock. "Leigh?"

Ruby gave me a key when I asked because the bar is closed tonight.

I turn the key and step inside.

"Magic!" Tweetie's voice sounds from behind us.

Rowan looks over his shoulder as a car pulls up along the curb, and my brother steps out of the building. The feeling of elation in my stomach is replaced by a lead balloon. I duck inside the building, trying to peek out through one of the windows.

"Why aren't you coming with us tonight?" I hear my brother ask.

"He's got regular pussy to attend to, that's why," Tweetie answers before Rowan can.

"I have plans, but I'll catch you next time," Rowan says.

"Let her come out with us and meet your new friend, Magic," Tweetie says.

"Give him a rest," I hear Henry, who must have joined them, say.

Rowan turns to me and ducks his head inside, frowning. I shoo at him in a gesture that says get rid of them.

"Next time," Rowan tells them.

"This better not be how it'll be when I move here!" Conor shouts, and I flip him off even though he can't see me.

"Don't call me from jail. I'm not picking your sorry asses up." Rowan walks inside, and I shut the door, flicking the lock.

Rowan stares at me for a beat. "You're acting weird."

"I just didn't want to be pulled into going out tonight." Another lie. I'm stacking them up like my mother now. I have to tell him tonight. I have to.

"Why do you have a key to the bar? How close have you and Ruby gotten?" He follows me as I walk over to the bar.

"What can I get you?" I grab a bottle and try to flip it, almost missing it, but I grip the handle right before it crashes to the floor.

"Leigh, what's going on?"

I pull out a glass for his vodka tonic. "I'm going to buy the bar."

His face looks a lot like Conor's did earlier, and my smile drops.

"You think I'm crazy?"

He shakes his head, seeming to recover. "No. I just didn't know it was something you wanted to do."

"I do." I search the bottles, finding the vodka.

"Okay. Ruby didn't pressure you though, right?" He sits on one of the stools.

"She actually made me think about it before she'd agree, but I really want to do it. I'm not going to buy it right away. She's going to let me train under her for a bit, and then we'll figure it out."

He smiles at me, blue eyes twinkling. "Awesome. Congratulations then."

"Really?"

He chuckles in that low, easy way I love. "Of course. I'm sure you'll do great."

My heart lifts that he so easily believes in me. That he thinks I can do this. "You're my first customer, so I'm going to make you your favorite drink."

I pick up the vodka and tip it to pour it into his glass, but his hand covers the rim, and I straighten the bottle, staring at him.

His gaze rises to meet mine, and he bites his bottom lip. "There's something I should probably tell you."

Shit. Has he been keeping secrets too?

twenty-two

Rowan

THIS ISN'T SOMETHING I SHARE WITH ANYONE. Other than Ruby and Jagger, no one else knows. Not even Tweetie or Henry. I like to keep this part of my life private because I don't like answering a lot of questions about it. The only reason I ever told Jagger was because he was adamant I tell him about anything that might come out in the press that could be perceived negatively. That if he was caught by surprise, he'd cut me off, and I wasn't going to risk not having the best sports agent in the business.

She places the bottle on the bar while I rise from the stool, rounding the bar to the other side—her side.

"Let me show you how to make my drink."

"Okay." Her voice is shaky.

I'm still not positive that giving her this information about me is the right call, but for some reason, I trust her enough to do so. I think she'll keep this secret, and I hope my judgment isn't wrong.

I fill the glass with ice by using the scoop and grab the soda nozzle. I pick up her hand and place it over the button, pressing the button for the club soda to fill my glass close to the rim. Grabbing a lime from the fridge, I drop it in.

Her hand holds the soda nozzle, and her eyes meet mine. "That's it?"

I pick up the drink and take a sip. "That's it."

Our eyes stay locked, and I can read the questions in her eyes.

"You weren't drunk that first night we met?"

I chuckle and shake my head. "Nope."

"Oh."

"Were you?" I didn't think she was. I knew she had a few glasses of wine but not so much that she was hammered.

"No. But I guess I figured..."

I place my cup on the bar top and broach the distance between us, stepping into her and caging her back to the bar with my hands on either side of her body. "Figured what?"

"That you were, you know...tipsy, I guess."

"Tipsy?"

"Okay, and horny."

I step closer to her, letting her feel how hard I am. "I am horny."

"Rowan." Her hands splay on my chest. "You were going to tell me something."

I could say the same thing to her. We're both keeping secrets from one another. And maybe I should say a secret for a secret, but I don't want to force her to tell me. I want her to trust me like I do her in this moment.

I bring one hand up, swiping her hair away from her forehead and tucking a chunk of it behind her ear. "My dad drank...a lot...and he wasn't a happy drunk."

She grabs my shirt in her fists but doesn't say anything.

"I did drink in college and some of the early years in the league, but I stopped a long time ago. Not because I had a problem, although had I let it go any longer, I probably would have. But I didn't like who I was. I didn't like waking up in the morning and not remembering what I did the night before. It made me feel out of control and a lot like my father, so I stopped drinking alcohol all together. The longer I went without it, the happier I was."

"Why hide it?" she asks, and I step back, leaning against the back of the bar.

"I don't want all the questions that go along with a decision like this. It's not people's business." I cross my arms, the defensiveness I've always felt showing. I force myself to loosen them to my sides. She can ask me whatever she wants now that I've told her my secret. "So far, I've been lucky that no one has noticed, and I'd like to keep it that way. I don't want people to dig into my past. They'll find all the police reports of domestic abuse. They'll find my father's death certificate stating he died of liver failure due to chronic alcoholism. They'll find a lot of shit about my life that I don't want random people to know."

Her eyes fill with pity. "I'm sorry you had to go through that."

"Yeah, that's the other thing I fucking don't want." I turn to leave the area behind the bar, but she wraps her arms around me, practically climbing on my back.

"Wait. Stop. I'm just so sorry that you've had to go through that. Especially as a young kid. Life isn't fair."

I cover her hands with mine because unlike the few other times I've discussed this with someone, I don't want to run away. Isn't that the problem with her? I always want to be with her. This infatuation stage of our relationship isn't losing momentum, quite the opposite, and it makes me feel out of control in my life. A feeling I don't do well with.

"Please don't ever tell anyone," I say in a soft voice as if there are people around.

"Never. I would never." When I circle around, she rises on

her tiptoes, grabbing my face and staring in my eyes. "I won't ever tell anyone. I promise."

"Thanks."

She places her mouth on mine, and I lick the seam of her lips. We don't rush our kiss, our hands running over the layers of our clothes as if we're naked. God, she's ruining me, and I'm just letting her do it, but the last thing I want to do is walk away from this.

I really hope Ruby doesn't have cameras.

Per usual, slow only lasts so long before the tension rises to a point that we're desperate to come together. Backing her up to the bar, I continue to kiss her, my hands manipulating the buttons on her blouse until I spread it open to reveal her bra-covered tits.

"I want to fuck these so bad," I say, taking the weight of them in my palms.

"Do it." She's practically panting already.

"Not now. I need to be inside you."

Her fingers run up and under the hem of my sweatshirt, slowly torturing me until her warm palms run along my back. "I love to feel your skin under my hands."

It's something I've noticed. Every time we're together, her hands find their way up along my chest or back. I don't mind one bit.

She rests her chin on my chest and stares up at me with those big caramel eyes of hers. The look on her face makes me think she might be ready to tell me whatever it is she's been holding back. But instead, she pushes up my sweatshirt and places kisses over my heart and around my chest.

Jesus, I think now she feels sorry for me.

Fuck. I just want to forget that I shared my most vulnerable admission with her.

I lower my body, swiping an arm around her middle and hoisting her up, taking her to the private room to fuck her on the table. Every time I'm in here with the guys from now on, this is what I'll be picturing.

I push through the door and drop her on the table.

"Condom?" she asks.

I dig into my pocket and hold up the one I had with me when I went down to meet her because I planned on taking her as soon as she entered my condo.

She pushes at my chest, and I stumble backward. Leaning back on her hands, her eyes peruse my body from head to toe and back up. "I want to see you strip."

I chuckle and hold the hem of my sweatshirt, lifting it up my chest. "Don't jump me."

She giggles, twirling her finger. "Keep going."

I strip my sweatshirt off, but don't continue. "How about I take an item off and then you take an item off?"

Without a word, she slides her arms out of the blouse, hanging it off her finger and letting it drop to the floor. "Your turn."

I shake my head. I don't have a lot of clothes left. I toe out of my slides.

"Shoes don't count."

"Well then." I pull down my sweatpants and step out of them, leaving me in—

"Well, well, seems you're sharing more than one secret tonight." She giggles, staring at my crotch.

I look down and holy fuck, how did I forget?

"I mean, I get the Captain America thing, but did you steal Bodhi's underwear by accident?"

My Captain America boxer briefs dampen the sexy vibe of our back-and-forth stripping game, but I'm not going to tell her how embarrassed I feel. Instead, I hook my fingers into either side and yank them down my legs, leaving me completely naked.

"Oh, I kind of liked it. We could make it a whole role plaything." She jumps off the table, shedding her pants. She's just about to do the same with her sheer baby blue underwear, but I raise my hand.

"Keep them on."

Her gaze floats up and down my body, landing on my dick that's pointing north and growing harder by the minute. "A bossy Captain America. I like it."

"Get up on the table."

She does as I say, and I walk toward her, fisting my cock. She watches me running my hand up and down my length. "You trying to make me forget about the whole Captain America thing?"

"Is it working?"

"Kind of."

I use my free hand and push her legs apart, my palm sliding up her inner thigh. She opens her legs wider, and I step in between them, releasing my cock to grab her ass and tug her to the edge. Then I take my dick in hand again, slide the thin fabric over, and run my tip up and down her slick center.

"Shit," she says, watching me.

Keeping one hand on her lower back and one hand on my dick, I purposely run it along her clit and back to her entrance, all while watching where I'm going to disappear in minutes.

She picks up the condom from next to her, opens it, and holds it out. I hold my dick at the base, and she rolls it over my length. Then she kills me as she slouches slightly, her ass hanging off the table, and guides my dick into her opening.

I slide inside, inch by inch, staring at her taking me in, at us connecting as one.

"Rowan," she moans.

I look up to see something in her eyes. Something I don't want to see. As playful as I tried to make this moment, it's still something more than our usual encounters.

I'm not sure if it's the fact that I told her something about myself no one knows, or if the feelings I've felt rushing over me these past few weeks are refusing to stay quiet any longer. My hand cradles the nape of her neck, and I inch forward, kissing her as I get as deep as I can. From there, things ramp up.

Our mouths are ravenous, unable to get enough of one another. Her legs wrap around me, squeezing my hips, and I continue to kiss her like the starved man I am for her. I want everything she's willing to give me.

The only sound in the empty bar is the wet slapping sound of me pounding into her and the strangled moans escaping our mouths.

She clings to me, her fingertips digging into my biceps. I really need her to come soon before I embarrass myself. I bring my hand to her clit and massage it in the rhythm I know she loves.

Her lips strip off mine, and her head rocks back, her back arching. "I'm coming."

Thank God because once her pussy walls clench around my dick, it strips me of the last of my willpower. I spill into the condom on a curse, holding myself inside her while her back falls to the table, catching her breath.

I'll never get used to how stunning she looks after she comes.

I take a moment while her eyes are closed and she doesn't know I'm looking at her to admire her beauty and the fact that she's kind of mine. I mean, I don't think she's seeing anyone else. Or fucking anyone else. I hope not. We never talked specifically about being exclusive. Shit, do I even ask?

I withdraw from her body, jealousy thick in my veins at the idea of her with anyone but me. I go to the bathroom and dispose of the condom, returning to find her still lying on the table, her hands on her stomach.

"You good?" I ask.

She nods and sits up. "Great."

But her words don't match the euphoric bliss I assumed she'd be in after the amazing sex we just had.

"You sure?" I pick up her clothes and place them on the table. I want to get her to my condo and lay her in my bed for the night, which I know is the wrong thing to want at this moment.

She smiles. "Yeah. It's just..."

I can't bear for her to tell me this is turning into something more, and she wants to bail, so I don't allow her to tell me. Instead, I pick up her clothes and hand them to her. "Let's go up to my place. I'm starving."

Using my stomach as an excuse, my delay works, and she doesn't tell me she wants to end this because she feels this is heading in the opposite direction than agreed on. That we're becoming more than fuck buddies.

"Don't forget your Captain America boxers."

"You think you're funny, do you?" I lift her and haul her over my shoulder. "I can do this all day."

"Did you just use one of his lines?" She laughs.

"Maybe. If I'd known you were a Captain America fan, I would've worn the boxers earlier."

I spank her ass with my hand, and she yelps, hitting my ass like a drum with both of her hands. A strange sensation lights up in my stomach, but I push the feeling away. There's no way it's what I think it is.

twenty-three

Kyleigh

"Do I have to answer it?" I whine like the younger sister I am when it comes to Conor and me.

My dad is standing on the other side of my apartment door. Doing this in public wasn't an option, but I wish we didn't have to tell him here. I don't need the reminder of breaking my dad's heart every time I walk into my living room.

"We should've done it at your hotel," I whisper to Conor as I walk over to the door. "Just a second, Dad."

"I'm staying at Tweetie Sorenson's actually."

I freeze and circle back around. Surely it's some joke. Two hockey players being roommates? Two hockey players who are worth millions? "What?"

"The place I bought won't be done for a few months because there are some renos to be done before I close, so he said he'd let me take his second bedroom in the meantime."

My dad knocks again.

"Ky?" Conor says, nodding toward the door. "Stop stalling and get the door."

I'm pretty sure I look like I did when he let it slip that there wasn't a tooth fairy.

He gets up off the couch. "What's with you?"

He walks over to the door, and I hear him say hi to my dad.

Conor is living at The Nest? Is the universe trying to screw me? Why didn't Rowan tell me? Then again, why would he? It's not really my business since he has no idea Conor is my brother.

I cringe. God, this is such a mess.

"Ky?" Dad says, his hand landing on my shoulder.

I turn and force a smile. He opens his arms, enveloping me in a hug. I try to commit this moment to memory because everything I know in this life is about to implode. I inhale his woodsy scent.

"How was the case?" Conor changes the subject, giving me a look after I separate from my dad that tells me I need to get a grip, and I'm acting like he's dying.

"We won." Dad sits down in my chair, his long legs stretched out in front of him. He rolls his neck. After every big case, you can see the stress and toll it took on him. I wish we could give him a few weeks to decompress, but that would just be delaying the inevitable.

Conor heads into my kitchen. "Beer?"

"To celebrate you coming home. Not my case." He sits up and rests his forearms on his knees. His salt-and-pepper hair isn't styled today like it usually is. His gaze lifts to mine. "We should plan a meal with your mom."

I tear my gaze away and stand, meeting Conor at the fridge. "I'll open up some wine too."

"Ky." My dad sighs. "I know your mom expects a lot from you. But she just wants the best. Nothing is going to change until you two talk this out."

My jaw clenches, and I glare at Conor because it's taking

all of my willpower not to spit out that she's a lying cheater. But my dad isn't and doesn't deserve to be told that way.

"We ordered some pizza," Conor says, opening my dad's beer and handing it to him.

"Okay, but—" Dad starts to say something else, but suddenly stops, and I'm guessing that it's because of the look Conor is giving him.

This is our family dynamic. I allow my mom to push and push me until I finally push back. Then I retreat and ignore the fact that I'm mad. Sometimes I suck it up, let her apologize, and we make up. But those times, she wasn't sleeping with a man who wasn't my father. It was always about her control over my life, my career, and my decisions. To my dad, this is no different than any other time, and he thinks we'll be one big happy family again soon. With Conor returning, he's probably excited for weekly family dinners.

My chest squeezes, and I have to force myself to keep my face neutral.

"Sorry I've been MIA while you're looking for a place here," Dad says to Conor. "I should've been helping you. Have you decided whether you're buying or renting?"

They sit in the chairs across from one another while I sit on the couch. Conor looks so at ease with his baseball cap on backward, his worn jeans, with an even more worn T-shirt. While I feel like a kink in a necklace and no matter how much I try to free the knot, the metal tightens.

"No worries, Ky helped out. I ended up buying. I'm hoping I'm here for a while." He shrugs. "I mean, I think I will be."

"You will. You're the best thing that could happen to the Falcons," my dad says.

"Besides Landry," Conor says, and my stomach feels as if a dozen helium balloons were let go.

My dad smiles. "That entire offensive line, but how is Rowan?"

"He's great. Solid. Has it all together like usual." There's a jealous note in Conor's voice that I'm not used to hearing.

"He's definitely got a good head on his shoulders. Doesn't let all that fame get to him."

My dad is right. I never would've imagined how grounded Rowan seems for being the player he is in the league. Not to mention how fucking hot he is.

"I can't wait to play with him again. But I'm staying at Tweetie Sorenson's until my place is ready. Funny enough, he lives right above Rowan."

"They live in the same building?" my dad asks.

There goes that dread washing over my body again. How am I going to get to Rowan's apartment without Conor seeing me? Plus, they'll be at Peeper's, and that's the bar I'm buying. Our time together is running out.

Conor's hasn't brought up the bar again, but I'm sure once he returns for good, he's going to want to insert himself into the situation.

"Yeah. Hensley and his son too."

My dad nods.

"They call it The Nest," I say before I think better of it.

Conor's head whips in my direction. "How do you know that?"

Shit.

I scoff. "Hello? I mean...everyone in Chicago knows."

Conor narrows his eyes, and I try to push away all the anxiety quickly overtaking my body language with the hopes that he'll believe me.

"They mentioned it in an interview on *SportsNight* when they told the three of them about your trade."

Thanks for the save, Dad.

Conor nods and strips his gaze off me. Thank goodness.

"So, Dad..." Conor sits up straight, setting his beer on the table.

My heart hammers like a pagan war drum, and I gulp down my wine. This is it. We're going to tell my dad. My heart is fracturing as I take one last look at him before he knows, then I stare at my lap.

"The reason Mom isn't here," Conor starts. "She, um..."

"I know you're having your differences, Ky. She's been so stressed out these last few weeks without you. I wish you'd just talk to her."

"That's not it, Dad," Conor continues and glances in my direction.

The hurt has to be overwhelming Conor, and he's always been there for me. It's time I don't let him handle everything in my stead. We're both adults now.

"Dad, um...a few weeks ago, I went to one of the weddings for Mom. And I had to stop by the office to grab something I forgot beforehand. Mom was there."

He shakes his head. "I keep telling her to stop working so much, but who am I to talk? With my cases, I'm at the office at all hours."

Listening to him defend her nearly breaks my heart.

"Yeah, no. That's not it."

"Sorry you guys were brought up by two workaholics." Dad chuckles.

"That's not it," Conor says and nods in my direction.

I suck in a breath and let it trickle out slowly. "She was with another man, Dad."

He's looking at me, but I don't think he's really seeing me. He's processing what I just said. Trying to decipher what exactly it is I'm saying. "Another man?"

"They were..." I swallow past the Sahara Desert that is my throat. "Kissing."

"Oh." He puts his beer on the table.

None of us say anything. He stares at the floor while Conor and I glance at one another, unsure what to do from here.

"I'm sorry you saw that," he says.

I'm not sure how to take that. Did he already know? Maybe just suspect something was going on?

"I need to talk to your mom."

He's so calm, but this is where Conor gets it from. Dad's going to process this and dissect it like he does his cases at work. He's always told us never to draw conclusions before looking at the facts.

"Did you know him?" he asks, and his jaw clenches.

"No," I say with tears in my eyes. "Dad, I'm so sorry." I slide to the end of the couch and lean forward to take his hand. "I can't believe she did this."

He squeezes my hand and stands. "Thank you for telling me, Kyleigh." I hate hearing him using my full name. "I know this couldn't have been easy for you two."

I stand and wrap my arms around him, pressing my cheek into his chest and wishing I could do something other than be the bearer of bad news. He runs his hand up and down my back as if *he's* consoling *me*. I step back, and he heads over to Conor, hugging him.

"I'm sorry, Dad," Conor mumbles.

Then Dad walks toward my apartment door.

"You don't want to stay for pizza?" I ask.

"Ky," Conor says.

Dad turns around with his hand on the doorknob. "No pizza tonight, kiddo. I have to figure this out with your mom, but what's happened doesn't change the fact that she's your mother."

My mouth slowly falls open, and I cross my arms. "She's destroyed our family."

Conor comes up beside me, putting his arm around my shoulders.

"She's the only mother you have, that's what I'm saying. It's our marriage, not yours. You'll have to separate the two. She didn't cheat on you. She cheated on me."

I huff. "No, Dad, you're wrong. She cheated on all of us."

Conor's hand tightens on my shoulder.

"You have every right to be angry. You both do. We'll talk soon." Dad opens the door, steps out into the hall, and shuts it behind him.

I turn into Conor's chest, and the tears stinging my eyes finally slip free while he holds me.

"It's going to be okay. He's going to be okay," he says.

"I hate her, Conor. Hate her."

He squeezes me tighter. "I know. I know."

I'm not sure what I would do if I didn't have Conor as my big brother. Which makes me hate even more than I already do the fact that I'm keeping a secret from him. I'm sleeping with his teammate and friend, and he has no clue. Hell, his teammate doesn't either.

But now is not the time for me to drop it all at his feet. His mom cheated on his dad too. And although Conor's great at hiding his emotions and moving forward to do what has to be done, I know he's as torn up as I am. How could he not be? Our family has always been the stable thing in our lives, our calm in the world's storms.

She took that from us. All of us.

twenty-four

Rowan

IT'S THE FIRST DAY OF PRESEASON TRAINING, AND yesterday was the first day I didn't see Leigh in I don't remember how long. A month maybe? So I'm at my locker, making sure I'll see her tonight. Hockey season is about to start, and our time together is going to dramatically decrease.

> I miss your pussy.

You. I want to say you, but I don't know how she'd take it.

> You dropping the whole horny thing then?

> I'm horny AND I miss your pussy.

> First line was better.

> Can I see you tonight?

There. It's out there. I'm actually asking instead of making sexual innuendos.

Sure.

When can you be at my place?

Want to come to my place for a change?

She's never offered her place before, but I'd love to see where she lives because I'm sure it says a lot about who she is. Then again, I'm not supposed to want to know more about her.

The two little devils on opposite shoulders argue—when are you going to own the fact that you want her for more than just sex? one asks. When she gives me a sign that she wants that too, the other one says.

Sure. Address?

She sends me her address, and I save it under her contact.

Send me a pic?

She sends me one of her knee cap.

I do love your knees, but I was hoping for a little higher up.

She sends me one of her outside thigh. She must be wearing a dress.

A little to the left.

She sends me a pic of her inner thigh.

Keep going.

She sends me a picture that cuts off right before the juncture of her thighs, and my mouth salivates for another one. Even with her panties still on. I don't care.

"Shit, is that the girl?" Conor asks over my shoulder, and my phone drops to the bench.

I push him in the chest and grab my phone before she sends anything more revealing, and these dipshits get a glimpse at her. "Fuck off."

"Relax, it's her leg, not her tits." Conor goes over to his locker. "You're in deep, huh? Getting all hot and bothered by a thigh." He laughs.

"He's a goner, but still in denial," Tweetie says across the locker room.

I check my phone, and she sends me one last picture of her one leg open and one side of her panties. God, I want to be inside her right now.

> I can't wait to lick you right there, but I have to get on the ice. Keep it wet for me.

I turn off the screen and put my phone in my bag, then finish getting ready. We all head out, Tweetie and Conor continuing to give me shit until their skates hit the ice.

"You know it's okay to like her, right?" Henry says, falling in line with me.

I skate onto the ice, drop the puck, and practice my stick handling. "It's not like that. We're just having fun."

He does the same as me, and I'm thankful because I really don't want to have this conversation.

"You haven't seen her yet?" I hear Tweetie asking Conor. "She's at the building all the damn time. Dark hair, great tits, and an amazing ass."

"Shit, she sounds hot," Conor says, skating toward the goal.

"She is. Too bad Magic found her first. I would've

snatched her away." Tweetie smiles wide at me, and I shoot a puck at him. It flies up and hits him. "Now you're acting jealous. Buy a ring already."

"How come I haven't heard anything much about her from you?" Conor asks, doing some warm-up stretches before we start hammering him with pucks.

"Because she's not my girlfriend. She's just a girl." I hate saying that about Leigh, but I'm not the type of guy who pours his heart out to his teammates.

Henry scoffs under his breath, passing me behind the net. I'm not sure why he has so much to say about it. I don't see him looking for the love of his life. Then again, he has to consider Bodhi as well.

"Hate to break it to you, but permanent pussy is pretty much a girlfriend," Conor says. "Are you stringing her along?"

I stand idle and knock the puck around with my stick. I'm not playing her. She could be playing me though I guess, which shouldn't hurt as much as it does right now. "It's a mutual thing. Neither of us want anything serious."

Conor looks at Tweetie, and they both laugh.

"What?" I glare at them.

"I guarantee she's hoping you'll change your mind. She's probably playing hard to get to keep you chasing. She thinks she can change your mind eventually." Conor shakes his head.

"She's not like that. She's different. Not a puck bunny." I argue in her defense because to me, she is different. So different from any woman before her.

"So, she didn't know who you were when you met?" Conor asks, raising his eyebrows.

"That's a hard ask. I'm Rowan fucking Landry." I play it off because she did admit that she reads the hockey blogs. Which means she knew my reputation—my false reputation—before I talked to her.

"Look who's pretending to be cocky now." Conor motions with a gloved hand my way.

Tweetie skates around me and steals the puck. "You should be cocky. Settling down at this stage of your career is really shitty to the rest of your crew."

I'm pretty sure Tweetie is joking, but there's something in the way he's trying to play it off like he thinks monogamy and settling down are a bad thing that I'm not buying.

"Exactly, I just got here. Come on, you can't prefer dinners in with your girl over a club filled with girls grabbing for your dick." Conor rotates his neck, cracking it.

I'm happy to see Coach coming out. He'll get me the hell out of this conversation.

"You guys sound like Neanderthals." Henry, being the disciplined player he is, skates back and forth, working on his footwork.

"You already strapped yourself down with Bodhi, so we gave up on you a long time ago." Tweetie shoots me the puck, and I skate behind the net and down to center.

"And you'll die a lonely old man." Henry raises his eyebrows. "Don't give Magic shit just because you already passed up on your soulmate."

Fuck, Hensley really went there.

Tweetie's jaw clenches, and I prepare for a showdown, but I get why Hensley said it. You come after Bodhi, he's gonna fire back. "She obviously wasn't my soulmate, and don't talk about shit you don't know about."

I shoot Tweetie the puck to give him something to concentrate on other than beating Henry to the ground.

"Back at you," Henry says, his mouth a firm line.

"Fine."

"Way to deal with your aggression, boys. I'm proud of you." Conor laughs. "I thought for a moment I'd be able to grab a unit at The Nest. Oh, can I tell you...my little sister knows what that place is called."

"Sister? I like sisters." Tweetie stops skating in front of Conor, whose eyes narrow.

"Not on your life. She already knows never to date one of my teammates. I made that clear a long fucking time ago."

"Jeez, it's like you're sweetening the pot. I like the challenge too." Tweetie grins. "And now you're living with me for the foreseeable future. Why don't we have a sleepover with her and get to know each other better?"

Conor's expression says it all—try it, and he's not going to be as gracious as Henry. I'm pretty sure you cross that line with Conor and that calm demeanor he usually displays will turn feral. Even in college when he'd mention his sister, it was obvious he was overprotective.

"Okay, boys, let's go!" Coach shouts.

Thank God.

Our first practice isn't bad. We're split into drills. I'm excited to be back at it even if my nerves about starting the season strong are always under the surface.

After my shower, I'm packing my bag, and Henry sits down next to me. Half the locker room has already cleared out. Conor and Tweetie left a few minutes ago to get something to eat. Henry has to get Bodhi, and I'm heading to Leigh's—right after I buy a box of condoms.

"If you want to talk, I'm here." Henry zips up his bag. "It looks like you're struggling with something lately."

I stare at my duffle bag between my feet. "I'm good."

"Rowan," he says, "you don't have to play her off to me. I get it."

I look beside me. "Who?"

He shakes his head. "Someone I used to know a long time ago. But we were young, and she needed to find herself, and it wasn't going to be following me around so I could play hockey. I let her go."

The thought of letting Leigh go feels like being crushed by a thousand-pound weight.

"I'm pretty sure she's going through something, but she doesn't want to talk about it, and I don't ask any questions," I say. "I'm not sure this thing with us is going anywhere. In fact, we both agreed that it wouldn't. I might have to let her go."

He nods. "Or you hold on tight and help her through it. This job isn't easy. Our schedule sucks during the season, and to start a relationship right now isn't ideal. But if you feel something for her, you should go with it instead of pushing it away."

I nod, but it's a step I've never taken, and that scares the shit out of me. "You just said you let yours go."

He huffs. "That was different. Like I said, we were young, and she had dreams she'd never fulfill alongside me trying to fulfill mine in hockey. My parents died young, and I was raised by my grandparents."

"Shit, I'm sorry." I frown.

He nods. "Yeah, but my grandparents enrolled me in the Big Brother Big Sister program, and Reed, the big brother who was assigned to me, took an active role in my upbringing. I was lucky to have him. I'm not sure where I was going with this...oh yeah, she's his stepdaughter and was my best friend until our teenage hormones took over." He chuckles, but it's forced. He clearly loved the girl. He pats me on the back. "Anyway, if you want to talk it out, I'm here. Regrets can live with you forever, but if you take the chance and fail, at least you know the outcome. That's what got me through this process of finding a spot in the league. I didn't want to let her go, but I would've regretted her staying here and never figuring out the person she was meant to be."

He walks toward the doors of the locker room. I hang my

head and blow out a breath before standing and picking up
my duffle bag.

My phone vibrates from inside with a text from my agent.

> Endorsement is all set. Ten o'clock on
> Saturday and plan for the entire day. It's all
> three of you.

I put a thumbs up and scroll to my text thread with Leigh.
The last picture is a glimpse of her black thong, but I really
wish it was her smiling face.

> On my way.

> See you soon.

I stare at the three words, and my stomach clenches.
Henry's right. The sex is off the charts, but deep down, I want
more than just her body. I want the part of her she's closed off
from me. I want to be the one to take care of her wounds and
heal her scars. And that just complicates things. The question
is, does she like complicated?

twenty-five

Kyleigh

WHILE I WAIT FOR ROWAN AT MY APARTMENT, MY phone rings on the coffee table. I lean forward from where I'm sitting cross-legged on the couch and see my mom's name on the screen. Anxiety zaps through my veins with the intensity of a bolt of lightning. What does she want?

I should answer it. Just get it over with. Rip off the Band-Aid like Ruby says, but I'd rather let it go to voicemail and not deal with her. Then again, I had the strength to tell my dad, and I did confront her when everything first happened. I can do this.

I snatch my phone off the table and swipe the screen to answer. "Hello?"

"Kyleigh." My mom says my name with the exhaustion of a parent who's been trying to reach their daughter all night because they didn't know where she was.

"Mom."

"You told your father?"

I've been good, Mom, thanks for asking. Yeah, I am still

upset about everything you did, I appreciate your concern. I'm
sorry you ruined our family too.

"I told you I would." I get up and pace in front of the television.

"I was going to do it, but he had that big case. It wasn't the right time. If you would've given me—"

"Mom, you had almost a month. And should never have cheated on him in the first place. A good wife would have ended the marriage before sleeping with someone else. Or talked to her husband and tried to fix whatever was making her unhappy."

She scoffs. "You think you're so smart, Kyleigh. You're twenty-five years old. You don't know what it's like to be in a long-term relationship."

I suck in a deep breath. "I know not to cheat on someone. Someone you supposedly love. Someone you market to the masses as the love of your life. Someone you say you can't live without."

She's quiet, but I hear her moving around. She's a pacer too, so I stop moving. I don't want to be like her in any regard. Then I walk in a small circle around my chair. The chair my dad sat in only a few nights ago when I told him the truth.

"It's complicated, and I don't expect you to understand. To you, we're just Mom and Dad. You don't see your father's faults. The hours he works—"

"Just stop." I squeeze my eyes shut. "He's my father, and I'm not going to listen to you defend your actions. What you did is unthinkable. There was a way you could have dealt with being unhappy that I would have understood. I'm not some naïve child, Mom. Yes, I am twenty-five, and I understand you see that as young, but I know not all marriages are rosy and perfect. But you get out of the marriage or try to fix it. You don't deceive someone."

She sighs. "I wish you'd meet me in person. I don't want to do this over the phone."

"Sorry, not going to happen." I become dizzy, so I sit on the edge of the chair and crack my neck back and forth.

"When are you coming back to work?"

I sit up straight in the chair, preparing myself for her reaction. "I'm not. I'm done."

"What? Kyleigh, you're going to take over my legacy."

I want to laugh out loud at the word legacy. I mean, yes, my mom does very well for herself. Her client list is extensive, with a long waiting list for consultations. But legacy is a bit much. "I don't want that. I've decided to—"

I almost slip up and tell her my plans, but she doesn't deserve to know what I'm going to do with my future. Let her sweat it out since she thinks I should run all my life's decisions through her.

"You're not going to waste your grandfather's money by not working, are you? That's not who you are."

"It doesn't matter what I'm going to do. It's my money. Like you said, I'm twenty-five, and it's mine now."

My grandfather left all the grandkids a small amount of money. It's not like a trust fund or anything I can live off, but enough for a down payment on a modest house or a nest egg. The only stipulation he put on the money for each of us was that we wouldn't receive it until we were twenty-five.

"But you'll just waste it," she says.

I thought I'd reached my limit with her weeks ago, but for some reason, her accusation that I'll be irresponsible with the money pisses me off. The only reason I can still pay my bills is because I'm responsible and have always put a portion of my paycheck into a savings account since I started working.

"No, I won't. I would tell you to trust me, but we both know you've never believed in me. You never let me forge my own path. Well, now I am, and I don't plan on that changing. I don't need you to micromanage me anymore."

I hear her breathing, but she says nothing for so long that I'm ready to hang up.

"You expect me to be perfect. I'm not, Kyleigh."

"Wrong, Mom, *you* expect *me* to be perfect."

"I made a mistake."

The heaviness in my heart lightens a little. That small piece of hope that she and Dad will fix this and everything I know in this world will be right again flickers then dies. Because I quickly remember, it won't ever be the same. I can't go back to the person or the life I had before walking in on my mom.

"Yes, you did." My voice breaks.

She scoffs. "So, you're just going to keep punishing me for it?"

"Punishing you?"

"Yes! You're going to ostracize me out of our family. Conor doesn't call me. Your dad moved out. And you're quitting on me."

My chest aches at the news that my dad has moved out. I make a mental note to call him tomorrow and see how he is.

"You did it to yourself." A knock sounds on my apartment door, and I know it's Rowan. "I have to go."

"Kyleigh, we have to fix this. You always ignore your problems, but I'm your mother. You can't just make me disappear out of your life like you're waving a magic wand."

I stare at the floor for a second. It hurts so much to think about losing my mother. And maybe one day down the road, I'll be able to be around her. I'm not sure I'll ever entirely forgive her, especially since she's trying to defend her actions, but I'm not even close to being there right now.

"I can do whatever I want to do, Mom. That's the great thing about being an adult. Bye."

My thumb shakes as I click End on the screen. I try to

calm my body, but my pulse is erratic, my limbs shaky, and I want to crumble to the floor and weep.

Rowan knocks again.

I shouldn't have answered the phone when I knew he was coming here, but I think subconsciously, I was hoping I'd pick up, and my mother would tell me what a huge mistake she made, how she regrets ever hurting my dad, me. Now Rowan's going to want to have sex, and I'm not sure I can use him to just push this away like I have every other time.

I walk over and open the door. When it swings open, his fist is raised to knock again. The usual smile he has when he sees me drops, and he steps inside, shutting the door and dropping his bags on the floor before wrapping his arms around me. I go willingly, clinging to him as tears fall, soaking his shirt.

The dam breaks, and all the pushing back of emotions becomes too much as I stand there sobbing in his arms. All I can do is let it out. Unfortunately, the timing couldn't be worse since I'm standing here with my fuck buddy who's probably thinking this isn't what he signed up for.

"I'm sorry." I back up, wiping my tears from my cheeks.

He steps forward, his arms stretched out, but I ignore them. "Are you okay?"

I nod, mentally laying brick after brick to build the wall back up. "Yeah, sorry, just got a bad phone call."

His gaze falls to the floor. "Do you want to talk about it?"

Yes! I want to tell you everything. Tell you who I really am. Tell you that I'm messing this up between us.

I want to ramble on and on, but if I do, he leaves. And I lose him. And I can't bear another loss at this moment.

"I'm sorry, I just don't think I'm in the mood tonight. Rain check?"

He nods, and I see the drugstore bag at his feet, next to his duffle bag. Condoms that won't get any use tonight. "Do you want me to leave?"

"I...I don't know," I say because I don't.

It's supposed to be just sex between us. I've never slept in the same bed as Rowan. We've been clear about where the line is, although I know he's slid in under my barbed wire at some point. Sure, maybe it's great that this thing between us has evolved. But I don't know how I could ever get into a relationship right now with where my head is, and he doesn't want anything more than what we have anyway. Letting myself think otherwise is setting myself up for heartbreak, and I've had about enough of that lately. Not to mention I've been lying to him about who I am, and I have no idea how he'll react when he finds out.

"I could hang out."

My shoulders sag. "Nah. I mean that's not part of the—"

"Listen." He takes my hand, guiding me over to the couch. His gaze runs over the room before landing back on me. "I'm still a friend. I think we've developed a friendship, right?"

"But—"

"But nothing. I want to. Let me stay and be the friend you need right now." His blue eyes implore me to give in, but I know it's because he's a decent guy, not because he's falling for me.

"I don't want to talk about it." I just want to mourn what I've lost. I'm done thinking of future scenarios of what my family dynamic might be going forward. I don't want people telling me I'll survive, I'll get through this right now.

"Fair enough. How about we order takeout and watch a movie?"

I sigh, and my shoulders slump. "Rowan, that's not our arrangement."

He presses his lips to my forehead. "Maybe we change the

rules. Sex doesn't have to be on the table in order for us to see each other?" He draws back with questions in his eyes.

Panic constricts my chest. "How about just for tonight?"

Something flashes in his eyes, and it almost looks like disappointment. "What's your favorite takeout spot?"

He pulls out his phone, and we order from my favorite barbecue place.

I cuddle into his side, and he holds me under his arm as we watch a comedy he chose to cheer me up. It's one of the best nights I've had with him, and I wasn't even screaming his name in ecstasy.

I'm in so much trouble.

So in over my head.

I'm not telling him who I am because the thought of losing him entirely makes me feel as though I can't breathe. But losing him is inevitable. Just not tonight.

twenty-six

Rowan

AFTER THE ENERGY DRINK PHOTO SHOOT, I ARRIVE back at the condo with Henry. Tweetie is meeting up with Conor at some club. I swear, the two of them are on a quest to meet every single woman in Chicago.

"Why aren't you going out?" I ask Henry.

"Not in the mood. I'm gonna shower and go get Bodhi and take him to his favorite pizza place. You wanna come?"

I stop on the sidewalk and look at Peeper's Alley.

Henry laughs. "Forget it, man. Go get your girl."

"Sorry."

He presses the security code into the pad by the gate. "Don't apologize. I like knowing I'm not the only one who wants a steady person in my life rather than women constantly coming and going."

"Maybe you need to go find that girl," I say, walking backward toward the bar.

"That ship sailed. See you tomorrow." He waves and disappears inside the gate.

I open the door to Peeper's and stand just inside the threshold, watching Leigh behind the bar. She's wearing her heartwarming smile and a T-shirt with the bar logo on it that stretches across her tits.

"Magic!" A woman I don't recognize comes over to me. She's probably in her early twenties. She looks back at her friends. "I told you bitches he comes here."

They're the youngest customers here by far, and they all have mixed drinks surrounding them—probably because Ruby refuses to serve seltzers. In her opinion, the girls stick around longer that way, and she's protective of us. I kind of like it.

"Do you want to get a drink?" The girl steps forward and brushes her tits along my bare arm.

"Sorry, I'm..." I'm what? I don't actually know. I'm not taken. Technically, I'm single. But I'm not interested in meeting anyone. "I can't."

I move away from her to walk toward the bar, but she steps in front of me. "Come on. I came all the way from Joliet. My friends and I are your biggest fans." She dips her chin and looks up at me through her lashes.

I look toward the bar. Leigh is watching us, and I don't see Ruby anywhere. She usually handles this type of thing for us, so we don't get bad press from the girls we're rejecting.

"I can do an autograph or a picture, but not a drink. Sorry."

She playfully pouts, her bottom lip drooping lower as if there's a weight attached to it the longer I don't relent. "Okay, a picture would be great."

I turn and walk over to the table.

"You're so much hotter in person," one of the women says. "I bet you get that all the time."

I don't say anything but move behind the girls since I tower over them and smile at their friend holding the camera.

"Wait! You have to be in it, Lizzie," a girl says and snatches up Lizzie's phone, going over to the row of men with strained beer bellies over their belts. They're a great group of guys who don't ever heckle us when we come in. I actually think they're more baseball fans than hockey. "Would you mind taking a picture for us?"

The man looks at the phone and back at the girl. "No." He circles back around to face the bar and television that's replaying a Colts game.

"I'll do it." Leigh rounds the bar.

Her long legs that I love to have wrapped around me look amazing in the short shorts. Thankfully, no younger guys usually come in here. I should make sure somehow that Tweetie and Conor don't come here after they get back tonight.

"Perfect. Thanks." The girl hands Leigh the phone.

"It's like finding a conch shell in the ocean, am I right, girls? The chances of you meeting Rowan Landry are insane." Leigh smiles too wide, overly friendly, positioning the phone to take a picture.

All the girls surround me, and I cough from the amount of perfume wafting around us.

"Put your arms around them, heartbreaker."

I drill my gaze into hers, and she laughs, then I position my arms out around the group of them.

"Everyone say, Magic," Leigh says.

"Magic," all the girls say in unison.

Leigh takes the picture, and I shift to move away, but she insists on one more. She proceeds to make me stand there for two minutes while she keeps having the girls switch poses and takes a bunch of photos.

"Perfect. You all look amazing." She hands the phone back to Lizzie.

"Nice to meet you," I say and walk around them, about to walk away.

"Listen, ladies, I'm so thrilled you got to meet Rowan Landry. But just so you know, now that you have your picture, you can't bother him while he's here, or I'll have to kick you out." The girl who originally came up to me opens her mouth to speak, but Leigh doesn't wait to hear what she has to say. "Sorry, I know I'm being a bear, but I need to keep them coming. You get it, right, girls?"

They give a response along the lines of, "Oh, totally."

"I'm sure they drive in a lot of business," another one chimes in.

"They do. Thank you so much, and for understanding, the next round is on me. Okay?" Leigh smiles at them all.

"You're so sweet," the Lizzie one says. "Thanks."

"Of course, and hang around, you never know if any of his friends will show up." Leigh looks all excited for them.

I leave the group of them and keep walking until I reach the private room reserved for those of us who live in the building.

Leigh follows me. "What can I get you, sir?"

"Your pussy. Preferably on my face." I swing my arm around her waist and tug her over onto my lap. "You're playing games."

"I'm using you to keep customers happy. Are you mad?" Her hand runs down my chest.

She's so beautiful. I wish she wasn't working, so I could take her up to my apartment for the night.

"No. As long as you don't get the wrong idea." I tuck a piece of hair behind her ear.

She tilts her head. "Wrong idea?"

"That I would want any of them."

She laughs and hops off my lap. "I know my worth."

"Come back." I hold out my hand.

"I have to work. I'll be right back with your drink." She goes to leave the room but stops and turns around. "Are you expecting anyone else to join you tonight?"

"Just me. Hoping for Tweetie?"

"Just wondering." A look of relief crosses her face, and she disappears into the bar area.

I turn on the television to *SportsNight*, trying to figure out why she wouldn't want my friends here. It would only drive more business for her. We never hang out with them. Actually, other than that one breakfast, we haven't spent time around them at all. But I guess that was part of the deal, wasn't it?

I might have to change that, so she feels comfortable around them. Especially if she's buying the bar in our building.

She returns with my club soda and lime, placing it in front of me. "Sir."

"Oh, I think I like this role play thing. Where's Ruby?"

"She just ran out to get dinner for herself. She'll be back soon."

Perfect. "So, you aren't closing?"

"I am."

My head rocks back. "I have to wait to have you?"

"Afraid so, big guy." She leans over, kissing me.

I place my hand on the back of her head, keeping her lips on mine as long as she's willing.

"She's working, get your mouth off her," comes Ruby's voice from behind her.

Leigh strips her mouth off mine, laughing and moving away as I grasp for her. My night was just ruined by a petite, red-haired woman with the attitude of a mobster.

I stay in the room watching *SportsNight*, and Leigh comes in and out, serving me refills. As the night wears on, my desire to have her increases every time I see her ass in those shorts.

I venture out of the room under the guise of using the

bathroom. If Leigh wasn't here, I'd be up in my condo, but even the few minutes every half hour that I get to spend with her is too tempting for me to just leave.

Ruby is behind the bar and talking to two men I'm fairly sure are regulars. There's no sign of Leigh, so I wait until Ruby turns her back to me, then I walk through the back door into the storage room.

Leigh is there on her tiptoes, reaching for something. "You need a step stool. How on Earth do you get this down?" she says, presumably thinking I'm Ruby.

I shut the door and press the lock.

She looks over her shoulder, surprise and delight in her eyes when she sees me. "Rowan."

I grab the box she's trying to get. "Here."

"What are you doing in here?"

I cradle her cheek, my thumb running down the front of her throat. Urging her back against the wall, I watch my thumb move over the delicate skin on her throat. "You know what I'm doing here."

"Ruby will kill us," she stage-whispers.

"Ruby is busy." I press my lips to hers, and she grabs the back of my shirt, sliding her tongue into my mouth.

That's my girl.

twenty-seven

Kyleigh

ROWAN GRABS MY HIPS, PROPPING ME UP ON AN empty keg. "You're really challenging my willpower tonight." His finger dips under the hem of my shorts. "I'm not sure about these."

"You gonna try to tell me what to wear?"

He chuckles, and his face lights up with an expression that reads "No because I care about my dick." It makes some tender part of my heart ache.

I'm falling for him. I've known it for some time, but tonight, while I ventured in and out of that backroom, the way he would smile at me as if I'm his entire world pierced my heart because I know I'm guaranteed to lose him.

First, I've been lying to him. Second, he has so much going on in his world other than me. He's a hockey icon, and I know from my brother being in the league that that's where his priority has to be in order to remain at the level he's at. I witnessed my brother let everything else fade away in order to play the sport he loves.

So right now, Rowan might want only me, but eventually, he'll grow bored, or the season will start, or he won't want anything serious. And I get it. Conor would be the same way. I can't change the rules now just because I fell for him.

"I would never tell you what to wear. But I only have you for a few minutes, and I want to make the most of it." He tips his head, lips falling to mine.

Rowan's tongue slides into my mouth, and I moan from wanting more than we can have right now. He takes it slow and easy, which only spurs a ravenous desire to have him right here.

My hands fly to the buttons of his shirt, which is a change from the usual T-shirts he wears. I unbutton the top two, but then his hand cups my breast over my shirt and bra. My fingers slide between the gap in the fabric, and I rip open his shirt, buttons flinging in all different directions. His fingertips flex against my skin.

He steps back, and I inch forward, not wanting his lips off mine.

"Fuck, that was hot." He stares down at me, and I run my fingertips down his impressive chest.

Returning to stand between my legs, he kisses me like a mad man. As though he can't breathe, and he's starved to have me. I match his intensity, until his lips trail down past my jaw and throat.

"Everything about you is so unexpected," he whispers.

My fingers clench over the waistband of his jeans, wishing I could rip his clothes off, see the impressive man he is.

"I never thought..." I stop talking because he doesn't need to know how much he affects me. How he bulldozed past my warning signs and won me over.

He flicks the button on my shorts, and my clit throbs with anticipation. "Tell me you're wet."

"Check for yourself."

His laughter vibrates along my skin, and he lowers the zipper, opening my shorts for his hand to slide underneath. I bolt up when his palm presses against my clit at the same time his finger swipes through my dampness.

"Fuck, Leigh, I don't have a condom and..."

I shake my head. "We can't here."

I rock back, my elbows resting on the edge of the shelf behind me, giving him access to get me off. He slows his pace, teasing my entrance and watching me.

"T-shirt up. Bra down. I wanna see your tits."

I love a bossy Rowan, so I do as he says. Once my tits are out for his viewing pleasure, he bends over me, sucking my nipple into his hot mouth.

"Oh fuck," I pant.

He moves to my other breast while his finger toys with me, elevating me to a place only he's ever been able to.

The doorknob wiggles, but he doesn't stop, plunging one then two fingers inside me while his thumb circles my clit. I have to press my lips together to keep quiet.

"Come on...come for me," he whispers.

He arches his fingers, and it's all I need before my climax rolls through me. I stifle a moan, sucking air in through my nostrils while my hips undulate against his hand.

Ruby bangs on the door. "Get out of there, you two. Find your own place to get kinky."

I'm too hypnotized from my orgasm to care what Ruby wants.

Rowan slips his hand out of my panties, and I physically tremble when I watch him lick my juices off his fingers with a satisfied smile.

"I feel bad." I eye the bulge straining the zipper of his pants.

"Don't. Seeing you get off is by far my favorite thing."

My heart flutters.

"Come on, you two!" Ruby bangs again, jiggling the handle.

"I really wish I could snap a picture of you right now. You look so fucking sexy."

I smile and hop off the keg to kiss his chest, palming his dick through his pants. "After I get off tonight, you're the first thing on my to-do list."

"I'm gonna hold you to that."

I pull my T-shirt down and button and zip up my shorts.

Before I look up, he's walking me backward to press me against the wall, something I've noticed he really likes to do. I don't mind being caged in by Rowan.

"Stay over. Spend the night with me."

I freeze and tip my head up to look up at him. He's not smiling as if it's a joke. And he's obviously not drunk—except maybe on lust.

"What?" I whisper.

"Spend the night with me."

"Um..."

He lowers his head, kissing my neck. "I'll beg if you want me to."

"But what about..."

"Please, Leigh."

I wince at him calling me Leigh, which oddly, I'm starting to like. But him saying that name only reminds me that I'm holding a secret back from him. But one last night with Rowan won't ruin me, right? Because the time has come to tell him the truth.

"Okay," I whisper.

He draws back, holding me around my waist and looks at me. He doesn't say anything, but he doesn't have to. Those gorgeous blue eyes of his say it all. I'm not the only one feeling something I shouldn't.

Which means I'll break both of our hearts tomorrow morning when I tell him who I really am.

twenty-eight

Kyleigh

Rowan walks me up to his apartment after Peeper's is closed, and I swear it's as if there's a butterfly exhibit in my stomach. It's full of flutters and excitement that I'm spending the night with him. But at the same time, there's a looming sense of loss on the horizon, knowing what I have to do tomorrow morning.

This is just one last night to remember him by.

I step in, and he shuts the door behind me. As usual, his arms wrap around me from behind. "I'm sure you must want a shower." He kisses the side of my neck.

"Are you offering to wash me?" I place my hand on the back of his head, not wanting his lips off my skin.

Tonight, I'm going to just go with all the signs of us becoming a couple. The lingering touches that aren't sexual. The sweet kisses. All the acts of intimacy. I'm going to enjoy them—just for tonight.

"That's my job."

I swallow deeply. This man.

"First, we need to get you undressed."

He steps back from me, reaching for the hem of my shirt before shedding it from my body and dropping it to the floor. Next, he undoes my bra, adding it to the pile. Reaching around me, he places light kisses along my shoulder while unbuttoning my jean shorts and lowering the zipper, pushing them down my hips.

Soon, I'm standing with my back to him, wearing only my underwear. I hear him moving behind me, and when his hands wrap around my stomach again, we're flesh to flesh, his hardening length pressing into my back.

"God, Rowan." There's so much I want to say to him, but I can't. Not yet.

"Let me live up to my promises." He walks us toward the bathroom, me in front of him, and I let him take control of my body.

He turns on the water in the shower, situates me in front of the counter and sinks to his knees. "I love the taste of your pussy. I think about it all the time." He brings his face to the apex of my thighs.

His fingers slide under the fabric on my hips, and he pulls my panties down my legs. I step out of them, and he leaves them at his side. Then he spreads me with his thumbs and french kisses my clit until I'm moaning.

He rises to his feet. Taking my hand again, he guides me into the shower. The water is warm, and the scent of his shampoo and soap fills the small space.

I'm not sure how long we're going to be able to stand naked and wash one another before we succumb to the need to have sex, but it feels nice as his hands work shampoo through my strands. Then I wash his hair. By the time we're on to the soap, our hands are slipping and sliding all over one another.

"I promised myself I'd control myself while we're in here,"

he says in a voice that tells me he's very close to breaking his promise.

I push him against the tiled wall. He slides his thigh between my legs, and I lean forward, kissing him. I grind along his muscled thigh, the friction on my clit tightening all the muscles in my core.

Steam fills the shower and his bathroom, and soon I can't take it anymore.

"Now. I need you right now."

He chuckles, leaving me in the shower to go grab a condom. He returns with one already on his dick, positions me so my back is on the wall, and lifts one leg around his waist before he plunges into me. It ends up being the best shower sex I've ever had.

A half hour later, I'm in his T-shirt and my underwear, snug in his bed, in his arms. I'm trying to force myself to stay awake so I can enjoy tonight as long as possible.

"Are you enjoying working at Peeper's?" he asks in the dark.

I shrug. "For the most part."

"I'm glad. The customers are nice to you?"

"Yeah. Though, I don't think a lot of them like the change of having me there. I guess they're a lot like Ruby in that way. But they've been polite. It's just boring having to refill beer after beer." I laugh because that's the only thing all the men there order.

"As long as you're happy. That's all that matters." His large palm rubs along my bare leg, his fingers slipping under the hem of his T-shirt.

I lift up off his chest, sitting cross-legged at his side. I can just make out his silhouette in the dark. "How was the endorsement thing? Tell me how it works."

He blows out a breath and stares at the ceiling. "It's kind of annoying. Just not my thing. Especially when there's the three of us. But it's done, and I guess now my face might be on a billboard."

"Oh, I think there's going to be a line of ladies climbing and risking their lives to kiss this beautiful face." I cradle his face with my hands and bend down to kiss him.

"You're the only one who gets the real thing."

My heart thumps double time. I pull back, and he doesn't look away.

"Leigh," he says, his hands sliding onto my cheeks.

My heart soars, but at the same time, bits and pieces are breaking off because if he's going to say what I think he's going to, I'd be so damn happy, but so undeserving at the same time. And I can't let him bear his soul to me when he doesn't know the truth.

The end is finally here.

My chest squeezes painfully. "Wait." I press my finger to his lips. "I have to tell you something. I—"

I'm cut off by the sound of a blaring fire alarm.

"Shit." His palms fall from my face, and he rushes out of bed.

"Is that the fire alarm?" My body stiffens because I cannot leave this condo until I tell Rowan the secret I've been keeping. What if my brother is back from whatever he's doing and is in Tweetie's apartment?

"Yeah." He turns on his bedside lamp and disappears into his closet before returning wearing a pair of sweatpants, then he tosses me a hoodie. "Put this on."

I grab it and watch him throw on a T-shirt, not getting off the bed. Sirens blare outside, and panic flares inside me that this is a real fire, not one we can ignore and stay in bed.

"Leigh, come on!" He's all dressed and grabbing his wallet and phone from the nightstand.

I shake my head. "It's probably a false alarm. I don't want to leave the bed."

He stares at me for a second as though I'm batshit crazy.

Walking to the window that faces the street in his family room area, I can see the red lights of the fire engine.

"Not a false alarm," he says, coming up behind me, holding my purse. "Come on."

I take my time putting on the hoodie, trying to think of something I can say to avoid leaving this apartment until we know for sure that we have to. He says my name again.

"I'm coming."

Pounding on the door startles me. "Magic! Fire. Let's go."

Conor. Oh shit. My only saving grace was if they were still out, but that hope crashes to the ground like a paper airplane.

I pretend to be looking for something, which uses up the last of Rowan's patience. He comes over and picks me up fire-fighter-style. "Guess I'm carrying you."

"No! I can walk."

"When we get downstairs." He opens his apartment door, and I try to pull his sweatshirt down over my ass so I don't give everyone a glimpse.

I should've predicted Rowan wouldn't put me in a position for anyone to see my ass. He lowers me to the ground right before he opens the security gate. I quickly put the hood up over my head and stare at the ground, shielding myself from everyone as he leads me out onto the road by the hand.

"Is there really a fire?" he asks someone.

"Daddy, look at all the lights." Bodhi sounds so excited. I'm sure this is like a movie for him.

"Yeah, bud. Pretty cool," I hear Henry say.

I stay at Rowan's side, allowing him to shelter me with my arms around him, face buried in his chest. Refusing to look up, I try to stay as inconspicuous as possible.

"God, I just got into bed," Conor says.

I hold my breath for a beat because he sounds really close.

"Me too, and now I'm gonna be up all night," Tweetie adds.

"Daddy, they're getting the hose out!" Bodhi shouts with excitement.

"It's at Peeper's," Rowan says. "Fuck. We should call Ruby."

I look over, and sure enough, they're breaking through the windows to get into Peeper's with their big hose. All of the firefighters are in full gear. This fire is real.

I step forward, but Rowan tugs me back, thankfully.

"Leigh," Bodhi says, and I freeze. "Isn't this awesome? At first, I was scared." He stands right in front of me, his clear blue eyes filled with excitement only kids can have.

"It is," I whisper and run my hand over his messy bed head.

"Oh, shit, sorry, Leigh. With all the commotion, I didn't even think." Tweetie steps closer to me. "So...you two are having a sleepover, huh?" His laugh is drowned out by the sound of another fire truck barreling down the street toward us.

I give Tweetie a little wave and look back down, sliding closer to Rowan, allowing him to hold me at his side. Can the firefighters just finish this up so I can get the hell out of here?

"So, you're Landry's girl." Conor steps up to my side. "Be polite and do some introductions," he says to Rowan.

No. No. No. Not like this. I have no idea what to do or how I can possibly escape the collision I can see coming from a mile away.

"Oh right. Leigh, this is Conor Nilsen, our new goalie." Rowan backs up, positioning me to free me from his side, but I grip his shirt with my fist as though we're at the edge of a cliff.

"Shy one, I see. Didn't get that impression from everything I've heard."

I'd punch Conor in the face right now if I didn't want him to know it's me.

"Not usually." Rowan puts his hand over mine, untangling my fingers from his shirt.

I give a quick wave to Conor. "Nice to meet you," I say in a high-pitched girly voice that sounds fake.

"What happened to your voice?" Bodhi asks innocently.

Damn kids, do they have to comment on everything?

I'm sure everyone is looking at me as if I'm some alien trying to remain unnoticed, yet making myself so noticeable because of my behavior.

"You too." Conor's tone is the same one I've heard when he has an encounter with someone rude.

Great.

I watch his feet move away, but they stop and turn back around, coming closer. "Your tattoo."

Oh shit. Why didn't I put socks on? That would've been the smart thing to do.

"Funny, I know someone else with that exact same tattoo in the exact same spot."

I stare at his slide-covered feet. I think he's getting pedicures. I shake that thought from my head. Not the time.

"Oh yeah, who?" Rowan asks.

"No need to be embarrassed. Let's see the woman who finally tamed Rowan Landry?" Conor's stance widens, and he crosses his arms.

My stomach pitches.

"That's a little extreme. I didn't need to be tamed," Rowan says. He backs up to offer me the space to turn and look at Conor for a proper introduction.

"What the fuck, Ky?" Conor tugs the hoodie of the sweatshirt off my head and our matching brown eyes land on one another. There's rage in his and apology in mine.

"What the hell?" Rowan pushes Conor back by the chest. "What the hell do you think you're doing?"

Conor stumbles but recovers like the athlete he is. "Me? You're the one fucking my sister!"

Rowan's head whips in my direction, face pale. "What is he talking about?"

I open my mouth but am unable to form any words.

"Oh, snap!" Tweetie says with glee. "And the sidewalk show goes from *Chicago Fire* to the *Maury Povich Show*. You *are* the sister!"

Jesus, does this guy ever shut up?

twenty-nine

Rowan

THERE'S NO WAY.

"You're Conor's sister?" I look at Leigh, but she doesn't say anything. She's fiddling with the sleeves of my sweatshirt, tugging them over her hands and shifting her feet. "Leigh?"

"Why do you keep calling her Leigh?" Conor asks. "Is that some cute fucking nickname you have for her? She hates being called that."

I turn from Conor and back to her. "Your name isn't Leigh?"

I step back, and finally her guilty gaze drifts up to mine. Wetness coats her beautiful caramel eyes. The pain I see there shouldn't cut me, especially right now when I'm the one who was made to look like a fool.

"It's Kyleigh. I—"

"Ky, what the fuck? I don't understand," Conor says. "Why are you with him?"

"Excuse me," I say, stepping up to him. "Is there something wrong with me?"

He puts his hand up in my face as if this isn't my business, but between him and his sister. "Um, yeah. The fact that you're using her for sex."

I balk. "You have no fucking clue what you're talking about."

"Hey, guys." Henry dips his head into our little trio. "I have a kid over here. Can we cool it with the f-word?"

I groan in frustration. "Why did you lie?" I want to ask her a million more questions, but I'm trying to stay calm because people are starting to come out of their apartments.

"At first...I didn't...he was in Florida." She points at Conor.

"That's not an excuse." My arms fly up at my sides.

"Did you know who he was when you met him?" Conor asks, interrupting my line of questioning.

"Hey, you'll get your turn. Right now, I get to ask the questions."

"Like hell." Conor steps in front of me.

I'm not usually a physical guy outside of the rink, but I fucking cared about this woman. And she's been lying to me this entire time.

"You know what?" I put up my hands and step back. "Have at it. I'm done."

"Wait!" Leigh or Kyleigh or whatever fuck her name is steps forward, but Conor blocks her from getting to me.

"He's not worth it. This is exactly why I made you promise to never get with one of my friends or teammates. They're all looking for nothing more than a quick fuck."

"Hello!" Henry shouts.

"Guys, we're causing a scene, and phones are starting to come out." Tweetie lowers his head into our widespread huddle.

"She wasn't that," I say because I'm an idiot who can't stop himself. "I mean..." Oh fuck it. I can't right now.

All this time I thought she wanted to tell me something, I never thought it was that she was Conor Nilsen's sister and that she'd been lying to me since the moment we met. Fuck, it hurts.

"So, here's the deal." A fireman who seems to be the chief comes over to us. When he takes off his gloves, his silver wedding ring shines under the streetlights. His name tag reads Bianco. He looks strong, and with the way he's built, I bet he models for those firefighter calendars or is auctioned off every year for some fundraiser. He takes in Tweetie, then looks at Conor, me, and Henry last. "Falcons?"

"Yeah," Henry says.

He rocks back and glances at the security gate. "You all live upstairs?"

"We do," Tweetie says, crossing his arms.

"Well, the fire is out. We're pretty sure it was electrical, but the water damage is extensive on the ground level. The sprinkler system was working, so it minimized any fire or smoke damage from extending beyond the bar. We called the owner and told them it's boarded up for the night, but that they can get back inside in a few days. You're all free to go up to your places."

"Thank you, firefighter," Bodhi says, staring up at the man as if he's a hero.

Chief Bianco squats and glances over at another firefighter, gesturing for something. "What's your name?"

"Bodhi," he says. "Is it fun to be a fireman?"

The tension dissipates from watching Bodhi be so amazed.

"It's a lot of fun, but a lot of hard work. Do you want to be a fireman one day?" Chief Bianco asks.

"Maybe." He looks at Henry behind him. "Or a hockey player."

Chief Bianco laughs, and the other firefighter comes over and hands him a plastic firefighter hat. Chief Bianco puts it on

Bodhi's head. "Here you go. You can be Firefighter Bodhi for as long as you want."

Bodhi's mouth falls open, and he turns back to Henry. "Dad! Look!"

"Say thank you," Henry says, nodding toward the chief.

Bodhi whips back around. "Thank you."

"You're welcome." The chief chuckles. "I know this was an inconvenience, but it could've been a lot worse."

He nods then walks away, heading over to an EMT standing by the ambulance and talking with a police officer. It's late and maybe I'm just tired, but I swear they all resemble one another.

"Come on, Fireman Bodhi, your bed is missing you." Henry takes Bodhi's hand and heads toward the building.

Tweetie stands idle between us, but surprisingly says nothing and follows after Henry and Bodhi.

"I'm taking you home," Conor says to his sister. I have no idea what to call her at this point.

"I'm not a child." She ignores him and walks over to me. "Can we talk?"

I blow out a breath and glance over to see people with their phones out. "Let's just go upstairs."

I step back and hold my arm out for her to go first. She walks by me. Conor tries to cut in front of me, but I slide in right behind her.

The three of us walk up the stairs and enter my condo. I wait for her to walk in, but I should've known Conor would follow. I'm not even sure I want to be alone with her right now. I'm upset and hurt, but anger simmers just below the surface from the embarrassment she's caused.

She turns around and faces her brother. "Conor, can you please just go?"

He crosses his arms and widens his stance as though he's

waiting for a fight or trying to intimidate me. "I'm taking you home."

She picks up her clothes from the floor and goes into the bathroom. "You're not."

The door to the bathroom closes, which leaves me alone with Conor.

Not wanting this to leak into the locker room, I figure it's better to handle this with him now. "I didn't know she was your sister, got it?"

"Now you do. So, I guess the question is, what're you gonna do about it?"

I've never seen this side of Conor before. Sure, maybe directed at someone else. He had a pretty big rift in college with this Trent guy who played for our biggest rival. Maybe at a bar once or twice when words would get thrown around in a drunken brawl, but he's usually pretty calm and level-headed.

As for what I'm going to do, I have no damn clue. As mad as I am at her, I'm still gut-punched seeing the aftermath of her secret coming out. I want an explanation, but at the same time, I don't care what she has to say. She lied. My head is everywhere and nowhere, and I need to step away from the situation and sort out my feelings before I can sit down and talk this out with her.

"Just let her go, man," he whispers, and I wonder if he sees it in my face that I don't know what to do. "She's in the worst time of her life right now. She's confused and not acting like herself. She's using you to escape her reality. I mean, she's talking about buying a bar for fuck's sake."

It's like he took out a dagger and sliced me, quick and clean right down the center of my chest. Maybe I don't know the real Leigh, or Kyleigh. He would know, wouldn't he? God, that word. *Use.* It guts me.

The bathroom door flies open before I can ask him any questions about what he just said. Kyleigh's dressed in her shorts and T-shirt, and my stomach sinks as she hands me my T-shirt and hoodie all folded up.

"I'd like to explain," she says.

My jaw clenches. I'm not ready to have this conversation with her yet. "I think you should go home."

The wetness that filled her eyes overflows, and a tear cascades down her cheek, then another one. "But—"

"Let Conor take you. I need time to think this over. It's a lot."

She reaches out, and I step back, her arm dropping to her side. Her mouth falls open, and the pain etched in her features unfurls something inside me that I can't navigate at this moment.

"Okay." She walks to the door, and Conor opens it, waiting for her to leave first. I don't even bother watching her go. I don't want to bear witness to it if it's the last time she'll ever leave my apartment. "I'm sorry, Rowan. I really am. I think I just got caught up in...us."

I close my eyes and take a deep breath.

The door shuts with a click that echoes throughout my empty place. I bring the clothes in my hand up to my nose, smelling our scents mixed together.

Fuck that.

I dump them in my hamper and sit on the edge of my bed for a second before I stand by my window and watch her get in an Uber, then I bolt out of the apartment. I can't stand to be haunted by her memory in my space.

thirty

Kyleigh

I'm standing at the curb, waiting for the Uber to arrive, when I hear the security gate open. I glance over my shoulder, berating myself for hoping it's Rowan. Conor's dressed in sweatpants and a sweatshirt with a backward hat on.

"I can get myself home," I say loudly enough for him to hear.

"We need to talk. And unlike other people, I'm not letting you go home by yourself at three in the morning." He stands next to me, his protective stance trying to showcase some sort of dominance.

"You know it's none of your business, right?"

His head rocks back in sheer disbelief. "He's my fucking teammate. And friend."

"He wasn't. At the time, he wasn't."

Thankfully, probably due to the time of night, my Uber pulls along the curb. Conor opens the door, and I huff, getting in, my gaze floating up to the window of Rowan's condo. He stands there with his arms crossed, watching me leave. I really wish he'd let me talk to him and tell him everything, but I also understand how big trust is to him, and I broke that. I knowingly broke that.

Rowan turns around as if satisfied I'm gone, and I slide into the car. Conor climbs in after me.

"I'm an adult in case you haven't noticed."

"You'll always be my little sister. Deal with it."

The Uber driver looks at me in the rearview mirror, recites the address, and I nod. He doesn't react to Conor, which means he must not be a hockey fan.

"I can live my own life. I don't need you or Mom telling me what to do." I stare out the window.

"So, when I got traded, you were already with him?"

How much information do I want to give him? I'm not sure. I really want Rowan to know everything first. "Yes."

"And with him means what? Because I've heard about the girl he's with, and it didn't sound much like dating to me."

Shit. Of course they've talked about me. Most likely Tweetie opened his big mouth. Rowan doesn't seem like the kind of guy to kiss and tell. "We had an arrangement."

A strangled growl erupts from deep inside his chest, and I watch his fists clench on his thighs.

"Oh my god, grow up. Your little sister has sex."

The Uber driver coughs into his fist.

Conor glances at the driver and sits there quietly, probably wanting to wait until we're out of here before he says anything else. He's used to having to stay guarded around strangers in case people overhear his conversation.

His silence makes the car ride awkward and uncomfortable. I really wish he would've let me go home by myself.

Finally, the Uber parks in front of my apartment building, and Conor gets out. I thank the driver, press the tip on my phone, and go to my building's door.

"I'm home. Bye."

"No way. I'm staying the night in case Landry's ass shows up here," he says.

I wish I had something pointy to stab him in the eye with. But I'm not going to make yet another scene on the street in the middle of the night, so I let him follow me up to my apartment. Once we're behind my apartment door, I decide it's about time we define our adult roles in our sibling relationship.

"Listen, I'm not twelve. I'm twenty-five years old. I can fuck who I want, when I want, and you can't say anything about it. I'm sorry that you found out the way you did. It wasn't my intention."

"It *was* your intention. That's the problem. You were purposely lying to me, to him, and to yourself." Conor opens my fridge and grabs a beer that's there from when my dad was here. He cracks it open, and I shake my head.

"You have no idea what I was thinking. I'm not having this conversation with you. The only person who deserves this conversation is Rowan."

His jaw clenches so hard I think he might crack a tooth. "I fucking hate it, Ky. He's my friend."

"So what?" I toss my purse on my small table and wind around him to the fridge.

"You don't get it, do you?"

I grab a water and twist the cap off with more force than necessary. "You're trying to control me, just like Mom. Well, news flash, no one is controlling what I do anymore."

"Listen to you. You're like a spoiled child. I mean, who buys a bar just because? You're not even you anymore. You think you have something with Rowan? Well, news flash to you, sis, he doesn't even know the real Kyleigh Nilsen. He didn't even know your name." He finishes half the beer, slips off his shoes, and stomps over to my couch.

He cannot be serious right now. He's going to sleep on my couch? Overstep much?

"Leigh is part of my name."

He stares blankly at me. "That's your answer? Some bullshit that it's part of your name? You never go by that, and in fact, you hate when people call you that."

"I said that once when I was in the fourth grade when Mrs. Trinton kept calling me that."

"Okay, so I'll call you Leigh from now on then. Hi, Leigh, I'm Nor."

I narrow my eyes and inhale deeply, my fist clutching my water bottle so tightly, water spills over the rim and down my hand, dripping onto the floor. "You're being a real jerk."

"Because you're about to fuck everything up for me here. This is the year. I can taste the fucking Cup, and you fucking Landry is going to screw it all up."

Good thing Bodhi isn't here to overhear that sentence.

"I should've realized this is all about you. Figures. My entire life has been about you."

He rolls his eyes. "Fuck off. You're so dramatic."

I put the cap on my water and slam it on the counter. "I'm sorry, did you have to go to all my sporting events? I must have missed that. Did you have to sit in the stands, or worse, get pushed to play with kids you normally wouldn't have because instead of being with your real friends, you have to befriend the siblings of your brother's teammates?" I twirl my finger. "Yeah, that was me." I point my finger right back at me. "And now you're going to come to Chicago when you've been gone for years and tell me who I can and can't see? You don't get to tell me what to do."

"See? You think you're seeing Landry?" He shakes his head. "Jesus, Ky, he's using you for sex. As soon as the season starts, you're gone." His words cut through the flesh and bone right through to my heart. "Not because he's a bad guy, but he's not gonna have time. And believe me, I know the guy. He carries shit from his childhood deep down, and he's told me more than once that he's not the marriage type. So, come down from the tower, Ky, he's not saving you."

"You're such an asshole!"

I stomp down the hallway and slam my bedroom door, flipping the lock. Then I crawl into my bed, curl into the fetal position, and let all the frustration surface, crying myself to sleep while wishing I could magically disappear.

thirty-one

Rowan

I KNOCK ON HENRY'S DOOR AT SIX IN THE MORNING, unable to sleep and tired of walking the streets of Chicago.

He opens the door and runs his hand through his disheveled hair. "I expected you earlier." Stepping out of the way, he holds the door open for me.

I'm sure Bodhi is sleeping, so I try to be quiet, toeing out of my shoes, and stepping into his family room.

"She's Conor's sister." I shake my head and run my hand behind my head, tugging at my strained neck.

"Unreal."

"I'm not even upset about that. I mean...I'm shocked, but she lied. For a long time."

He sits down and extends his legs, resting his feet on the ottoman. Bodhi's toys have all been put in their designated bins, and books are stacked on a shelf under the television in the console. "Yeah."

"You know how hard trust is when you're in this profession. I was a fool."

"I wouldn't say that."

I look at him. The bags under his eyes show how little sleep he got. I probably shouldn't have come here, but I didn't want to be alone with my thoughts. "I've never opened myself up like that. I told her things I don't tell anyone. I—"

"Let her in?" He arches an eyebrow.

I nod and collapse into a chair. "And she took all that with her lie and tossed it in the garbage."

"Mehhh..." he says.

"She did."

"I think she got caught up. I think you both did."

I lean back in the chair and rest my ankle on my opposite knee. "That's no excuse for lying."

"No, it's not."

Jesus, could the guy give me more than just a few words, maybe offer me some advice?

"How about we have a conversation?"

He chuckles. "We are."

"No, I'm spilling my guts, and you're just giving me one-word answers. Tell me what I should do."

"And what good would that do?" he asks. "It's been what...four hours. You think you're ready to be done with this? Make a decision? Have you even talked to her?"

I shake my head. "Conor took her home." I nibble on my bottom lip. "I couldn't talk to her after I found out. I'm angry, and I don't like to talk to people when I'm pissed. I like to be by myself."

Another practice I picked up because of my father, just like the not drinking thing.

"Makes sense."

I point at him. "See, shit like that. Say something else."

"What do you want me to say?"

I grow more irritated. "You're smart. You clearly have a good head on your shoulders. You adopted Bodhi. Have somehow figured out how to be a great single dad and play hockey professionally."

"Aww, thanks. You think I'm a good dad?" He smiles.

I pick up a stuffed elephant in the bin next to me and toss it at him. "I'm serious. This is why I don't get this deep. I hate feeling all this shit stirring inside me."

"Feelings? Yeah, they can suck." He clucks his tongue.

I grab a stuffed turtle and chuck it at him. He catches it. Asshole.

"I should just break it off, right? I mean, it's going to fuck up the locker room dynamic. Conor's and—"

"Why are you thinking about Conor?"

I give him a duh look. "He's her brother."

"But you said that didn't matter to you. It was the fact she lied. Conor isn't a factor in your decision."

He's got to be on something. Took a sleeping pill after the fire and is still out of it even if he looks all right.

"Of course he matters. It will affect all of us. Maybe the damage is already done, already splintering us, who knows. She's hurting now, and if we don't get past this, I broke her heart. If we do get past this, he'll be pissed that I'm with her, probably just waiting for me to fuck up and break her heart. Either way, I'm screwed."

"Conor's a smart guy."

I look up and throw my hands in the air. "It's that kinda shit response that's only making me angrier."

"Sorry." He shrugs.

"Henry," I say, growing more and more irritated.

He chuckles and sits up. "Listen. It's only been hours, and it's six a.m. on a Sunday. Give it a day. Or two. Whatever you need. Time and distance can change a lot in your head."

"You want me to feel like this for days?"

He rolls his eyes. "I hate to break it to you, but if you don't get past this with her, that feeling of dread and longing and yes, heartbreak, is going to last a lot longer than twenty-four hours."

I slouch down into the chair with a groan. "That girl you were saying had to find herself...how long did that feeling last for you?"

He huffs and shakes his head. "It's still there. Sure, it's dulled a little. The edges aren't quite as sharp. But it can resurface with a vengeance at the mere mention of her name or a flash of her picture."

"I'm screwed then!" I scrub my hands down my face. "You should've warned me."

"Warned you?"

"Yeah, friend to friend."

"What would you have done?"

What would I have done? I'm not sure. Stopped seeing her. But looking back, I never would've listened to him anyway.

"Yeah, that's what I thought," he says.

A bedroom door creaks open, and Bodhi comes out wearing the same pajamas I saw him in in the middle of the night. His new firefighter hat is on his head.

"Did I wake you, buddy?" I ask, earning a death glare from Henry.

"I can't sleep." He climbs onto Henry's lap, laying his head on his chest.

Damn it, what is this new feeling in my chest? I've never wanted kids, but I wouldn't mind a little cuddle right now myself.

Henry points for the blanket behind my head, and I pick it up and toss it to him. He lays it over Bodhi. "If you want my advice—"

"It's the reason I'm here."

"Give it a little bit. You'll get the clarity you need. Let the anger simmer down so you can think rationally." He runs his hand over his son's shoulders, and he kisses the top of Bodhi's head.

We sit there, him watching his son and me watching the two of them. I have to give it to Henry. Who adopts a kid who needs a home when he's a young professional hockey player? An amazing person, that's who.

Bodhi bolts up, his eyes open, and the blanket falls to his lap. "Where's Leigh?"

Just when she wasn't at the forefront of my mind.

"She's..." I start, but what do I tell him?

"She was sad when the fireman was here. Did you make her sad?" His blue eyes stare at me, and I hate the feeling of disappointing him.

"No, he didn't," Henry answers for me.

"Did you break up?" The worry lines on Bohdi's forehead just about do me in.

"Bodhi, not our business," Henry says.

"I like her," Bodhi says, like a declaration. "She taught me how to draw a sun on the sidewalk. She gave me a kiddie cocktail downstairs. With extra cherries!"

Henry looks at me over his kid's head.

"If you broke up, does that mean Daddy can date her?"

Henry laughs, but quickly tries to stop, failing miserably.

"No," I answer.

"Why not? Mrs. Brewster says you have to share. That sharing is the nice thing to do because you want to spread happiness. If something makes you happy, it would probably make someone else happy to play with it too."

I raise my eyebrows at Henry, and he tries to hide his smile.

"I'm not sure it's the same with people," Henry says. "Right now, Rowan likes to play with Leigh, and until he puts her back on the shelf, we have to wait our turn. You wouldn't like it if I took your favorite toy out of your hands while you were playing with it, right?"

I roll my eyes. "Just when I complimented you on being a great dad."

He flips me off behind Bodhi's back.

"Put her back on the shelf, Rowan, so Daddy and I can have her."

Even I can't hide my laugh, although thinking about casting Kyleigh aside doesn't sit well. Actually, it doubles that sinking feeling in my stomach, then turns into a jealous sort of anger thinking about her being someone else's.

Henry is right. I need to give this some time.

"I don't think Rowan is a good sharer." Henry can't fight his smile.

I pick up a Falcon stuffed animal and throw it at him.

But he's not wrong. When it comes to Kyleigh, the only thing I know for sure is, there's no sharing.

thirty-two

Kyleigh

IT'S SUNDAY AFTERNOON.

Rowan hasn't texted.

Rowan hasn't called.

Rowan hasn't come over.

I bury my head under the covers and ignore the splintering sound of my shattered heart.

thirty-three

Kyleigh

I t ' s W e d n e s d a y , a n d t h e r e ' s s t i l l b e e n n o w o r d
from Rowan. Every day I tell myself that he just needs time,
but I'm starting to think I'll be waiting forever. Since he's at
training, I go over to Peeper's Alley to check on Ruby. I
brought reinforcements in case I run into Rowan, even
though I'm not expecting him to be there.

"You could've warned me. I'd have worn my rain boots."
Alara steps into the bar behind me.

The windows are boarded up, and for the first time that
I've seen, the Peeper's Alley sign isn't lit up.

"Ruby?" I say, walking farther into the building.

She pops out of the back room. "Hey. Can you believe
this?"

I frown. "I'm sorry I haven't come earlier."

She waves me off. "Please, I couldn't get in until yesterday, and then it was filled with insurance people. The
restoration people are supposed to show up sometime today
too."

I want to hug her, but Ruby isn't really a hugging kind of person.

"Hi, Ruby, I'm Alara." Alara puts her hand out between them, and Ruby stares at it.

"Who's this?" she asks me. Always on guard with new people, this one.

"This is my best friend, Alara. She came in case..."

Ruby's lips press into a thin line. "Yeah, Tweetie really lives up to his name. He was down here yesterday telling me what went down. I'm sorry." She genuinely looks upset.

"Well, ultimately, it's my fault. I lied." I give her a sad sort of shrug.

"Landry still giving you the cold shoulder?"

I nod.

"If it helps, a big birdie with blond hair told me that he's sucking it at preseason training. That he's got that same droopy look on his face you do." She points at me.

"I really wish he'd talk to me."

"He's a tough one. Has some issues deep down. Hell, a psychologist could buy a beach house in the Hamptons if he was their patient."

"Ruby!" My mouth drops open.

"Damn, maybe I should work with adults, not children," Alara says.

My head whips her way.

"I'm kidding." She raises her hands, but we both know she's thinking about the money.

"You were helping him get past his issues. And if he can't see that, it's his loss." Ruby pats me on the shoulder.

"What can we do to help?" I ask, wanting to change the subject.

"Leave."

My eyebrows draw down. "What? Why?"

"Because this one looks like she's ready for brunch at

Tiffany's, and you're heartbroken, which means you're going to take it out on what's left of this place."

Alara raises her hand slightly, with a look as though she's afraid to speak. "In my defense, had she told me where we were going, I would've dressed appropriately."

"You're not in grade school, stop trying to be the teacher's pet." Ruby walks behind the bar. "Come here." She points at me, then her finger shifts to Alara. "You stay."

Alara looks like a disciplined puppy who got too excited and jumped on the guests.

"I'll be right back," I say.

"Yeah, I'll just, um, stand here on the wet wood floor, swollen from the water, and hope the electricity is turned off. Don't worry about me."

She pulls a small laugh out of me. At least it's a baby step from being depressed all the time.

I follow Ruby past the bar, and I don't look into the private room for fear I'll see a hologram of Rowan taking me on the table like he did that one night. We walk past the storage room and the empty keg is still there, triggering the memory of him asking me to spend the night with him. How perfect it all seemed then. Why didn't I tell him sooner?

Because you're a chickenshit conflict-avoider.

At the loading dock by the alley, she pulls over two empty kegs and pats one for me to sit on. She sits on the other, putting her ankle on her opposite knee and her forearms on her thighs. "Listen. I'm not selling the bar."

"What? Why?" I'm surprised, especially after the fire. I get that she'd have to use the insurance money to make it decent again, but we could be partners and make it something new.

"Seeing it destroyed made me realize how much I'd miss it. It's like a husband—it drives you crazy, but at the end of the day, you love it, and it's been good to you. A lot of people find solace here, a comfort they can't find anywhere else. That was obvious to me when our regulars reached out to me after the fire. So, you're off the hook."

She stands as if that's the end of the conversation, but what am I supposed to do now?

"Off the hook?"

"Yep. Go find another hobby." She waves me off.

"Ruby..." I'm set to argue even though I feel a sense of relief set in. I was going to honor my commitment to her, but working the bar late at night and serving the same beers to the same men wasn't really doing it for me. It was fun at first, something different, but I can see it getting old quickly. And I think maybe she knew that.

"Oh, stop it. I'm not going to apologize. This is my bar. Find something else."

My throat tightens, and my nose tingles. I want to cry because there's so much more to Ruby than what she shows the world. "If you ever need someone to cover a night shift—"

"I'll call someone else. Now go. I don't need a lawsuit when your friend slips and breaks an arm because of those ridiculous shoes she's wearing." She shoos me away.

I nod, and we walk back out to the main bar.

"It was nice to meet you, Ruby," Alara says.

"Get your lips off my ass," Ruby says in response.

Alara crinkles her eyes at me, surely confused as to why Ruby is so mean. I laugh because it's just her way. You learn to love her though.

"Hey," Ruby says before I turn to leave. "Don't give up—he hasn't."

I smile, and tears well in my eyes. I've cried more in the last month than the five years previous. If this thing with Rowan isn't fixable, I might never see her again because it would hurt too much to come here and run into him. All the memories that would float to the surface would crush me every time.

"Bye, Ruby." I raise my hand.

"See ya, Leigh." She winks and circles back around, walking toward the back hallway.

"Well, she's a peach," Alara says once we're outside.

"Yeah. She is."

"I'm starving. Let's go eat," Alara says, already on her phone and probably calling an Uber.

I look at the security gate. I can almost see him there, standing with his back to the brick wall, head buried in his phone, waiting for me.

Alara tugs on my sleeve. "I knew this was a bad idea. Come on."

Twenty minutes later, we're entering our favorite place to go for cheesesteak sandwiches.

Alara goes right to the crane machine game in the waiting area, next to the poker machines. I'm guessing it's so the kids can try to win a stuffed animal while their parents gamble.

I drag her away by the sleeve. "No, you don't. You waste so much money on those things."

"You're right, but just once isn't going to hurt."

"We're eating first." I walk over to the hostess. "Two please."

The place is a bar-slash-restaurant, heavy on the bar.

We're seated in a booth dangerously close to the crane machine, and I groan knowing she's going to leave me to go play that game at some point. I purposely sit so I'm facing the machine and not her.

The waitress comes over and takes our drink and meal order. Alara waits until after the drinks are delivered before bringing up what I know she wanted to. I'm surprised she had the patience.

"So, you're free of the bar. Let's toast to that." She raises her glass.

"What am I going to do now? That was my future."

She raises her eyebrows. "Um...no, it wasn't. And you know it."

I shrug. "Okay, I ended up not really caring for it, but I'm not qualified for anything else now."

She hems. "You're qualified to design clothes."

I down my lemon-lime soda, ignoring her. "That's not me anymore."

She rolls her eyes. "Okay, we'll save that topic for later."

"What do you mean?"

"Nothing." She shakes her head. "Let's talk about you getting caught. How are you? I'm thinking you just hang up the towel if he hasn't reached out yet. Maybe he wasn't who you thought he was."

I sigh and frown. "No. He was. I know it. He never made me feel like just a piece of ass. He was sweet and—"

"Which could just be his thing until he's done with you."

"You weren't there," I say. "You didn't see his face when he found out I was Conor's sister. Hell, when he found out my name is Kyleigh." I cringe at the memory.

"Conor is an ass, and you can tell him I said that. Leigh *is* part of your name."

My head sways right and left because I fought Conor on it too, but he's right. I've always corrected people when they shortened my name to Leigh.

"Well, he's not really talking to me either, so...there's that too." I shrug.

"If I cared, I'd say he's busy with preseason training, but I don't. Fuck Conor."

I laugh, which feels really good, although once I'm done, that same gruesome terrible feeling resurfaces.

"Ruby is right. It'll be his loss if he chooses to not talk to you at the very least."

I love Alara, and I couldn't ask for a better friend, but the night Rowan admitted to me what his dad was like and the fact he doesn't drink because of it, I saw how vulnerable he was. How uncomfortable it made him to share that with me. How deep that hurt was burrowed inside him and that we were only scratching the surface with his admission. And I repaid that trust by continuing to lie.

Sure, it was because I was afraid to lose him, lose what we had. Every time I thought about confessing, I thought just one more day, one more time, one more moment with him before it all fell apart. But it was selfish, and I don't blame him for not wanting to hear me out.

Our cheesesteaks come out, and I drown my anxiety and sorrow in the deliciousness of meat, cheese, and bread.

"God, I love these things," Alara says with a moan. "One final treat."

I put down my sandwich and wipe my mouth. "Final treat?"

A strange look crosses her face, but she waves me off. "You know me. I'm always starting a diet."

"You don't need to. You're taken. I'm the single one." I push my cheesesteak away from me.

"Shut up." She pushes it back.

We continue eating. The last thing I want is to feel this way again, so I won't be looking for a man any time soon. When we finish, she grabs a dollar bill from her purse and slides out of the booth with a mischievous smile.

"Alara!"

"Just once." She puts up her finger without looking back at me.

I watch from the booth. Sure enough, the metal crane

picks up the stuffed animal, but it drops it almost immediately.

"No!" she shouts, and more than a few pairs of eyes turn toward her.

She comes back over to the table, but I grab her purse. "You're done."

"Just one."

I clutch it to my chest.

"Please. It's right there. Taunting me." She looks back at it.

I open her purse and grab her wallet. "You need to join a support group." I slide my fingers into where she keeps her bills, but I feel something else.

"Come on, before someone else gets to it." She holds out her hand.

"What is this?" I pull out a ring. A diamond ring. A *new* sparkling ring. "Alara, what is this?" My mouth drops open.

She sighs, and her shoulders sink. "Nothing."

I just stare at her without saying anything.

"It wasn't the time to share my news. You're hurting, so I'm hurting."

My eyes widen. "Is this an engagement ring?"

She nods.

"Oh my god! You were keeping this from me?" I stand and wrap my arms around her, filled with joy and excitement for my best friend. "I'm so happy for you."

"But—"

"No." I step out of her embrace and grab her left hand, sliding the ring onto her finger. "Don't worry about that. You're getting married!"

She nods, a big smile transforming her face. "I am."

"Sit." I gesture for her to take the seat across from me as I get back in the booth.

She glances at the machine but sulks and slides into her side of the booth.

"Tell me all the details."

Apprehension is visible in the lines of her face. "First, now that you know, I have a favor to ask."

"It's fine if you want my mom to design your dress." I would never stand in the way of Alara having the dress she wants for her big day.

She shakes her head and grabs my hand. "I want you to design my dress."

My stomach flips. "Oh."

"Think about it, okay?"

I think about it for a moment and nod before wiggling forward in my seat. "Now tell me everything."

She does. And I'm truly happy for my best friend. She deserves all the happiness in the world, and although my belief in marriage has faltered, I was hopeful that my feelings for Rowan might be leading in the direction of conquering that disbelief.

I'm not sure I'll ever get there with anyone else though, so I'm going to enjoy this moment through my friend.

thirty-four

Kyleigh

IT'S BEEN ALMOST A WEEK.

I've almost called him twenty times a day, but I can't find the nerve.

So I go to the store to buy a new sketchbook and start fresh, wondering if I'm even in the right headspace to design my best friend's wedding dress.

Eventually, I'll have no choice but to move on, but I can't find it in myself to do so.

thirty-five

Rowan

THE LAST PLACE I WANT TO BE RIGHT NOW IS AT A fucking preseason practice. Seeing Conor is only a reminder of Leigh...er... Kyleigh. Fuck, will I ever not think of her as Leigh?

Seeing Conor across from me in the locker room, I now see all the similarities between them. The same caramel-colored eyes, and their hair color is close except she has some highlights. It's also in the structure of their noses. Damn it. I tear my eyes away because it causes a heaviness inside me when I think of her.

"You okay?" Henry approaches me, voice low.

You'd think we're all at a funeral home with how quiet the locker room is. I'm unsure if word got around, although I don't think Tweetie or Henry would say anything to anyone who's here. It's our business. What happens at The Nest stays at The Nest.

"I'm good." I put on my helmet and walk out of the locker room to get away from Conor.

I want to ask him if she's okay. Is she still upset? I shouldn't give a shit, but I do. I also know where he stands on the topic of our...former relationship, I guess. My only saving grace is that today I'm set to work on passing drills, which means I won't be shooting pucks at Conor.

When my skates hit the ice, I already know it's going to be a shit day. I'm exhausted from no sleep.

It's been almost a week, and I haven't reached out to her. Every time I pick up the phone, my thumb hovers over her name. I've even gone back and read some of our text exchanges. Then I'll think about how long she lied to me. How I told her about my dad. Sure, I didn't go into detail, but I opened up to her, and she continued to lie.

"Let's go, Landry. You're dragging today," Coach Buford shouts.

Tweetie, Henry, and I pass among ourselves, but I'm slowing us down.

During the water break, they stick near me, leaving Conor with the other group of guys. Our eyes catch for a minute.

"You gotta get her out of your head," Tweetie says.

I down some water. "Does it look like I'm not trying to do exactly that?"

He holds up his hands and looks at Henry, as if he's the one to guide me. Then again, there's a reason we call him Daddy.

"Have you talked to her?" Henry asks.

I shake my head.

His forehead wrinkles. "Fuck, Rowan, why not?"

Tweetie plays with the puck and his stick, doing tricks we've all been doing since we were kids.

I shrug.

"That's not a reason."

"I'm not your kid."

Henry shakes his head at me. "Fine, suit yourself. It's your life, and you're old enough to take responsibility for your fuckups. And if you let her go, you're fucking up."

"Says you."

"We talked about this. She lied, yeah, and it sucks. But you guys weren't in a relationship. It was all supposed to be fun and games. She didn't owe you anything. She didn't have to tell you who she was when you were just messing around. Sure, once Pinkie got traded"—he shrugs—"she should've come clean, but I also know from an outsider's point of view, that's when things were shifting between you, no?"

I shrug. I hate how perceptive he is. Does that happen automatically once you become a dad? I think back on my own father and know the answer—no.

"Admit it. You fell for her. That's the only reason you're hurting so much. The reason your game fucking sucks. The reason you're moping around. You did the one thing you always swore you wouldn't do, and you fell for the woman."

"So what? She ruined it."

He laughs and claps me on the back. "Cut it out now then."

"What are you talking about?" I take another gulp of my water because our break will be over soon.

"Cut out your heart because you're refusing to listen to it. Fuck it, right? It's just your life and your happiness. Being stubborn is way more important than that."

"Who are you?"

"I'm your mind begging you to listen to your heart. Shit, man, we get one life, and happiness isn't guaranteed. Why are you just throwing your chance in the gutter? So what? She lied about her name, but she didn't lie about who she is. You saw the real her. You fell for the woman she is. A name doesn't mean shit. The fact she's Pinkie's sister doesn't mean shit. The only thing that matters is how she made you feel—about her and about yourself." He pats me on the chest, just over the heart.

Then the whistle blows, and Henry skates away.

It's a struggle to admit to myself that she made me feel on top of the world. I've accomplished a lot in my life, but nothing compares to how it felt to have her in my arms. See that smile on her face when I stepped into a room. Admire the flush on her skin when she came.

I try to do the drills.

I try to focus on my job.

But as I skate around and practice my footwork, my head isn't in it. I end up stopping after one drill, and I'm standing with my stick in my hands, watching Conor. It's so great that he's back in my life in a big way, and it sucks this is going to put a dent in us remaining close.

As soon as he showed up, it was like it'd always been between us. He told me what was going on in his life, and I tried to give him my best advice. It was like no time had passed at all.

Wait...I think back to the conversation I had with him at Peeper's.

Fuck.

My sister found out my mom is cheating on my dad. Like witnessed her and the other guy making out in my mom's office.

Yeah, well, my sister doesn't handle things like this very well, so she's an emotional mess.

Fuck. That's why sometimes I'd see Leigh staring into corners. She was struggling with something huge.

The rest of practice, my head is swimming with the decision of what to do, but one thing I know for sure is that after this, her apartment is my first stop. She's been hurting, and I didn't know it then, but I know it now.

Henry's right, what the hell am I doing?

I'm not only torturing myself, but her too. At least I think

I'm torturing her, but I won't know until I see her. I've pushed past fear my entire life. Fear of coming out from under the bed or the kitchen table. Fear of standing up to him. Fear of not being good enough to make the top league in my area. Fear of not getting a scholarship to college to play. Fear of not getting into the league. Fear of not coming through for my team. Fear isn't some new emotion, and it's never stopped me before. Ever.

By the time practice is over, I'm ready to run to her damn apartment in my gear and skates, but I force myself to take a beat, shower, and change.

Right before I'm going to walk out of the locker room, I stop at Conor's locker. Most of the players are still dressing.

"Can I talk to you outside?" I ask him.

He looks up at me from digging into his bag, still in his white towel. "Say it here."

I cock my head. "Seriously?"

I watch his Adam's apple bob, and he studies me for an awkward moment. "Fine."

I go out in the hallway to wait. Conor comes out two minutes later with a white T-shirt and sweatpants on. He crosses his arms and widens his stance like he's been doing since this whole roller coaster began.

"I'm sorry," I say. "Had I known she was your sister, I wouldn't have started something."

He drops his arms to his sides. "Thanks."

"But..."

He crosses his arms again when he hears my tone.

"I can't turn back time. I can't change the outcome."

Conor's eyes narrow. "What are you saying?"

I inhale a breath. "I like her. A lot. I fell for her. And as your friend, I'm sorry it upsets you, but I'm not backing down. I want her in my life."

His eyes burn holes into me. "She's going through a hard time. You're taking advantage. She's vulnerable right now."

"She's stronger than you think."

"Don't act like you know her better than me."

I don't say anything because I'm not sure what to say to that. "It's her mistake to make, but I don't think it's a mistake."

"She bought a bar. She's a fucking fashion designer, and this entire thing with my parents has screwed her up so bad, she bought a bar. That should tell you something."

"If it makes her happy, I don't see the harm."

He huffs and looks down the hallway. "You're gonna hurt her."

"You have no say in this," I say. "It's her decision. I just wanted to be upfront with you."

"Fuck you." He cocks his fist back and punches me in the face.

"Shit." I cock my jaw and hold my cheekbone, then hold up one finger. "That's your one shot." I walk down the hallway, cheek throbbing.

"You're throwing away your chance at the Cup. This will poison the locker room," he shouts after me.

"Only if you don't let it go."

He growls, and I push open the doors to outside. Thankfully, my Uber is already waiting. I slide in, give him Kyleigh's address, and pray she's home.

thirty-six

Kyleigh

I'M SITTING CROSS-LEGGED ON MY COUCH, MY sketchpad on a pillow on top of my lap with *Southern Charm* playing in the background. I draw a few lines and tear off the piece of paper, crumpling it and tossing it into the growing pile on the floor.

A knock sounds on my door. Since I'm not expecting anyone, I almost don't get up to answer it. Someone probably let a solicitor into the building.

"Leigh...Kyleigh."

Oh my god. Rowan.

I toss the pillow and sketchpad off my lap and look down at myself. Of course he picks the day I'm in sweats and an oversized T-shirt, no makeup and my hair thrown up in a messy bun.

I tiptoe over and look out the peephole. There he is, and holy shit, his eye is swelling, and there's a bruise forming on his cheek.

I swing open the door. "Rowan!"

He walks in. "I'm sorry. I'm an asshole."

I shut the door behind him, taking in his face in horror. "What happened?"

"I should've come sooner." His eyes are imploring.

"Your eye." I go to the freezer, grab a cool pack, and wrap a dish towel around it. "Did something happen at practice? You take an elbow?"

I place it on his face, and he winces, covering my hand with his, and I quiet the flutters in my stomach. *Don't get excited, we don't know why he's here.* Just because he walked in with an apology doesn't mean he wants to be with me.

"Your brother happened."

"Seriously?" My mouth drops open.

He shakes his head. "Let's save it for later. Can we talk?" He grabs my hand and leads me over the couch. His gaze falls to the sketchpad as he moves the pad and pillow out of the way. "What's this?"

I shake my head.

"Yeah, later," he says and waits for me to sit before he sits next to me. "I'm—"

"No. Let me explain." I blow out a breath. "Keep the ice pack on, okay?"

He lowers it to his lap. "I'm fine."

"Just." I pick it up and put it back on his face. "For a little bit." He smiles at me, and goose bumps cascade over my skin. "What?"

"You care about me still. I haven't completely blown this, have I? On the way over, I thought maybe I'd lost you."

"Oh jeez," I say, surprised. "I owe you an explanation."

He doesn't say anything, and I gather the courage to tell him what happened the day we met.

"The night I met you at the wedding is the same night I walked in on my mom with another man. I was in a bad head-space and thought a night with you would distract me from my troubles. My mom is a popular wedding dress designer and my mentor. I worked for her. Life as I knew it shattered like glass at my feet that day. Everything I believed, everything I grew up to depend on was gone. My parents were always the ideal couple to me. Something I aspired to be a part of. My mom even used our family as part of her branding for the business—one big happy family."

He slides closer, his hands covering mine to stop them from shaking. I grip his calloused hands, and my body calms as it always does when we touch.

"But you were nothing like I thought. I figured you'd be the usual cocky, arrogant hockey player. I mean you're so good and so well-known, I assumed you'd only want to spend one night with me, so what was the harm? Conor was playing in Florida. But I wasn't sure if you'd remember me or if Conor would have ever referenced me in college, so I lied about my name, and I'm sorry. I just wanted that one thing for myself that night, even if it was selfish."

He nods, and his thumbs run over my fingers.

"Then when you saw me at breakfast and asked me to continue the arrangement, I wanted to because when I was with you, all that crap in my life didn't exist. It all disappeared, and I liked not having to feel all that pain. But I also liked you. As time went on, I didn't want us to end. By the time Conor was traded, I was invested. I'd already fallen for you, and every time I saw you, I told myself to tell you, to come clean, but I didn't want it to end. I'm sorry. I know I lost your trust."

He studies me for a moment before he speaks. "Can I ask you a question?"

I steel myself. "Anything."

"Was it just the sex? The sex that let you forget?"

I sigh and give him a sad smile. "I wish. These past six days, I so wished that was the case because if it was, you'd be replaceable."

"Well, I don't know about that." He smirks, and something unknots in my chest.

"It's you, Rowan. Your humor, your kindness, your supportive nature, it's all of you. The entire Rowan Landry package." He opens his mouth, but I put up my hand. "No, I purposely used your full name because being a hockey player is a part of you, and I lo...like him too."

He places the cold pack on the table. "I should've let you explain that night. I automatically put up my defenses and shoved you aside. That was so wrong, and I'm sorry. I'm so sorry, Le...Kyleigh."

I smile. "I'm the one who lied. Had I told you the truth earlier, we could've dealt with it together. I'm sure the shock—"

"Stop making excuses for me. I know what I was feeling for you. I just disregarded it, and that wasn't fair to you. I'll never do it again. I promise." He releases one of my hands and places his hand on my cheek. "And I always make good on my promises. Do you forgive me?"

I nod. "Do you forgive me?"

He nods. "That's why I'm here. These last six days have been miserable, but I'm most upset that I failed you, and I need to make that up to you."

"You didn't. I failed you."

"We failed one another."

I'll never fault him for needing time to sort out his feelings, although it was torture waiting. "Rowan—"

He leans forward. "No." He shakes his head then presses his lips to mine and pulls back. "I love you, Kyleigh Nilsen. Will you be my girlfriend?"

I giggle, and tears spring to my eyes. He loves me.

Rowan draws back.

"Could you have asked me when I had mascara on at least?"

He tucks a stray piece of hair that's escaped my messy bun behind my ear. "You're the most beautiful I've ever seen you right now."

"Good line," I say.

"If you'd rather me be a jerk…"

I grab his shirt and bring him to me. "I love you too, and I'd love to be your girlfriend, Rowan Landry."

His lips land on mine, and I release his T-shirt, wrapping my arms around his neck.

"We're gonna need a bed for this." He picks me up bride style and walks us to my bedroom.

He lays me down on the mattress, and I grab the hem of my T-shirt to take it off, but he covers my hand with his. "That's my job." Kneeling on the bed, he lowers himself over me, resting his weight on an elbow and pushing more stray hairs from my face. "You're so stunning."

He runs his hand down my torso, between the valley of my breasts, and fiddles with the hem of my shirt. Then he draws his hand up and under, his palm skating over my flesh, raising my shirt inch by inch. I suck in a breath when his hand covers my bare breast.

"Oh, I like this. New rule, no bra whenever I'm over." He tweaks my nipple, and I run my hand along his strong bicep and corded forearm.

"Rowan," I say, almost as if this is a dream, and he's not really here. A half an hour ago, I felt despondent. Now, I couldn't be happier.

His gaze floats up to mine. "You snuck up on me."

"You did, too. At a time when I didn't believe in love or forevers."

He kisses my forehead. "You're the best surprise of my life."

Tears spring to my eyes, but I don't want to cry. I don't want to ruin this moment between us. His hand moves off my breast, and he swipes away a tear that slips down the side of my face. "You're killing me."

"No. I'm just loving you," he says.

I run my hand through his hair and rest it on the back of his neck, pulling him down to kiss me. He doesn't rush our kiss. We're not tugging and ripping clothes off one another. We take our time and explore because now we know we have all the time in the world to be together. There's no longer an urgency based on the fear that we're going to lose this. I've never felt so at peace.

He kisses every inch of my skin, and my hands roam every inch of his.

Once we're naked, and he's between my legs with a condom on, we stare into each other's eyes as he pushes inside me. The thrusts aren't hard and fast, but languid and thorough. We're not screaming or grunting, we're moaning and sighing.

My fingers run lazily down his spine, and his mouth barely leaves mine except to take me in. When my orgasm climbs to the point I can no longer hold it back, I come staring into the blue hues of his eyes, knowing he'll always catch me.

His orgasm follows mine, and he jerks then stills but doesn't withdraw, instead staying inside me because he doesn't want this moment to end. We both don't want the connection we feel in this moment to be over.

I'm not naive enough to think that our life will be perfect from here on out. We'll have our arguments and disagreements, but I will forever remember that we have moments like this where we cherish and love one another. That will get us through the hard times.

If someone would've told me the night I met him that we'd be here, I'd have told them to have another shot of tequila. But in our case, I'm so happy to be wrong.

thirty-seven

Rowan

"This is our first preseason game. We squash this now." Tweetie, being one of the eldest on the team and a captain, tries to tell Conor and me what to do.

"I'm more than willing, but he's the one holding the grudge." I nod at Conor.

"You're sleeping with my sister."

"I'm *dating* your sister."

He glares and sucks in a deep breath. "You do your thing, I'll do mine."

"Fine."

"Shit, guys, we need to come together as a team. This is our year, and we'll never get there if you two don't stop coming at each other."

Conor steps closer to me. "Tell him to stop 'dating' my sister." He puts the word dating in air quotes.

I step closer to him, the two of us now less than a foot apart. "Tell him to get over it. I'm not going to hurt her."

"Tell him history says he's going to break her heart."

I laugh. "Tell him she's different."

The fuck if I'm going to tell him I love her. I was his best friend once. He should trust me. I've always been there for him.

Conor's jaw clenches. "Tell him if he was my friend, he would've let her go."

"Fuck this." I turn to walk away, but Tweetie pulls me back. "Tell him I'm with his sister and to deal with it because that's never. Going. To. Change."

Tweetie grunts. "Damn it, guys. Coach is gonna think I'm a horrible captain if I can't get you two to figure this out."

I appreciate Tweetie trying. I'm not sure why Conor can't get over the fact that I'm dating Kyleigh.

She told me she tried to call him, but he won't pick up her calls. Then she apparently left a voicemail cursing at him for ruining my pretty face. I shook my head at her and couldn't fight the smile. She's really something.

I'm about to turn and leave when Coach Buford calls me into his office.

"Shut the door," he says.

Fuck, don't tell me I just got traded or some shit. I'm not even sure what would happen with Kyleigh.

"Sit down." His furry gray eyebrows scrunch. "Word is you and Nilsen aren't getting along. I don't like dissension in my locker room."

"Why isn't he in here?" My lips press into a thin line.

"Because he's not the one dipping his dick where he shouldn't be."

I huff. "I don't remember signing a contract about who I can and can't date."

He stares at me long and hard, but I don't back down. "I've been a coach a long time. Probably should've retired years ago. Wife would've been happy if I had. But I keep coming back because I want to make something of this team. I know this is our year. We're set up for success. But if there's a fracture in the team, our success will turn to failure. Is she really worth it?"

"She is." More worth it than he can imagine. "How long have you been married, sir?"

"Too long..." He lets out a long breath.

"And I assume she's the love of your life."

"My only real love."

"Well, that's how I feel about Kyleigh. I wish she wasn't Conor's sister, but I can't do anything about that. She's my only real love. A once-in-a-lifetime love."

He taps his pen on the table and gives me a long, drawn-out stare. "You damn hockey players, you're so stubborn." He stares at the ceiling for a beat. "Fine. I'll give this a little leeway, but the minute it starts to affect this team, we're going to have a long sit-down. Go." He points at the door.

I head back into the locker room without saying anything to anyone. Conor glances at me but quickly shifts his gaze in the other direction.

I can't say it doesn't hurt. I can't say that I don't want him to see us together. That maybe he'd get on our side if he can see how much she means to me. That I'm not in this for her tits and ass, but her heart. The tits and ass are definitely a bonus though.

I dress and hear my phone vibrate in my bag.

Good luck tonight.

I see that she changed her name in my phone to KY-leigh. Little smartass.

Thanks. You offering any incentives to do well tonight?

How about a blow job for every goal?

> That's definitely an incentive.

What can I say? I'm a pretty awesome
girlfriend.

> The best.

I can't wait to watch you on the ice,
knowing that you're mine, and you're taking
me to bed tonight.

> Are you trying to make me go out there with
> a hard-on?

No. I don't want those puck bunnies to see
what they're missing.

Henry claps me on the shoulder. "Time to go, man."
I nod.

> Gotta go. I'll be looking for you. You're in
> the suite, right?

Hell no. I'm front and center. I want to
watch my man up close.

My nervousness kicks up a level.

> Love you.

Oh, and my dad's beside me. Eek.
Love you!

Hell, the father of the woman I love is sitting in the stands
while his son hates my guts. This should be fun.

We get on the ice, and we're first line.

Ten seconds into the game, I've got the puck, skating
toward the goal. I pass it to Tweetie, and he shoots it to Henry.

I skate behind the goal, Henry passes it to me, and I manage to get it past the goalie, the red buzzer lighting up.

I do my celly, and Tweetie and Henry celebrate with me.

I take off my glove, skating by Kyleigh and placing one finger up in the air. She laughs, her head rocking back and exposing her neck. She's wearing a Falcons sweatshirt, which is great, but I really want to see her in my jersey. The man next to her is tall, with a thin frame and salt-and-pepper hair. I recognize him from all the parents' weekends during college and the times he and his wife came to our games. I'm going to have to introduce myself to him tonight with the hopes that Conor hasn't shit-talked me too much.

"Stop eyeing her. You'll make it worse," Tweetie says under his breath.

"I'll lick the fucking glass just to piss him off."

Tweetie blows out a breath. "One of you has to be the adult here."

We both get off the ice, letting another line come on. At least Conor is on the ice the entire game tonight, so I don't have to speak to him on the bench.

We end up winning two to zero.

Conor leaves immediately after showering, and by the time I get outside the locker room, Kyleigh is standing by herself.

"Dad went with Conor, but he said to tell you congratulations, he loved seeing you play."

I wish I could have met Mr. Nilsen as Kyleigh's boyfriend, but I guess next time. Right now, I just want to get us home. "You gonna come home with me?"

"Is that even a question?" She walks in front of me, and I admire her ass in her tight jeans. "Technically, I owe you one, right?" She lifts her hand with her pointer finger extending in the air.

I walk up to her side and smack her ass, grabbing it right after. "That's right, and I can't wait to collect."

"Fuck, I like this sex after the adrenaline of a game." Her back falls to the mattress and she blows out a huge breath.

The pink blush coats her soft skin, and it makes me want to take her again.

I go to the bathroom to dispose of the condom, and she gets off the bed. When I return, she's got one of my T-shirts on and the pizza sits in the middle of my bed.

"I hope you're not like one of those guys who doesn't eat in bed because if you are, I might have second thoughts about us." She takes a big bite of the pizza in her hand.

I grab some shorts and go into the kitchen before returning with two waters. "You can do whatever you want in my bed." I sit on the edge and take a piece of pizza myself.

"Oh, I feel so special."

"You are." I lean forward and wait for her to kiss me.

We eat our pizza and drink our water, filling it with talks about my one goal. Henry got the other one.

"I have a question, and if I'm overstepping, please tell me." She stares at her pizza instead of me.

Shit, this is serious. "What?"

"You never mention your mom..."

Like my father, my mother isn't something I bring up a lot because of the pain it causes me.

"She died right after I graduated from college. About a month after."

"Oh, Rowan, I'm so sorry."

I drop the piece of pizza I'm eating in the box. "You deserve to know about my childhood." I broach the subject I usually avoid.

"Not if you don't want me to."

"I want you to know. It's just that I've never really talked to anyone about it. Probably should've gone to therapy at some point in my life." I take a sip of my water. "Like I said, my dad was an alcoholic and an abuser. He would hit my mom, intimidate her, verbally abuse her. Verbally abuse me too. He got sick when I was in the sixth grade but continued to drink. Eventually, his organs gave out, and he died in a hospital with my mom still by his side."

She slides closer, putting her arm around me and her head on my shoulder.

"I was happy he was dead. It meant he couldn't hurt her anymore. Because she never would've left him. He made us lose our house. The sheriff showed up one day to evict us because he'd been out of work for a year and was lying to my mom about paying the mortgage. He beat her so bad one night in a drunken rage that her friend had to take her to the hospital. She lied and said she tripped over one of my toys, but I'm sure they knew. Her other bruises that were half healed revealed her lie for her."

She grips me tighter. I hate telling her all this shit. I know she grew up in a household where she felt safe, and I don't relish exposing her to anything different. When she went to sleep at night, she wasn't worried about being woken by the sounds of glass breaking, shouting, and sobbing.

"My dad is the one who wanted me to play hockey. He got me into it. Came to games drunk and screamed at the refs, coaches, me. If I didn't perform up to his caliber, I heard it the entire way home while he banged his fist on the steering wheel."

I hate thinking about how scared I was to mess up on the ice back then. It felt like literal life and death.

"So, the day he died, it was a huge relief for me. I felt lighter. And although she had to work a lot, and I traveled to games and tournaments with a lot of other families, she always made sure I could play hockey. I'm not sure if it was because my dad wanted me to or because she knew how much I loved it, but she never took it away from me. I felt guilty for a long time because I didn't find any joy in it until after he died."

"I'm glad you were able to find your love for the game after he was gone. It sounds like it was hard to find enjoyment when he would ride you so hard."

I nod. "Yeah, I had some great coaches. I'm pretty sure everyone in my area knew about him. The sports world can seem small at times. But everyone was always nice to Mom and me. Jack's family took me in as one of their own through high school and never asked my mom for hotel room or food reimbursement. That's why I was at the wedding." I smile at her.

She kisses my cheek. "Thank God for that."

"Definitely." I swallow the lump in my throat. "She never told me she was sick. Didn't want to worry me when I was finishing up college. I kick myself now because I knew something was up when I saw her the winter before graduation. She looked frail, but she worked so much that I assumed that's what it was. She told me she'd been taking on a lot of hours. She called me a week after graduation and told me she was sick and wasn't going to get better. I flew home and sat at her bedside until she died." I blink back tears when I remember how frail she looked on her deathbed. "I never got to give her the life she deserved. I never got to take care of her. Allow her to stop working, repay her for everything she did for me."

Kyleigh rises onto her knees and crawls into my lap, laying her head on my chest. "I hate that you had to go through that. Especially alone."

I hold her in my arms because somehow, she makes the pain bearable. "It's life, I guess."

She doesn't say anything, and we hold each other for a long time.

I hate the feeling that things are great now, but they might not stay that way. It's one I was well-acquainted with before my dad died and he'd have a good week or two in a row. Life is unfair and unpredictable, and sometimes you get the shit end of the stick.

thirty-eight

Kyleigh

THE FALCONS ARE BACK FOR THEIR LAST PRESEASON game at home, and I arrive with my dad, sitting in the seats that Conor gets for us. I felt a little like a traitor when Rowan volunteered to get me seats, and I turned him down, but I want to sit with my dad.

With our popcorn and drinks, we sit down in front of the glass. I take off my sweatshirt, and my dad raises his eyebrows.

"I'm sorry, but Conor can deal with it."

"But his jersey?" My dad looks exhausted with the fight his two children are in.

"Rowan's important to me, and I want to support him." I sit down.

Dad folds himself into the seat next to me. "I know. I do. I tried to talk to him, but he swears you've lost your mind, and Rowan is taking advantage of you."

"Not true. Conor should trust I can make my own decisions."

I eat my popcorn, hoping I'm here before the warm-ups.

Rowan does this one stretch where he thrusts his hips that I love to watch.

My dad doesn't say anything for a while, and I hope that means he's going to drop the subject.

"By the way, I wanted to talk to you about something. I don't want to spoil your night, but it seems the only time you have for me are during these games." I open my mouth, but he interrupts me before I can say anything. "It's fine. I remember the early days."

"Sorry, I'll try to reach out more."

He shakes his head. "It's fine. It's nice to see you happy. But you should know that your mom and I are getting a divorce."

It's not a shock, but my stomach clenches anyway.

"And I think you should talk to her. Hear her side. She's your mother."

My hand stops midway to my mouth with the popcorn. "Um...no thanks."

When I think about what my relationship with my mother will be like moving forward, I'm unsure what to expect. I don't see myself never talking to her again, but I'm still so angry.

"Look at me, Ky." My dad turns to me in his seat. Most of the people around us are busy eating and talking and not paying us any attention, so I meet my dad's gaze. "I made mistakes too. A marriage involves two people, and it's not an easy road. Which you'll find out for yourself one day when the time comes. I'm not excusing her actions, and yeah, I'm still mad as hell, but she's the only mom you're ever going to have. I'm asking for you to try to find some common ground between you for your sake, not hers, because this will affect you down the road. And it'll trickle down to your kids when they ask you about their grandmother."

A pain so sharp it feels as if I've been slapped across the

face shocks me when I realize that if I'm lucky enough to marry Rowan, my mom will be their only shot at having a grandma. It makes me sad for my imaginary future kids. To only have one set of grandparents who won't even be married.

"I get it, Dad." I sigh.

"Do you? I'm glad. Just lunch or something."

"I'll think about it." I'm definitely not going to give him an affirmative answer because I don't know if I can do it. "And I'll think about it harder if you stay tonight so I can introduce you to Rowan."

"I know Rowan," my dad says with a chuckle.

"Not as my boyfriend."

He smiles and knocks his shoulder against mine. "No, I don't. I look forward to meeting him as such."

"Thanks." I give him a big smile and dip the side of my head onto his shoulder.

The lights go down, and the music ramps up. Strobe lights sweep across the audience and ice. Adrenaline fills my veins as the mic guy announces the players. When he introduces Rowan, I smack the glass and shout while my dad does the same when Conor is announced.

After the introductions, Rowan positions himself in the face-off circle. He gets the puck, in full control, and passes it to Henry. Henry skates back and forth around the defenseman, keeping the puck in his control.

"He's gotta get it out," Dad says, always acting like a player or coach when he watches the games.

Henry shoots it to Rowan, who passes it to Tweetie. I see the reason for his nickname. Rowan is so smooth on the ice. I swear at one point he's so fast I missed a play where he had the puck, and then it was gone.

The three of them hammer it out with the two defensemen from Detroit, and Rowan goes behind the net when the puck gets free. Henry gets there first and spots him, shooting the puck his way.

The puck hits Rowan's stick, and right away he does a wraparound and gets it by the goalie, the red light lighting up and the buzzer going off. He raises his fist in celebration and skates around, coming toward me.

I put my hands on the glass, jumping up and down and cheering. He skates past and blows me a kiss. I could melt into a puddle.

He skates over to the bench, and a new line comes on the ice. Dad elbows me and points toward the Jumbotron. I look up, and there's a picture of Rowan and me with a heart on one side of the screen. On the other side is a picture of Conor in the net with a scowl. The caption reads, "Big Brother Doesn't Look Happy."

Seriously, who got wind of this? This can't be good for the team. I haven't read a hockey blog since Rowan and I solidified our relationship because I don't want to read about myself being bashed. The minute Rowan demanded to put a picture of us on his social media, I tried to tell him it wasn't a good idea. I wasn't looking forward to having every flaw and insecurity of mine being criticized and judged.

I look down the ice to see Conor staring daggers at me, but I don't care. He needs to grow up. Can't he see that he's the only one miserable here?

After the game, I'm waiting with my dad where the players come out.

Conor is first, and he heads over to our dad, shaking his hand. "Thanks for coming." They give one another a hug.

"Great game. You saved a ton for them."

"That's my job." Conor positions his duffle bag on his shoulder. "Enjoy the seats, sis?"

"I did. Thank you."

"Landry can't get you any? Shouldn't you be in the wives and girlfriends' section?"

I bite down, and I think one of my teeth might crack. "I wanted to watch it with Dad."

"Good cover." He turns to our dad. "Want to go grab something to eat?"

"Um..." Dad glances in my direction.

I loop my arm though my dad's. "Sorry, he's spending tonight with his other child and her boyfriend. You're welcome to come if you can behave yourself and not throw a fit like a toddler." I smile sweetly at him.

"Come on, you two. This is ridiculous." Dad sighs.

"Maybe if your boyfriend understood the first rule of being a best friend, I could join you."

I inhale a calming breath. "He didn't know."

"Oh right. I forgot, *Leigh*, you let him fall for you, and then you told him. Oh no, wait...you waited until he found out himself."

I narrow my eyes. "He forgave me, so maybe you should too. And you should understand that there's this thing called free will, and you can't dictate what people can and can't do."

"I assume I'm interrupting," Rowan says, coming up behind me.

I slide my arm out of my dad's and wrap my arms around his neck, placing a big fat kiss on his lips. *Take that, Conor.*

Rowan takes my arms from around his neck and lowers them, staring over my shoulder. I assume at my brother. Oh, no, I am not going to act any differently for him.

Rowan puts his hand out in front of my dad. "It's nice to see you again, Mr. Nilsen."

Dad shakes his hand. "It was always Troy. No need for formalities just because you're dating Kyleigh."

Conor grunts, and Rowan looks at him.

Rowan slides his hand into mine. Thank goodness, I was worried for a moment.

"Pinkie, I'm heading out. You coming?" Tweetie hollers where he is down the hall with two girls at his side.

"Dad?" Conor raises his eyebrows.

"I'm gonna go to dinner with Kyleigh and Rowan. You go ahead."

Conor pats my dad on the back. "Thanks for coming. I'll call you tomorrow."

His eyes throw daggers at Rowan and me before he heads in Tweetie's direction.

"You can thank me later," Tweetie shouts at Rowan.

Rowan's gaze follows Conor. I hate to see the hurt in his blue eyes. Their friendship was important to him, and Conor's letting it go because of me.

"Where should we go?" Dad asks.

"I have a place I think you'll both like. Let me call to see if they can get us in." Rowan walks away with his cell phone to his ear.

"There's a lot of tension," my dad says under his breath. "It can't go on like this forever."

"Then talk to your son." I'm done with my brother's bullshit. I'm happy. I'm living my life, and I'm not going to stop because Conor thinks he knows better than me.

Rowan walks back over. "We're in. I called an Uber to take us."

"I like this treatment," my dad says.

I rise on my tiptoes and kiss Rowan's cheek. "Me too, Dad."

We go to the restaurant, and Rowan is charming and affectionate and wins my dad over easily. Then we head back to my place and make love. Life is great. Other than my jerk of a brother.

thirty-nine

Rowan

THE GUYS ARE GOING OUT. ALL THE GUYS BECAUSE Henry's got a babysitter.

When they leave, I head over to pick up Kyleigh at her place.

I knock on her door, and when she answers, my jaw just about hits the floor. "I'm not sure about that dress." I place my hands on her hips and walk her backward into her apartment, kicking the door shut behind me.

"You seem to like it." She gives me a sexy grin.

"What's not to like?"

She steps into me, and I grab her ass with both hands, my lips falling to hers. I miss her so much when we're not around one another.

I miss the way her nails run down the back of my head while we're kissing. I miss the way she rises on her tiptoes and steps into my arms. I miss the way she tips her head back and lets me explore every inch of her.

She's perfection, and she's mine.

"I think I need to remind you who you belong to tonight."

Her laughter rings out through her apartment. "I like this alpha thing."

I lift her and place her on the couch. I catch sight of her sketchpad and a few pieces of fabric spread out on her coffee table.

Her legs open with the slightest touch of my hands on her inner thighs, and she anchors herself with her hands linked behind my neck.

She's hot every day of the week, but tonight in this short tight dress, she's breathtakingly gorgeous. I'm afraid I could get into a few fights if other guys try to touch what's mine.

"Actually." I step back and untwine her arms from my neck. "We're going to wait until after."

"What?" She leans forward, grabbing the bulge in my pants.

"Yeah, I'm going to tease you tonight." I take her hand off me.

She hops off the edge of the couch. "Oh, you just wait and see who is going to be doing the teasing. You'll be taking me in the bathroom or the alley within an hour of us being at the club."

"You do know I thrive on competition, right? Tell me I can't hold out, and you'll be naked, begging for my cock, and I still won't give it to you." My hand goes to her cheek, and I nudge her against the wall by the front door, my leg between her legs, forcing her to open them.

"Game on, Landry."

I chuckle and stare at her lips. I'm suddenly regretting my decision to wait rather than taking her on the couch. "Okay, Nilsen, if you're gonna play that way." I lean forward, running the tip of my nose down the column of her neck and back up. "You just missed out on having my mouth on yours with all your smack talk."

She cups my dick through my pants again. "And you missed out having my mouth wrapped around your dick."

"Fuck, you play dirty." I cage her against the wall, wishing we could stay in the entire night.

But we've already spent too many nights in our places, in our beds. She deserves to be wined and dined, and although it's not a fancy restaurant tonight, it is showing the world that she belongs to me. That she's someone important in my life.

I step back and link my hand in hers. "Let's get out of here before we don't go at all."

She giggles, grabs her purse, and we walk down her apartment stairs to the SUV I ordered.

"Wow. Fancy. No Uber."

"No Uber," I say, opening the door for her.

We arrive at the club, and the people waiting in the long line outside watch the driver pull the tinted SUV up. I step out first, holding my hand out for her to take. She glances at the people with their phones pointed at us. I really hope she's stopped reading those hockey blogs because she could be the world's hottest model and still people will find fault just because she's mine.

I wrap my arm around her waist and escort her to the bouncers. One opens up the rope, and I tip him for letting us in.

Tweetie said they have a VIP section reserved. I know Conor will be here, and I'm hoping we can squash some of this tonight. That he'll see me with his sister, see the way I am with her, and know that she's safe with me. When Tweetie brought up this plan, Henry was just as skeptical as me.

The club is crowded and dark, so I slide my palm down Kyleigh's arm and link our hands, keeping her close behind me as I wind us through the people. Her other hand hooks into the back of my pants. There's something about the gesture that I like. Maybe she's not only mine, but I'm hers. Or she trusts me enough to keep her safe. It's a powerful feeling when you can offer someone that feeling of security. But maybe that's just my fucked-up state of mind from never feeling safe my entire childhood. I probably cherish that feeling more than most.

"Magic!" Tweetie shouts, and heads whip in my direction.

I bump fists with him when we reach him. "Thanks for being discreet."

He laughs before tipping back his glass. I pull Kyleigh to my side.

"Hey, Kyleigh." Tweetie gives her a hug, then whispers something in her ear.

Her gaze shoots to the couch. I follow her line of vision, and sure enough, there's Conor drilling holes into both of us with his eyes—mostly where my hand rests on her hip.

We enter the VIP area, saying our hellos, and I introduce her to the guys she doesn't know. I get her a glass of wine, and we stand on the edge of the VIP lounge and talk to my teammates and any of their significant others who are here. Kyleigh leans into me. I wrap my arm around her stomach, holding her back to my front.

But I can't help feeling as though Conor is watching us, and when I look up, sure enough, the woman next to him—who is trying her hardest to garner his attention—sighs and slumps down in the circular booth, crossing her arms in a pout. I shake my head at him. He needs to get over this.

Kyleigh turns toward me, her lips kissing my neck. "Let's dance," she says in my ear over the loud music.

I pat her ass and stand straight, taking her glass and putting our drinks on the table next to us. Before we get a chance to head to the dance floor, Conor walks past, shouldering me as if he wants me to know he's pissed.

Yeah, I already got the memo, asshole.

I tell Kyleigh to stay in the VIP section while I venture out to talk to Conor. I weave through the crowds, guys giving me high fives and girls stepping in front of me to try to grab my attention. Finally, I push open the back door where I saw Conor go and enter the alley beside the club. He's walking toward the street.

"Conor," I shout.

He stops and slowly circles back. Once he sees I'm alone and Kyleigh isn't with me, he walks back my way. "What do you want, Landry? You can go fuck my sister on the dance floor now, I'm leaving."

"We're a couple, and I'm sorry if it bothers you, but when are you going to stop being such a dick about this?"

"I'm the dick?" He points at himself. "You know the bro code—don't fuck the baby sister!"

"Where's that written?"

"It's common sense. I'm your teammate, and even if I wasn't, you're my friend. Hell, at one time you were my best friend, and I was fucking excited to come back here and build that back up. And we were until I realized the girl you're fucking is my sister. I heard what you said about her. You implied that she was just a fuck."

My stomach sinks, and I run a hand down my face. "I said that because I didn't want to hear Tweetie's shit. Hell, man, I love her. She's all I think about. She's all I want. She's all I see."

I swear that only seems to make him angrier. "Until when? Until you're on the road, and she's back home, and you haven't seen each other or spent any real time together for weeks? Some woman will give you a little extra attention. Will she be all you see then?"

Anger boils inside me like a cauldron over the fact that he thinks so little of me.

"Nice best friend you are." I pocket my hands so I'm not tempted to punch him like he did me.

He leans forward. "A leopard doesn't change his spots."

"What the hell does that mean?"

"You forget, we were best friends. How many girls' hearts did you break in college, Mr. Heartbreaker?"

"Fuck you. None."

"That's what you say, and maybe that's what you think, but I was there with you, seeing you with different girls. No one held your interest longer than a night or two. You'll get bored of her just like you did the rest. Or decide she's getting too close to your issues and back away."

I want to stick up for myself and say that he's referring to the college version of me. Throw stones that he wasn't innocent either. But I'm not that twenty-year-old kid anymore. I'm almost thirty and have done a lot of growing up since then.

He looks over my shoulder and eyes me again. "Six years ago, I saw my mom with another man at a hotel bar. I confronted her, and she told me it was a mistake and that she was wrong to risk her marriage. Guess what? Here we are six years later, and she did it again. Like I said, a leopard doesn't change their spots."

I'm too shocked to say anything. The gasp behind me confirms I'm not the only one who heard him.

"You never told me!" Kyleigh rushes to my side.

I put my arm around Kyleigh because her world just got crushed again.

"You were nineteen, Ky. In your first year of college. You didn't need to know. Mom came to one of my games and told me she and Dad were having troubles. She threw around the word divorce. I believed her remorse and kept her secret."

Kyleigh steps in front of me. "We're a team. We're

supposed to get through this shit together, but you took it upon yourself to try to deal with it alone and not fill me in."

Conor throws up his hands. "What would you knowing have accomplished? Nothing. But you're being a fool if you think that Rowan is some changed man. That you have some magic pussy he can't live without."

I cock my fist back and punch him in the same spot he did me, right across the cheek and eye. "Don't you dare speak to my woman like that. Good luck stopping the fucking goals now."

The back door of the club opens, and Tweetie and Henry walk out.

"For fuck's sake! Take your frustration out on the other team's goalie. Jesus," Tweetie says with his hands pushed into his hair.

"Come on." I take Kyleigh's hand and step in front of Conor, who's holding his eye. "You either respect our relationship or keep your distance. I'm done with this shit."

We walk out of the alley and head back to her place. I had hopes that Conor would change his mind and see that I love and care for his sister, but I think we both need to realize that might never happen.

forty

Kyleigh

WELL, THERE WAS NO TEASING LAST NIGHT BETWEEN Rowan and me when we got back to my place. There was just me crying and him holding me because pretty soon, I fear he and Conor will be rolling around on the ground, beating the shit out of one another.

The news Conor shared about our mom didn't sit well, especially since I agreed to have lunch with her today. Knowing she cheated on my dad at least twice makes me want to cancel. Knowing Rowan will be there with me is the only reason I haven't canceled yet.

"I know this is hard, and the decision is yours." Rowan slides closer to me in bed, his fingers running down my arm. "But she's the only mom you have, and coming from someone who lost his, I think you should give reconciliation a chance, whatever that looks like."

Rowan's been patient and not offered a ton of advice on the matter of my mom.

I turn and bury my head in his neck, clinging to him. "We're so happy, I just want to stay in our little bubble."

His calloused palms run down my back, and he kisses the top of my head. "I wish I could take all the pain away. I hate that you're hurting."

I see it in his eyes—he hates all of this as much as I do. This should be the happiest time of our lives. We're embarking on a new beginning, we love one another, but my family is slowly draining all that newfound happiness away.

"I guess I should get ready." I groan.

"Probably."

I kiss his collarbone and slide out of bed. He doesn't try to grab me or get me in the mood, but rather remains my constant center of support.

I take my shower and slide into a dress suitable for brunch at the restaurant my mom picked. Rowan wears a button-down and a pair of slacks that make him look like the sex symbol he is.

We walk into the restaurant, and my mom looks up from a corner table that overlooks the Chicago River as we make our way over.

"Kyleigh, I love this color on you," she says, standing and putting her hands on my upper arms, looking me up and down, then she hugs me. "Love looks good on you." She smiles over my shoulder at Rowan. "And Rowan, how nice to see you again. You've really grown up and turned into a man." She hugs him. I watch Rowan stiffen before relaxing when she lets him go. "Sit, you two." She gestures to the empty chairs with her hand.

We sit, leaving the fourth chair empty, and watch the water traffic on the river.

"Thank you for meeting with me," she says, placing her hands on top of mine on the table.

I slide mine out and place them in my lap. "Sure."

She sits back and positions the linen napkin over her lap. The waitress comes over, and I order a mimosa while Rowan orders a coffee.

"We do love our mimosas," my mom says, smiling at Rowan. "So, I hear Conor isn't playing nice." Her lips turn down in a weird fake frown.

I'm not sure why she's acting so fake. "I don't want to talk about it."

"You know he's always been so protective of you, but that's what a big brother should do."

"He's taking it to the extreme," I say, unwrapping my silverware and laying my napkin in my lap.

"You can't really blame him." She looks at Rowan. "When Kyleigh started to go from little girl to all grown up, the boys noticed. They'd say things to Conor about Kyleigh's..." she leans in over the table, "boobs and stuff. You know how boys can be."

Rowan doesn't say anything but looks at me.

"I was four years younger. That's kind of gross."

She waves me off. "Not in high school. Once you were in college and we'd go to his games. Rowan knows what I'm talking about."

"Let's talk about something else," I say.

The waitress brings over my mimosa, and I take a large sip, wishing I hadn't agreed to this brunch.

Even if the guys Conor played with were saying things about me, it doesn't excuse how he's acting toward Rowan and me. He hasn't even taken the time to see us as a couple, to see how much we care for each other.

"What do you want to talk about then?" my mom asks.

Since the brunch is a buffet, we don't have to order and can go up and get food whenever we want.

"How about you cheating on Dad? Twice."

Her fake smile falters, and she looks at Rowan and back at me.

Rowan places his napkin on the table, sliding his chair back. "I'm going to be outside. I just remembered I have a phone call to make. It was nice seeing you, Mrs. Nilsen."

"Oh, please call me Val."

"Nice to see you, Val." He leans over the table to give me a kiss on the cheek. "I'll be right at the bar," he whispers in my ear.

I nod. I probably should've come by myself, but I would never have walked in here without the encouragement and support of Rowan.

"I really wish you'd keep our family affairs private," my mom says once he's out of earshot.

And there's my real mom.

"Rowan is a part of my life."

She rolls her eyes. "For now, but come on."

I shake my head, not wanting to get into a fight about this. She doesn't have the first clue about anything regarding Rowan and me.

"You want to say your piece, so say it." I sit back in my chair, cross my legs, and set my hands in my lap.

She brings her mimosa to her lipsticked lips and lowers the glass after she takes a sip. "I understand you're upset. Obviously the fact that you and Conor aren't talking didn't stop him from letting you in on our secret."

"Aren't secrets the problem? I didn't know this family had so many of them."

She twirls her champagne glass at the stem. "I don't expect you to understand. You're still in the beginning phase of love. Where you're his entire world. But there will come a time when it feels as if you're invisible to him. When you're no longer his shiny new toy. When you have kids and he only sees you as a mother and not a woman. Your father worked all the time. Cases took him away from our family for months at a time. I threw myself into my work once you and Conor were old enough." She glances toward the river at a tour boat going by with tourists staring at the skyscrapers, snapping pictures.

I watch a family of four getting their picture taken. The dad is secure in the back with his arms around his wife and his son, the little girl standing in front. The mom's hand is on the daughter's shoulder. Picture perfect. I had that once too, but now that image is gone, ripped away from me.

"Then you leave him. Or work it out. You don't cheat on him. How many men were there?"

She exhales an annoyed breath. I take that to mean more than the two I know about. "For someone who kept her own secret, it's a little unfair you can't put yourself in my shoes."

"You're honestly comparing my lie to you cheating on Dad?"

"It's the same thing. You were scared, so you kept a secret from him. Despite what you might think, I didn't want to hurt your father. It's not so easy to tell the man you once loved that you're not happy. I didn't want to blow up our life. You and Conor are my everything."

I scoff and roll my eyes.

"You are. But I lost myself in being a mother and a wife. You guys left home, and I didn't know who I was. I thought after you left, your dad and I would reconnect. That we'd find one another again, fall back in love. But while I tried to book vacations and date nights, your dad threw himself into his work. And I get it. It was the easy thing to do for him. The house was empty. There were no more practices to carpool to. No more footsteps running down the stairs. It was just silence."

"Still, Mom..."

"It's not an excuse for what I did. Not at all. I'm not saying that. I'm just trying to tell you a little of what I was struggling with. I know this isn't an easy fix, and I want to do the work to fix my relationship with you kids. I love you, and I love Conor. Sadly, your dad and I have decided to get a divorce, but I think we'll both be much happier, and in the end, it's the right decision."

"Says you." I grip the napkin in my hands.

She extends her hand toward me, but I don't take it. "In time, you'll realize it too. I know you only see us under the lens of your mom and dad, but we were once like you two." She eyes the empty chair to my right. I open my mouth to respond, but she quickly continues. "That isn't me saying you'll be sitting in my seat down the road. It's just to tell you that we were once two young people very much in love. And maybe we didn't nurture that love but ignored it and let it die. And then we didn't take the time or effort to try to bring it back to life." She shrugs. "Those are what-ifs that I can't keep thinking back on. I have to move forward with my life. For myself. You and Conor are all grown up. It's time for me to figure out who I am."

Hearing her confession is hard, but I am happy she's finally being real, even if I still don't agree with what she did.

I reluctantly move my hands up to the table and let her take them.

"I know that hoping you'll come back and work with me is futile, but I do hope you find your love for design again. You're exceptionally talented. And if you ever do want to come back, the door is always open." She squeezes my hand and retracts hers, picking up her mimosa and sipping it. "I love you, Kyleigh, and I'm sorry you had to see me with someone other than your father. I can't imagine how painful that was."

I push back the tears and nod. I'm not sure what to say.

"Thank you for hearing me out," she says.

"Thank you for being so transparent."

I am thankful she told me where her head was. Why she did it. Every other time I talked to her, I felt like she wasn't taking ownership for her actions, and she was being impulsive and immature and selfish, but I understand a little more now. I'm not sure how we'll ever get to the place we were before, but it makes me want to at least have some sort of relationship with her.

I'm just not ready to think about what the future looks like for us. One day at a time, I suppose.

"I know I've been hard on you, tried to direct you to live the life I thought you should. Not that there's a blessing in this, but I think all of this coming to light has really helped you find yourself. Figure out what you want in this life. And it's something I should've allowed you to do a long time ago."

"Thanks, Mom," I say, really looking her in the eye for the first time during this brunch.

She glances over my shoulder. "Will you stay for brunch?"

I'm not sure I want to honestly, but it would be a step in the right direction.

"Let me go get Rowan." I slide the chair back and leave her, weaving through the tables.

Rowan slides off the stool when he sees me coming and opens his arms. I step into them, and he envelops me, squeezing me tightly. Tears sting my eyes.

"Are we leaving?" he asks.

I pull back from our embrace. "I think we're going to stay."

His easy-going, sweet smile tips the corners of his mouth. "Okay."

I take his hand and guide him back over to the table.

And we have brunch with my mom. It's awkward and

uncomfortable at times, but it's also a little comforting and a step in a new direction.

I'm not sure where it will take us, but I think I'm okay with that right now. She's right—I'm finding myself, and it feels really good.

forty-one

Rowan

TODAY IS THE FIRST GAME OF THE REGULAR SEASON.

I wake from my nap and find Kyleigh on the floor of my family room, her legs stretched under my coffee table, her sketchpad out and a row of different colored pencils in front of her. Music plays lightly from my speaker. She's made herself at home, and I fucking love seeing her so comfortable in my space.

After my skate this morning, I asked her to come over and work here so I could have some time with her before heading back to the arena. She must've come in while I was napping now that she's got the codes to get in.

I walk around and swing my leg around her, sitting on the couch and straddling her from behind. I eye her design, a wedding dress that I assume is for Alara. Kyleigh's starting to find her passion again. She's made me stop more than once at a fabric store, and she talks about the design she's thinking when she sees a fabric or pattern she likes or points out a store-front and compares it to how she'd set up her own store.

"How was your nap?" she asks, continuing to work.

"Not nearly as good as when you're in bed with me." I kiss the top of her head.

"And your nerves?" She puts down the pencils and pushes the table away from her.

"High."

Chuckling, she slides out and comes to her knees in front of me, her hands sliding up my thighs. "Are you one of those athletes who thinks you shouldn't have sex before a game?"

I stare at her between my legs, and my cock strains against the fabric of my shorts. "Definitely not."

"So..." Her palms slide up my thighs, up and under the hem of my shorts. "Can I help take those nerves away?"

I lean back. "Do your worst."

Her hand reaches my hard cock, and she wraps her fingers around me.

"God, those hands are so fucking talented."

She smiles at me, her other hand sliding under the elastic waistband, tugging and freeing my dick. Her thumb runs over the tip, spreading my pre-cum around the top.

"I love your hands on me, but I really want to be inside of you."

I take her hand in mine, guiding her to stand. Her hand slips off my dick, and she stands between my legs. I push her jogger pants down and smile because she's not wearing any underwear.

"We're both commando?"

"Easier access," she says with a shrug. "On the way over, I really hoped you weren't one of those athletes who swears off sex on game day."

She steps out of her pants and straddles me, rubbing her wetness along my dick.

"Even if I was, I think you'd be a game-changer." I fist the bottom of my cock and guide it into her slick opening. She sinks down on me, and we both moan.

Turns out Kyleigh has an IUD, and we both got tested after we discussed ditching the condoms.

I'll never get used to being bare inside her. She's the first woman I've not used a condom with, and there's something special about not having that thin layer of latex between us. It brings us closer not only physically, but emotionally.

She rocks forward, and my fingers dig into her hips, allowing her to take control. I push away all the anxiety that's been hijacking my brain today. The fact that this is my first full year on the team. That we're one of the teams favored to win the Cup. Conor is still giving me the cold shoulder. The tension in the locker room is high and I can't shake the feeling that I'm a shitty teammate.

All of that disappears, and I realize that all I care about is Kyleigh. Seeing her behind that glass. Seeing her after the game. Seeing her in my bed.

"I love you," I say, grazing my fingers up her spine to the back of her head, guiding her lips to meet mine.

She kisses me slowly and languidly, each of us taking our time while her hips move like the slow roll of ocean waves at low tide.

I never thought I was made for commitment. Worried that the evil I was bred from would overtake me. But all I want to do is love and support Kyleigh. I could never do to her what my dad did to my mom. It's a soul-deep knowing. We'll face problems like any couple, but I'll always be a united front with her. She's found the man inside me I didn't know was hidden, and I'm grateful for that because without her, I'm not sure he would have ever surfaced.

Her hips speed up, and I lower my thumb to her clit, taking her over the edge.

Her cry echoes through the room, and I lift my hips off

the couch, driving deeper. She digs her fingertips into my shoulders. Watching her come is still my favorite thing ever. The way her mouth slowly parts, her eyes flutter shut, and her head lolls back. It's beautiful, and it's a fucking thrill to be the one to give her that.

Her eyes slowly open, and she smiles. "I love you."

She's perfect.

I continue to push inside her, my dick unable to hold back now that she's even wetter from coming. My climax hits, and I pump and still inside her, grunting as I come hard.

She falls to my chest, and I hold her to me, never wanting to let her go. She's all mine.

Everyone is in their heads when I get to the locker room before warm-ups. Mine is on Kyleigh, wanting to win this game and get back to her.

Tweetie sits down next to me as I get myself ready. "Hey, I think, um...Conor isn't in a good headspace. He saw Kyleigh come through the gate this morning. Knew she was going to your place."

"She's my girlfriend."

He sighs. "Yeah, I know. That's the point. His head is really twisted, man. I'm sure it doesn't help with all the shit going on with his family. I know he went out with his mom the other day. Came back and acted like a fucking bear." He shakes his head. "This season is really important to all of us, and I worry he's gonna fuck this up for himself and us. He's so angry, man."

"What do you want me to do? With the things he's said, the way he's been acting, I'm done. I can't have Kyleigh be part of that poison."

Tweetie looks at me and shakes his head. "I love this whole

fall-on-the-sword thing you got going on with her. And I appreciate the mile-high pedestal you've put her on. But this is the Cup we're talking about."

I stand up from the bench and stare down at him. "I want to win the Cup. I do. Don't think I'm not invested in this team's success, but Kyleigh trumps it all. It's up to him to make it right at this point."

His eyes dig into mine, and I'm surprised to find a hint of understanding in his gaze. I figured he'd be chest to chest with me, arguing that I'm wrong.

"I guess we're screwed then. You and Conor are going to take us all down with you."

I don't say anything and walk out the door.

"Daddy, we gotta come up with a plan," I hear him say right before the doors shut behind me.

The fans are sprinkling in. The arena will be packed tonight. I skate around the ice a few times, making sure I feel good, then I fall to my knees and do my warm-ups. Conor is a little farther down the ice from me. Tweetie and Henry arrive later than everyone else.

"About time." Coach Buford gives them a stern warning glare.

Henry skates over to me, and Tweetie heads over to Conor.

"I'm supposed to smooth this over, but..." Henry falls to his knees and does his hip flex stretch.

I roll over to my back. "It's his problem. I don't know why I'm getting the lecture."

"Tweetie doesn't like dissension in the team. He thinks if there are problems in the locker room, it trickles out into the game."

I agree with Tweetie, but Conor is being a selfish prick. And if he thinks I'm such a bad person, then what does that say about his trust in me? That there isn't any.

"You should double-team Conor then." I get up with my stick and skate away.

"Come on," Henry whines, following. "Bodhi acts more grown up than you two idiots."

I pick up a puck with my stick and start the team on some warm-up drills.

Conor skates toward the net, ready for us to take practice shots at the goal.

I practice my stick work, not trying to score a goal, but skate behind the net. I catch sight of Kyleigh coming down the stairs and a laugh bubbles out of me. Not only is she wearing my jersey, but she's got my number in glitter on her cheeks. Plus, she's decked out in the team colors, navy blue and light blue.

Instead of continuing my drill, I skate over to her, cursing the plexiglass that's blocking my lips from hers. I blow her a kiss, and she puts her hand on the glass. In her palm is a small handwritten note cut into the shape of a heart.

You got this. You're the best in the league.

I want to hug her because she somehow knows exactly what I need to hear right now.

She waves me off and puckers her lips at me.

Feeling regenerated, wanting to show her the man she chose and make her proud, I take the puck to the center line, skating in toward the goal when it's my turn. Conor's in the net, and when he spots me coming close and I'm about to knock the puck in, he skates out a bit, puffs out his chest, and I fall to the ground.

Throwing my stick to the side, I get up and grab his jersey.

"Whoa. Whoa!" Tweetie slides to a stop, pushing us both back by the chest, but it's too late.

My gloves are off, and my fist flies toward Conor's face.

"You piece of shit. Is that your solution? To take me out before the first game even starts?"

"Guys, come on." Henry joins in with Tweetie's effort to keep us apart, but Conor drops his gloves and swings, his fist colliding with Henry's jaw.

"Fuck, man!" Henry shouts.

"Taking us all down, huh, Nilsen?" I pull him closer to me with my fist on his jersey.

Tweetie and the rest of the team huddle around us, everyone grabbing to pull us apart. But this has been a long time coming, and it's about time we hash this out the hockey way.

forty-two

Kyleigh

I SIT DOWN IN MY SEAT, WAITING FOR MY DAD TO join me.

"Holy shit. Did you see that?" someone behind me says.

"What?" another guy says.

"Conor Nilsen just chest-bumped Rowan Landry onto the ice. And now it looks like...oh man, they're fighting."

My gaze flies to the rink. Sure enough, Rowan has Conor by the jersey and is punching his side. The fact that Conor is in full gear gives him the advantage, especially since Rowan doesn't even have his helmet on yet.

I can't see Conor's face, but Rowan's red, and he's clearly pissed off.

Tweetie gets between them, but they somehow fend off every other teammate trying to get them to stop. I bang on the glass, but that's useless. They're not paying one lick of attention to me, only each other.

I cringe, watching two men I love so much being so violent toward one another. The fear inside me that I'll have to choose between them rises to the surface. What if Conor never comes around?

The fans around me are cheering and yelling, laughing, thinking this is entertainment. It's sickening.

Shouldering my way through the crowd, I watch Conor take off his helmet. Rowan doesn't come to his senses but waits for Conor to remove it before they start up again, which pisses me off.

The coaching staff come out onto the ice and the players divide into two groups, one pulling at Rowan and the other at Conor.

I run up the stairs and try to make my way to the locker rooms. I stop and talk to a security guy standing by the entrance, telling him who I am, but he looks at me as though I'm trying to pull one over on him.

My phone rings in my purse, and when I pull it out, I see that it's Rowan. Thank God.

"Rowan," I say purposely loudly so the security guy can hear me, but he rolls his eyes as though I'm playing some game.

"It's Henry. Rowan is in Coach's office getting his ass chewed out. Listen, I was talking to Tweetie—"

"Get your ass in here!" Tweetie shouts in the background.

"I'm trying to, but no one will let me through." With narrowed eyes, I glance at the security guy.

"Hold on." It's muffled, but I hear Henry telling someone to come get me and bring me to them. "Okay, a guy named Ron is on his way. Meet him by the front entrance at the bottom of the stairs."

I nod even though he can't see me, and I start walking. "Are they okay?"

"If you're asking if they're injured, another black eye apiece, but no broken bones or anything. Probably some bruises you can nurse back to health. On Rowan, not Conor. Obviously."

I grit my teeth. "Obviously."

"Well, the rest of us have to go back to warm-ups. I expect they'll be out by the time you get here. I hope you can talk some sense into them. We've tried everything on our end. Good luck, Kyleigh."

Henry hangs up, and I feel as though he's sent me on a mission he doesn't think I can accomplish. Not that I blame him. These two men are some of the most stubborn alive.

I go down the steps to the front entrance, and a lot of fans are just now coming in. I watch families and smile at every Landry jersey I see, then scowl at the Nilsen ones, although it's always weird seeing people wearing my brother's jersey.

"Kyleigh?" a man says softly from next to me. He's shorter than I was expecting, with thinning dark hair and a kind smile. "I'm Ron."

"How did you know it was me?"

He looks at my jersey. "It's my job to know." He nods toward an elevator. "Let's go."

I follow him to the elevator and down a long hallway. He doesn't say much except how exciting the first game of the season is. He doesn't say anything about the fact my brother and boyfriend are ruining everyone's big night.

He opens a door for me, and I step into a small room with a couple of tables and chairs. Rowan is on one side. Conor on the other. Neither is looking at the other.

Rowan's gaze drifts up, and instead of his usual smile, he looks like a scolded child. Coach Buford must have done a number on them.

"Thank you, Ron." I give him a weary smile.

"My pleasure." He shuts the door behind him when he leaves.

I stand with my arms crossed, my gaze drifting from one to

the other. "Hello, boys. And I say boys because you're acting like twelve-year-olds on a playground."

"He tried to take me down," Rowan says louder than necessary.

"You're embarrassing me by acting all cute with her." Conor nods at me.

"She's my girlfriend."

"Okay. For the next five minutes, neither of you can talk. You're both going to listen. Understood?" Neither of them says anything. "I'll take your silence as a yes." I slide onto the table. "Conor."

He glances up, but the annoyed expression on his face tells me I might not get anywhere with him. And I realize I won't —unless Rowan isn't in the room.

I hop down from the table. "Actually, Rowan, I need you to give us a second alone."

"No."

I set my gaze on him, trying to convey nicely that he needs to do what I'm asking.

"Is this how your relationship works? It's a dictatorship?" Conor adds his two cents, and this is exactly why Rowan needs to go.

I walk across the room and put my hands on Rowan's shoulders. "This is a brother-and-sister thing. Wait outside, and I'll come get you when I'm done."

He looks at me as though he's trying to see if he should listen to me or not. Ultimately, he kisses my cheek and walks out of the room.

Once the door is shut behind him, I go over to a chair by Conor and sit, crossing my legs. "I'm not sure how much clearer I have to be, Conor. I love him, and he loves me. And I get that you've seen a side of him I never did. I understand that when you were in college, both of you," I lean down to grab his attention, "*both* of you never had a serious relationship and probably took advantage of being the big guys on campus."

He rolls his eyes. His own reputation isn't exactly squeaky clean.

"But he's not that guy anymore. He's sweet and kind and caring. Especially with me. Neither of us thought this would happen. We thought we'd...okay, you're not going to want to hear this, but we used each other for sex. But during that, a friendship formed, then our hearts got caught up in it."

Conor scowls at me, arms still crossed. "You're in no place for a relationship."

"I agree with you. I wasn't in a place for a relationship. Finding Mom crushed me on a level I never thought was possible, but Rowan built me back up. He allowed me the freedom to explore what makes me happy. I'm even sketching again now. You think I'm all broken pieces that he's taking advantage of, but he's been picking up the broken pieces slowly, putting them back in place. And if you'd spend any time around us without being so bitter about us, you might see that for yourself."

His eyes don't stray from the carpeted floor. "I get that I'm overprotective, but I've heard guys say so much shit in locker rooms about the girls they're seeing. The idea of my sister being the subject of some of those conversations." His hands clench into fists. "Some of them discard the women and...I just know that if he hurts you, I'm going to destroy him."

I smile at him, although he hasn't looked at me yet. "What if he doesn't?"

"Doesn't what?"

"What if he never hurts me? What if we get married and have kids and are happily married until we die hand in hand at the same time? Well, I get to die one minute before him, so I never have to live on this earth without him."

He chuckles—despite himself, I think.

I knock my foot into his calf. "You like Rowan as a friend, right? Like, he's always been a good guy to you?"

"Until now."

I roll my eyes. "If I wasn't your sister, what would you tell him?"

"I don't want to play these games."

"Just tell me."

He seems to think about it for a beat. "I'd probably think it was cool how you guys got together. That he found someone, if that's what he wanted."

"And if he wasn't your best friend, and you never played hockey with him?"

"I get it, okay? I get it, but I still don't like it."

I stand, pick up my chair, and put it right in front of him. "Look at me."

His gaze floats up to meet mine. Finally.

"I'm all grown up, Conor. You can't protect me from everything. I'm going to make mistakes. I don't think Rowan is one of those, but if something changes, and he breaks my heart, I'll put on my big girl pants and deal. Sure, it will hurt and that will suck, but I'll get through it. You don't have to worry about me. But this thing between you and Rowan is not only ruining our sibling relationship, it's ruining a friendship between the two of you *and* destroying your entire team. Is it really worth that?"

He sighs and lets his head rock back before meeting my gaze again. "He's good to you?"

There's so much worry in his eyes that it melts away some of the irritation I've been feeling toward him.

I nod. "The best."

"And you're good?"

I laugh. "The best, and I'm not buying a bar, so you can relax about that too."

He lets out a big breath. "It will take some getting used to."

"I know."

"But I'm kind of sick of being mad all the time." I laugh, and he tips his head back. "Call the bastard in here."

I stand and hold out my hands. "Not until we hug this out."

He stands, and I press my cheek to his chest, wrapping my arms around him although he's still wearing his pads.

"I love you, Conor. Stay out of my personal life."

He chuckles. "Point made."

I pull back and cross the room, sticking my head out into the hall when I open the door. Rowan is leaning against the wall, and I tell him to come in.

He walks in, and Conor stands and puts out his hand to him. "You hurt her, and I give you two black eyes and a knee to the crotch."

"What do I get if I don't hurt her?" Rowan asks.

My brother looks at me when he answers. "An amazing woman to love."

Tears well in my eyes.

"Deal." Rowan shakes Conor's hand, and they both kind of crack a smile.

It might be a longer road than I hope, but this is a step in the right direction.

Conor walks out of the room, leaving me alone with Rowan.

"What did you say?" he asks.

"I have magical ways, you know that."

He bends down, and when he's mere inches from my lips, he says, "You know your brother will never get a chance to knee me in the balls, right?"

"Duh, I'm the only one who can touch your balls now."

He chuckles. "Damn right."

He kisses me. After, we walk out into the hallway and find Ron at the end, waiting for me.

"You'll get her to her seat?" Rowan asks him.

He nods. "That's my job."

"Thanks, she's really special." Rowan looks at me, and more pieces of my heart lift from my chest and float into his hands. "See you after the game?"

"I'll be waiting."

Our eyes stay on each other.

I push at his chest. "Go score some goals." I wink.

"Oh, I plan to. Gotta impress this woman in the stands."

"Really?" I ask, playing along with his game.

"I'm thinking about making a deal with her."

My head tilts. "What would that be?"

"If I score a hat trick tonight, she moves in with me." He places a chaste kiss on my lips. "Wish me luck."

I watch him walk down the hallway toward the ice, Landry in big white block letters across his back. I'm certain one day we'll share that last name and, if we're fortunate, see a smaller version of ourselves do the same. I can't wait to see what the future holds.

epilogue

Kyleigh

"Why can't you just move in here, Magic, and then I can take your place at The Nest now that the deal on my place has fallen through?" Conor asks, picking up a box off my kitchen counter.

"Because we love you so much, we want to be in the same building as you." Rowan slaps my brother's back.

I try not to make a big deal of them messing around with one another, but it's good to see.

"So, I'm stuck with Tweetie then." Conor grumbles, heading out the door.

"Hey, it's a gift that I'm allowing you to stay with me. Be grateful."

"You only like him staying because he brings girls back to your place." Rowan walks out of my apartment with another box.

Tweetie looks at me. "They act like I don't have game."

"Did you know Rowan doesn't like to share?" Bodhi asks next to me, helping me box up some of my books.

"He doesn't?" I ask.

"No. I told him I wanted Daddy to have a turn with you, and he said no." Bodhi puts the two books he's holding into the box.

Rowan steps back into my apartment, obviously overhearing our conversation.

"You'll understand it one day, Bodhi," Rowan says, picking up another box.

"Meany," Bodhi says and looks up at me. "But I'm glad you're living with us. We can chalk more."

"Definitely." I tap his nose with my finger.

He puts his arm around my neck and rests his head on my shoulder.

"Your kid is encroaching on my territory," Rowan says to Henry when he returns.

"He's kind of a chick magnet," Henry says.

"Well, he's ruining your game then." Tweetie laughs.

The four of them take another round of boxes down.

They're on a winning streak right now, and the locker room is free of tension. Conor and Rowan aren't where they were before, but we can all sit in a room together, so that's progress. With time, I know they'll get closer.

My parents' divorce is about to be finalized, and I've had a few meals with my mom since our brunch. I guess all of us Nilsens need time to get used to our new normal.

Once my apartment is all packed up and only the furniture I'm leaving behind remains, I take a moment for one final walk-through.

"Having second thoughts?" Rowan stands in the doorway of my bedroom, leaning against the doorframe with his arms crossed.

"No." I walk over to him and run my hands along his sides to behind his back, hugging him. "Just thinking of how different I feel now."

His hand runs down my back. "Different how?"

"I feel more at peace. Excited for my future..." I rest my chin on his chest and stare up at him. "Our future." I shrug. "I can't explain it. I think I'm mourning my old life because it feels like we're starting a new chapter. But then I'm anxious, because with a new chapter, there's uncertainty."

He nods. "We'll weather the storms together and appreciate the rainbows after."

I lightly push him in the stomach. "Okay, Mr. Inspiration."

"I like that a helluva lot better than Mr. Heartbreaker." He chuckles and holds me tighter, swaying us back and forth. "Let's go home."

I circle in his arms and take one last look at my old bedroom.

We walk out of my apartment, and I slide my key under the door for the landlord, who said the next tenant is new to the city and would love to have the furniture I'm not taking with me.

Once we're both in the vehicle, Rowan pulls the small moving truck away from the curb. I rest my arms on the window, staring at my apartment building until he turns a corner, and it disappears from view.

I straighten in my seat, and his hand lands on my thigh, squeezing it. "You okay?"

I nod, tears forming and slipping down my cheeks.

"I'm starting to feel I forced you into this."

"No." I shake my head, wiping my tears. "I'm so happy. Really. I think it's all just hitting me. I'm no longer that single girl who went from believing in happily-ever-afters to thinking they were bullshit, then back to knowing they exist."

"Definitely not single." He makes a right with the truck. "And we're proof they exist."

I place my hand over his on my thigh and interlock our fingers. "Okay, I'm not going to cry anymore."

He chuckles. "As long as they're happy tears, I won't pull this truck over."

"They're happy. I promise."

We share a smile at a red light before he has to continue driving.

We pull along the curb by The Nest, and I notice there's a new sign for Peeper's Alley, with a "Grand Re-Opening Tonight" banner under it.

"Oh, it looks so good." I step out of the truck as soon as it stops.

"And now I lost you to Ruby," he grumbles right before I shut the door.

I walk toward the bar.

"Don't worry, sis, we got all your shit!" Conor shouts.

I wave, opening the door to the bar that might have been mine at one point. There are new wooden floors, and the tables are now bar-height with new stools. Everything in here is shiny and new.

"It looks amazing," I say to the empty room.

Ruby comes out from the back. "Aren't you supposed to be driving into the sunset or some shit?"

I break the distance, my hand running along the new vinyl stools that no longer have any tears in them. "Are you excited?"

"To kick out girls trying to get to the guys? No."

I laugh and smile, knowing she really is happy. "Well, I can't wait to come down tonight."

"You live a sad life."

"I know."

That earns the tiniest rise at the corner of her lips. "Now go. I'm busy." She shoos me out with her hands.

I point at a neon sign for a seltzer company. "Serving seltzers now?"

"Mind your business." She walks toward me, still waving at me to leave.

"Okay. I'm going, but I'll see you tonight."

"Uh-huh," she says.

I walk out of the bar, and all the guys have a box in their hands, like a row of ants going toward the security gate that Bodhi is holding open.

After they move me in, Rowan's second bedroom is filled with my things. Everything but my clothes and toiletries.

"Happy?" Rowan asks me.

"So happy."

"Good." He kisses my forehead. "Now come to bed with me. We need to christen our new place."

"I think we've done that a couple times over already."

He falls down onto the bed, his body bouncing off the mattress. "Didn't you hear? We have to do it, like, five times on every surface for it to be considered christened."

I place my knee on the bed, and he grabs my hips, rolling me over onto my back.

"Well, in that case..."

"Sorry, such a chore, right?" He rolls his eyes.

I giggle. "What a drag, but if we must." I slide my hands under his shirt.

We christen the bed, the shower, and the kitchen counter before we have to stop and get ready for the Peeper Alley's grand re-opening.

"Could you keep it down?" Conor asks when he runs into us on the stairs. "I'm trying to deal with the fact that you two have sex with each other, but I don't need to hear my sister screaming your name." He puts his hands over his ears and makes a sound.

"You can't hear us." Rowan wraps his arm around me.

"Tweetie and I were walking up the stairs after lunch. Yes, I did."

Conor opens the security gate, and the three of us walk out onto the street, turning to head into Peeper's.

"I've tried to get her to quiet down. She's an animal."

I smack Rowan in the stomach.

Conor pretends he's going to throw up.

Rowan opens Peeper's door for us, and we head inside to an already crowded bar. The usual guys are lined up on the stools by the bar, but there's a younger crowd in here too. There's one table with four girls near the back, which grabs my brother's attention.

Rowan and I beeline it to the back room and find Henry and Tweetie playing darts.

Alara and Justin show up, and I talk to her about the progress I'm making with her wedding gown.

A few other players that the guys asked to join us arrive.

The room becomes pretty packed, so I'm sitting on Rowan's lap while he complains to my brother and Henry about not having any bathroom counter space anymore.

He secretly loves it.

My brother's eyes go to Rowan's hand running up and down my thigh a few times, but he doesn't say anything.

The night is going great until midway through when Tweetie walks back into the room with a woman. She's cute, her brown hair curled in waves. She's dressed in jeans and a sweater, nothing crazy. Not Tweetie's usual type, but maybe he's maturing. One can only hope.

"Hey, everyone! We have a guest," he announces, and I'm not sure why he has to introduce us to his woman for the night when he never has before. "This is Jade."

Henry's head whips so fast in their direction he could be a robot. He's on his feet immediately.

"Oh," I say, seeing a side of Henry I never have before.

"Jade?" Henry asks with disbelief.

"Get your ears cleaned. I just said that." Tweetie shakes his head.

"Hi, Henry," she says.

All the tension that dissipated after Rowan and my brother made up fills the room again.

"You guys know each other?" Tweetie asks, forehead wrinkled.

Conor shakes his head. "Yeah, Captain Obvious."

"Yeah," Jade echoes.

"That's her," Rowan whispers in my ear.

"Who?"

He smiles at Henry. "The one he let go so she could find herself. Seems like she's found *him* now."

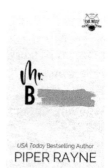

Is the saying, "If you love something let it go..." true for Henry and Jade? Is Jade back for Henry? So many questions to be answered in the **childhood friends to lovers, second chance and single dad hockey romance** coming next!

CLICK HERE if you love a hero who never stopped loving his first love.

Who is more protective, Rowan or Conor when the gang plays pickleball and Kyleigh gets hit on? Plus, Bodhi has a concert at school, and wait until you see who they run into. CLICK HERE for the bonus scene!

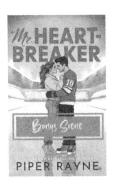

Please note by downloading the bonus scene you are agreeing to join our newsletter if you're not already a subscribed member.

also by piper rayne

The Nest

Mr. Heartbreaker

Mr. B (Title to be revealed)

Mr. S (Title to be revealed)

Mr. C (Title to be revealed)

Kingsmen Football Stars

False Start (Free Prequel)

You Had Your Chance, Lee Burrows

You Can't Kiss the Nanny, Brady Banks

Over My Brother's Dead Body, Chase Andrews

Chicago Grizzlies

On the Defense (Free Prequel)

Something like Hate

Something like Lust

Something like Love

Plain Daisy Ranch

One Last Summer

The One I Left Behind

The One I Stood Beside

The One I Didn't See Coming

The Baileys

Lake Starlight

The Problem with Second Chances

The Issue with Bad Boy Roommates

The Trouble with Runaway Brides

The Drawback of Single Dads

Modern Love

Charmed by the Bartender

Hooked by the Boxer

Mad about the Banker

Single Dads Club

Real Deal

Dirty Talker

Sexy Beast

Hollywood Hearts

Mister Mom

Animal Attraction

Domestic Bliss

Bedroom Games

Cold as Ice

On Thin Ice

Break the Ice

Chicago Law

Smitten with the Best Man

Tempted by my Ex-Husband

Seduced by my Ex's Divorce Attorney

Blue Collar Brothers

Flirting with Fire

Crushing on the Cop

Engaged to the EMT

White Collar Brothers

Sexy Filthy Boss

Dirty Flirty Enemy

Wild Steamy Hook-up

The Rooftop Crew

My Bestie's Ex

A Royal Mistake

The Rival Roomies

Our Star-Crossed Kiss

The Do-Over

A Co-Workers Crush

Hockey Hotties

Countdown to a Kiss (Free Prequel)

My Lucky #13 (FREE)

The Trouble with #9

Faking it with #41

Tropical Hat Trick (Novella)

Sneaking around with #34

Second Shot with #76

Offside with #55

Holiday Romances

Single and Ready to Jingle

Claus and Effect

Merry Kissmas

cockamamie unicorn ramblings

The first book in a series bears the most pressure. You're setting up a world that you want readers to love, so it's a delicate balance of bringing in new characters that will interest readers, as well as giving them enough of the couple.

Let's be honest: Sports romance is about the team and the brotherhood between teammates. We've always strived to include a lot of locker room scenes, ballbusting and other scenes with all of the heroes (and some where we leave you hanging until it's time for their book).

If you've read us for a long time, then you were pretty excited to see Tweetie from the Hockey Hotties series in this book. But we hope we surprised you when Henry from Smitten with the Best Man showed up! If you don't remember him and Jade, he was the little boy that the hero, Reed, was a Big Brother, and Jade was the heroine, Victoria's daughter. We absolutely love bringing these younger characters into books and being able to flesh out an entire backstory for them.

Let's see what changed from plotting to page...

They were going to be enemies-to-lovers, but we've written a lot of slow burns recently, so we decided we wanted to get right to the good stuff on this one. LOL So, we made them strangers with benefits, turned friends, turned more. Other than that, we're not sure there was much that changed, surprisingly. There were times we thought the book would never end, but every scene we wrote needed to be included for their journey to be complete.

We fell head over heels for Rowan and Kyleigh and we hope you did too. It might have been how they knew something was different about the other one, and the slow burn of their feelings growing. Plus, all the sex. That's always a bonus.

As always, we have a lot of people to thank for getting this book into your hands...

Nina and the entire Valentine PR team. The organization, the promotion, the way you keep us on point with deadlines. We appreciate you SO much!

Cassie from Joy Editing for line edits who took our book three days late since it turned out to be a little longer than planned coupled with our crazy summer schedules. LOL, we appreciate you always being willing to work with us on extensions.

Ellie from My Brother's Editor for line edits and proofing. We give you barely any time, but you always come through.

Hang Le for the cover and branding for the entire series which is always top tier. Your talent and eye is unmatched. We even did a little something different this time around.

All the bloggers who choose to read us when you have so many options out there. We're appreciative and honored to be on your list of must-reads and love reading all your reviews, edits, and more.

All the Piper Rayne Unicorns who support us every day, all day. We'd be lost without you answering our polls and telling us what you love and hate. We strive to give you the best Piper Rayne experience, and we can't say much else except that you're awesome!

Readers who have an abundance of books to choose from, thank you for picking up one of ours. We do hope you enjoyed the story and want to continue in the series.

What really happened between Henry and Jade? We're seeing a he falls first and hard second chance storyline in their future. Are you too? See you there!

xo,

Piper & Rayne

about piper & rayne

Piper Rayne is a *USA Today* Bestselling Author duo who write "heartwarming humor with a side of sizzle" about families, whether that be blood or found. They both have e-readers full of one-clickable books, they're married to husbands who drive them to drink, and they're both chauffeurs to their kids. Most of all, they love hot heroes and quirky heroines who make them laugh, and they hope you do, too!

Printed in Great Britain
by Amazon